T0195553

DON'T SPOIL IT

JOLI

authorHOUSE®

AuthorHouse™
1663 Liberty Drive
Bloomington, IN 47403
www.authorhouse.com
Phone: 1 (800) 839-8640

Published by AuthorHouse 03/04/2020

ISBN: 978-1-7283-4843-8 (sc)
ISBN: 978-1-7283-4842-1 (e)

Library of Congress Control Number: 2020903940

Print information available on the last page.

ACKNOWLEDGEMENTS

First and above all giving thanks to God for allowing me to bring my dream to fruition. With God, I acknowledge that all things are possible and without him I could have in no way completed *Don't Spoil It*. I am eternally grateful.

I must thank my children for putting up with the long hours I devoted to writing and giving me "quiet time" to process my thoughts. I know it wasn't always the idea atmosphere when I had papers all over the table and demanding solitude hours. To my daughter, thanks for reading over the novel and giving me constructive criticism. I appreciate and love you much.

Thank you Alyce Williams. You are an excellent Language Arts teacher whom took the time to read over my novel and look at some typos as well as point them out to me. I appreciate all of your help Alyce, knowing it was time consuming as you juggled between reading *Don't Spoil It* and teaching 6th grade Language Arts students.

My friend Tynesia Watson. Thanks for everything. Thank you for reading over the novel and pointing things out to me that I missed. Thank you for all the support and feedback. I appreciate you and if the book becomes a movie, you can play the part of Rhonda.

My sidekick Orgea Howell. You have been such an inspiration through this process. You were more excited than I was. You read the novel, gasped, laughed and encouraged me from the very beginning. You were a strong motivator and I appreciate your help. You were so genuine in your desire for me to move forward. When this novel becomes a movie I will reward you by letting you play the role of Nikki.

Last but not least, a special thanks to my readers. I appreciate you taking time to relax, kick back and enjoy this erotic novel that is sure to capture your attention from beginning to end. I hope that you will enjoy reading *Don't Spoil It* as much as I enjoyed writing it.

Joli

Chapter One

◇◇

"Um! Yeah! Oh Baby...that feels so good. Give me that magic stick." She rotated her body in unison with his while he held her legs over his shoulders. It had been approximately three minutes since he had put his semi hard magic stick into her. He insisted on calling it the magic stick even though the magic had been long gone. Usually five minutes was all it took before his eyes started rolling into the back of his head and he was doing the jerk.

"Ah Yeees! Yeeees Bay...bee! That's it. You're making Daddy cum. Augh! Whew. Daaamn! He clutched her arms as his body jerked and she could only see the white of his eyes. He pressed himself hard into her before collapsing next to her, trying to catch his breath. Rhonda looked over at the large digital clock that hung on the wall above her walk-in closet. 4:20 in the damn morning.

Bernard rubbed his hand up and down her arm. "Did that feel good to you Baby?"

"Yeah! You always make me feel good. I'm going to jump in the tub and get myself cleaned up. I won't be long. I love you." Bernard use to be good for at least ten minutes. Lately it seemed that as soon as he put his little five-inch magic stick into her sweetness, he would shoot off and his stick would fall, spilling his fluids all over her inner thighs. She kissed him before walking into the bathroom that adjoined their bedroom. The nice round marble Jacuzzi tub with gold knobs sat in the middle of the room. It matched perfectly with the marble floor. The gold and marble vanity held her makeup, oils, and perfume. The hidden drawer on the side held her toys.

Rhonda stood in front of the full length gold trimmed mirror. Her hands roamed her smooth caramel skin. Bernard's cum felt sticky between her thighs. She opened the hidden drawer and decided on her new toy. She had purchased the "Rabbit" last week at a pleasure party her friend Brandi hosted. She had tried lots of toys before; even another "Rabbit" but this one was waterproof.

After filling the Jacuzzi, she stepped into the warm water with relaxing oils and bubbles. Rhonda laid her head back and bent her knees as she opened her legs. She inserted the toy inside her. The rabbit was a dual stimulating toy. The false dick rotated inside her giving her body pleasure, while the rabbit ears worked her clitoris. She needed to cum.

Bernard no longer satisfied her sexual appetite but he was good to her. He provided her with a lavish lifestyle and he loved her unconditionally. There was a time when he actually pleased her. Even though his magic stick was not large, he used it well and always made sure that she was satisfied before he got his. She used to love it that her husband made it all about her.

Rhonda was twenty-three when she met Bernard. The Zodiacs were having a dance at the Post. Rhonda had gone there to meet the girls. She, Brandi, and Shemeka had hung out since tenth grade. They confided in each other and knew each other's inner secrets. Rhonda ordered a rum and coke while she waited for her friends to arrive.

Brandi was the first to arrive and headed straight for the bar. She didn't notice Rhonda seated further down on the other end. This was not a good sign. It meant that she and Anthony were having some sort of issue. Every time they had problems, Brandi seemed to think the solution was in a Bahama Mama. Rhonda couldn't imagine what the problem might be since Anthony was scheduled to be released from the Federal Penitentiary in about three months. Rhonda picked up her drink and moved to where her friend was seated.

Brandi had a shape that anyone would kill for. Her ass was nice and round and firm. Plenty of white men had tried to date her but Brandi chose to only date black guys. She was often called a traitor to her race or a nigga lover but it did not deter her. When she was in high school, black girls would get angry with her because they hated to see her with the good looking black guys but Brandi continued to do her thing. Rhonda and Shemeka thought she was cool for a white girl and were the first to befriend her. Soon the three were best friends.

Shemeka was always the last to arrive on the scene. She was homely and reserved. The first boyfriend she ever had in her life, cheated on her their senior year in high school, getting another girl pregnant. A year after graduation, he married the girl, and Shemeka was heartbroken. She went from one bad relationship to another. Finally, she decided that she was meant to be single and that all men were cheaters.

The three women were seated at the bar when Bernard walked in. All eyes were on him. He was casually dressed and when he smiled there was something so sexy about the gold tooth in his mouth that it made him look desirable. Bernard walked to a table where two other guys were seated. They greeted each other and smiled.

Ten minutes after she arrived, the bartender gave Rhonda another rum and coke along with a note. He looked in the direction of Bernard's table. "Compliments of the gentleman." Rhonda unfolded the note and read. *If I may approach, please wink.* She smiled as she told Brandi and Shemeka what the note said.

"Go for it girl." Brandi took another sip of her drink. "What do you have to lose?"

"Besides your panties" Shemeka looked at her. "You know how I feel. They all want one thing."

"Don't listen to her. How will you ever know what could have been if you don't give it a shot?"

Rhonda looked towards the table where the men were seated and winked, not quite sure which gentleman she was winking at. Bernard slid his chair back from the table, got up and walked towards the bar as Al Green's *I'm So Tired of Being Alone* played in the background. As he approached Rhonda, his lips curved into a smile. She was even more beautiful up close. Her smooth caramel-skin, her radiant smile, pearl white teeth and shoulder length kinky twist complimented her size 14 body frame.

"May I have this dance?" he asked as he extended his hand. Rhonda slid down from the bar stool and let Bernard lead her to the dance floor. They slow danced and he whispered in her ear. "You're beautiful. Too beautiful to be at a dance with your girlfriends. Where is your significant other?" He swung her around and looked into her eyes.

"Girls' night out." she answered.

"Does that mean you have someone?" Bernard held her tight as he pressed the side of his face to hers.

"No! If I had someone, I wouldn't be dancing with you. Had someone once, but he didn't know how to treat me."

Bernard pulled her close into him. "He has to be a fool. Or maybe he has a psychological problem. No man in his right mind would mistreat someone as precious as you. I know that I wouldn't."

Rhonda relaxed as Bernard led her around the dance floor. She actually felt warm and protected with his arms around her. When the music stopped he walked her back to her friends. They enjoyed several more dances that night. When the party was over, he had her telephone number and she had his promise to call.

Bernard taught the Exceptional Children's class at the middle school. He had a passion for students with learning disabilities and his class covered a variety of disabilities ranging from the learning disabled, to the emotionally behavioral disturbed.

His parents were killed in a plane crash during his junior year in college. He was an only child and inherited his parents' large estate. Bernard was careful not to get serious with the first woman he met. He was selective about the women he dated and never invited any of them to his home. He wanted to be accepted for who he was and not for what he had. He knew that his style of living would entice any woman and there were gold diggers out there.

Rhonda was different from any other woman that he had dated. She was wholesome and lively. When they were together, he could feel that she was genuine. This was the woman that he had to have in his life. She was his soul mate. After only nine months of dating, Bernard asked Rhonda to marry him.

"Oh damn!" Rhonda moaned quietly. Her entire body trembled from the orgasm she had just gotten. She washed her body and stepped out of the Jacuzzi. As she toweled dry, she thought about the conversation that she would be having with her husband shortly.

During their four and a half years of marriage, they had experimented a lot in the bedroom. Bernard was six years older than Rhonda and had introduced her to several sex acts. He was not the first man to taste her sweetness, but he was the first man to make her climax from the act. He told her that he hated the word pussy and would always refer to her vagina as sweetness. It was too good and sweet to be referred to as anything else. He insisted that she refer to his male body part as, the magic stick; after all, it really was magic and he could make her cum no matter what position he put her in.

Bernard seemed to lose interest in making love about a year ago. He very seldom approached the subject. Sometimes, she would ask and he claimed to be too tired. Other times, he would ask her to play with his magic stick. "Get it right for Daddy." But even after stroking it with her hand and licking it, the magic stick would only get semi-hard. Rhonda found herself wondering if he was having an affair or if he simply no longer found her attractive.

The five-inch rock hard magic stick that she had become accustomed to riding, no longer existed. It would barely get hard. There were times when Bernard seemed determined to please her and he would try to force it in. This would hurt because his knuckles would press against her sweetness.

Bernard finally faced the fact that there was a problem. He was thirty-five years old, a healthy man, and yet he was unable to please his wife as he once had. He went to the doctor for a complete physical, and a blood test revealed that he was diabetic.

As Rhonda climbed into bed with Bernard, she decided in her mind that it would be best to get right to the point. She wasn't being satisfied and it was not fair for her to have to pretend. She was young. She would be twenty-nine years old on her birthday and it was not right for her to get out of bed with her husband and have to take care of her own needs. She loved him. Bernard was a good man, but she owed it to herself to ask him for a separation. She made up her mind that it had to be done. Not tonight though. It could at least wait until morning.

The conversation would never take place. When Bernard pulled Rhonda into his arms, he had a proposal for her.

Chapter Two

◇◇

R honda pretended to be asleep when Bernard got up to get ready for work. After he was dressed, he walked over to the bed and kissed her on the forehead. She waited until she heard the garage door close before getting up. She sat on the side of the bed recapping the conversation she had with her husband the night before.

She had every intention of asking him for a separation. He had decided to take the relationship to another level, in a totally different direction. When she climbed into bed he pulled her into his arms and told her how much he loved her.

"Baby, we need to talk." He kissed her. "You know how much I love you. There is nothing that I would not do to make you happy. I'm no fool Rhonda. I know that you have not been satisfied with our love making for a while. Do you think I don't know about your toy drawer?"

She gasped. She had no idea that he realized she was doing herself. She was not ashamed. She would have loved to bring the toys into the bedroom. She was just surprised that he knew about it.

"I know that my diabetes plays a huge part in all of this." He continued. "But I feel like we need to try something different. I want you to be satisfied as well as me. We use to be open to different things. We have tried almost every position there is. Now I want to try something else."

"Something else like what? What are you talking about Bernard?"

He had gone on to tell her about how he heard some of the guys talking about a threesome. They said it had added variety and stamina to their sex life. It even made them stay hard longer. He insisted that it would be all about pleasing Rhonda and that he wanted them to bring another woman in with them just as a trial.

She had objected to the idea, telling her husband that she is not gay and did not want to be with another woman. "No Bernard! I'm not doing that. Are you crazy?"

"Baby, just listen. You don't have to do anything that you are not comfortable with. We will all be experimenting. If you don't like it, we can stop at any time. It will be your call. This might be the thing we need to save our marriage Boo. Pleeease Baby. I love you and I don't want to lose you."

Rhonda could not deny that the marriage needed to be saved. She was on the verge of taking a break when he came up with this proposal. The night had ended with her telling him that she would think about it and let him know within twenty-four hours. Until then, he would not pressure her.

Damn! She thought. *Why in the hell didn't I just tell him fuck no and be done with it. I don't even know what to do in a threesome. I'm not putting my mouth on a damn woman. I wonder who he has in mind. He said it would be all about me so what does that mean? Is he going to bring some woman in to eat me out while he watches us? I guess that he'll beat the hell out of his magic stick while he watches.*

She was so engulfed in her thoughts that she had completely forgotten about Brandi. The doorbell stunned her. Brandi had taken an annual leave day to get some rest after her trip. She had gone to West Virginia to see Anthony for the weekend. She had tried to talk Shemeka into riding with her, but Shemeka declined saying she was going to spend the weekend cleaning her house.

Brandi had finally settled on taking Anthony's cousin Denise with her. Denise was not one of her favorite choices but the trip was too long to take alone. At least Denise was supportive of the relationship. She was not like some of the other people in his family who acted like he was too good for Brandi. They thought that people should stick with their own race. She sometimes wondered if they had forgotten that Anthony was a convicted felon. They were not doing anything for him and no other woman, neither black nor white would make the sacrifices for Anthony that she had made.

"Just a minute." Rhonda spoke into the intercom. She slid into her bedroom slippers and threw her robe around her before pushing a button to unlock the door so Brandi could come in.

Brandi looked exhausted. Rhonda and Shemeka both had tried to get her to slow down on the visits. She tried to visit Anthony at least twice a month. The trips were expensive and cost her a lot of money that she could not afford. When she got low on money her family refused to help her. They told her that she would have money if she didn't spend so much time running up and down the road to see a convict who was only going to get out and break her heart as soon as he got his walking papers. They were not the only ones. A lot of people had advised Brandi that she was making a mistake. Her grandfather hurt her worse than any of them. "Of all the damn fools they have walking around here, you go and get you a nigga that's locked up. You disgrace our family."

"Grand-daddy, I love him. I have always been your little pumpkin and I have always respected you. Until now. If that's the way you feel, then I have nothing for you. Good-bye!" She didn't see him again until they called to tell her he was in the hospital. He had suffered coronary heart failure and was asking for her. Shemeka and Rhonda had encouraged her to go. He told her that he loved her and begged her to forgive him. After that, he took his last breath.

Brandi never believed any of the negative things people had to say concerning Anthony nor their relationship. He loved her too much to ever hurt her. He wasn't like some of those other men in there. She had witnessed firsthand how some of those men had different women visiting them and how they juggled to keep the women from bumping into each other. Some of them only wanted a woman so they could have someone to visit them and put a few dollars on their books. Although Brandi sometimes put money on Anthony's books, she felt like she was investing in her future. After all, he was going to be her husband.

Rhonda was glad that Brandi had taken the day off. They could catch up. After washing her face and brushing her teeth, Rhonda prepared coffee, and bagels with cream cheese. The two sat down to catch up on what was going on in their lives.

Brandi's visit with Anthony had gone well. They had made plans for the future and what they would do once he was released from prison. He would spend six months in a Half-Way House, but she would pick him up and take him on job searches. She understood that he would have to lean on her for a while. People were not jumping over one another to hire convicted felons. She didn't mind being his backbone as long as he was faithful to her. Brandi was not going to tolerate that running around stuff. Not after all that she had gone through with him. She explained to Rhonda how sweet he had treated her at visit and how glad she was that she had gone.

Rhonda vaguely heard what her friend was saying. Her mind kept drifting back to the conversation that she and Bernard had had the night before. *What would it be like to be with a woman? Could a woman really make a difference in her relationship with Bernard? Would she enjoy it?*

"So tell me girl. What happened?" Brandi got up to pour another cup of coffee. "What was Bernard's reaction when you told him that you wanted to separate? Did he get upset or what?"

Rhonda looked at her coffee cup as she stirred the coffee with her spoon. "I didn't tell him."

"Why? You said that he is not satisfying you. What are you going to do? Oh yeah. Go the rest of your life with your friend Mr. Rabbit."

"Isn't that what you are doing while you wait on Anthony? I don't see you getting tired enough to stop running up and down the road."

"That's different and you know it. But it's your life."

"Brandi, I'm not sure what I will do. Bernard loves me. I am sure of that. Look at all I have. He wants me to be happy. There is nothing that he would not do for me. Besides, we are going to try to rekindle our romance."

"I hope it works for you. All I want is to see you happy."

"And I want the same for you. We better stop all of this talking if we are going to make it to the department stores." Rhonda stood.

Rhonda, Brandi, and Shemeka usually confided in each other about almost everything. This was a little different though. She didn't feel comfortable about mentioning Bernard's suggestion of a threesome. There was no need to share that bit of information with anyone. They would only try to advise her but the end decision would be hers.

Brandi cleaned the kitchen while Rhonda showered and put on her Apple Bottoms jean suit. The two had agreed to spend the day shopping.

In the lingerie department, a sexy two-piece leopard negligee caught Rhonda's eye. It came with black fishnet stocking. Rhonda told Brandi she would buy it as a special treat for Bernard.

"Well that's one way to rekindle things. One minute you are ready to separate from this man and the next minute, he deserves a treat. What's up with you?"

"Nothing's up with me. If there is a chance for me to make my marriage work, then I want to do that. I love my husband." After the two had finished shopping, they stopped by O'Charley's for something to eat before departing.

Chapter Three

Bernard glanced at his watch. It was 7:40 p.m. Twenty minutes before Nikki was scheduled to arrive.

After he came home from work last night, Rhonda had agreed to meet Nikki. She refused to commit to a threesome but said she would at least meet the woman and then they would take it from there. In return, Bernard had agreed not to pressure her. Although she didn't ask Bernard, she wondered how he had met Nikki and how she had been chosen as the woman that would resolve their marital issues. She decided that she would ask him later. Depending on how things went.

Rhonda curled up on the lounge chair in the den. She sipped on Hennessey and sprite. Rum and coke was her drink of choice before she married Bernard. He turned her on to Hennessey and sprite and she found that to be a much milder drink. The room was candlelit and Bernard set out a tray of fried mushrooms, a cheese tray, and assorted finger sandwiches. He put in a Luther Vandross CD and Rhonda closed her eyes as she listened to the duet by, Luther and Beyoncé, *The Closer l Get to You.*

"Sweetheart, I love you so much." He walked over to her and kissed her on the forehead. "This is going to work. You'll see. Ask any questions that you want to ask. If you want to make a list of rules, we will follow the rules or we can do this by ear. This is all for you. It's for your pleasure. All I want is for…" He didn't finish his sentence. The doorbell rang.

Rhonda took another sip of her drink and relaxed on the lounge chair. Bernard went to the door and walked back into the den with a dark skinned woman who stood about 5'8 inches tall. She was not at all what Rhonda had expected. Nikki was thick with shoulder length hair; she wore a short skirt, which revealed the biggest thighs that Rhonda had ever seen in her life. Bernard had always been attracted to small women. How was this woman going to help their sex life? Maybe that's why Bernard had chosen her. Maybe he wanted to use a woman who he would not be attracted to. Maybe this really was about her.

"Sweetheart, this is Nikki." Rhonda stood and extended her hand to Nikki who ignored it and gave her a hug.

Damn! She smells good. Rhonda thought. "Nice to meet you. Please! Have a seat. What would you like to drink?"

"Gin with grapefruit juice on the rocks. Thanks." Nikki sat on the loveseat across from Rhonda. Bernard went to the bar to fix her drink. The women enjoyed eating from the trays he had prepared. She drunk her gin in three gulps and Bernard refilled her glass.

As the three conversed, Rhonda discovered that Nikki was the single mother of a three-year-old daughter. She worked as a real estate broker. She met Bernard when she got a flat tire one morning on her way to work. She was attempting to drive to a service station a few blocks away. Bernard flagged her over and changed her tire to keep her from messing up her rim. He would not accept payment. Nikki encountered him again when she was at the school talking to one of his coworkers who was searching for a house. She explained that she had serviced a lot of the teachers who worked at the school.

Rhonda wondered how Nikki had gone from being stranded to being a possible inclusion in a threesome. Bernard seemed to read her mind and explained that Nikki was once involved with one of his dawgs. They would often go to Bernard's room during his planning period for alone time. She wondered which one of the guys had been kicking it with this big boned woman.

Bernard explained that he wanted to give the threesome a trial run on Friday night. If at any time, either of the participants felt uncomfortable with the way things were going, they could stop at any time. Since no one stipulated any rules, they decided that they would make up the rules as they went. Friday night would be more like a 'get acquainted night'. It would give everybody a chance to get comfortable with each other. If it went beyond that then they would take it on to another level.

It would be a first time for all of them. Nikki said that she had been stressed out and dealing with some things. It would be a way for her to relieve some stress. She said that she had never been with a woman before but had always been curious about it. "What about you Rhonda?" She asked. "Have you ever thought about being with a woman or wondered what it would be like?"

"No, I never really thought about it. When Bernard approached me with the idea, I refused at first because I am not gay. I only decided to consider it because…well I guess that maybe I am curious now."

Bernard refreshed the drinks for the women. "Ladies will you please excuse me for a moment? I want to get out of these clothes and put on something more comfortable. I won't be long." He placed his drink on the bar before leaving the room.

Rhonda leaned back in the lounge chair and rubbed her eyes. She was not sure if she had had one too many to drink or if her eyes were playing tricks on her. Nikki was sitting wide legged on the loveseat and she didn't have on any panties. She was hairy as hell. Big black curly hairs. Nah! She had to be drunk. This couldn't be happening. Nikki licked her fingers and parted the lips of her pussy. Her clit stuck out like a child licking their tongue out of their mouth. Rhonda tried to ignore her and look away but her eyes roamed back to Nikki who had closed her legs. *What the fuck is she doing?* Rhonda thought. *And why in the hell is my shit getting moist like this?*

Nikki broke the silence. "Bernard said this is something he wants to do for you. He must love you a lot. He said that he wants to make sure you are satisfied and you enjoy yourself. I have never done anything like this before. I hope that it will be a fun experience."

"I don't know" Rhonda answered. "We'll see. We are only going to do it one time anyway. It's not like this is going to be an everyday thing." She took another sip of her drink and could feel herself getting a buzz. She decided not to have any more to drink. She looked at Nikki.

Nikki had her middle finger back in her pussy. She was going in and out of it like that was something, natural to do. "Um" she moaned. "Um!" She opened her legs wider to go deeper. She started rotating her body and working her fingers. Rhonda was fixated on her. She was thick as hell but the way she moved her body made Rhonda hot. She didn't know why but she was turned on. All of a sudden Nikki stopped.

"May I use your restroom?"

"Sure. It's down the hall. Second door on the left"

Nikki got up and stopped in front of Rhonda. "Stand up please."

Rhonda stood. "What's wrong?"

"May I feel you?" She started breathing heavily and looked at Rhonda for permission to touch her.

"No!" she responded. "No! We're not doing anything. Are you crazy? Bernard will be downstairs in a minute. He just went to freshen up and change clothes. Go ahead and use the restroom. It's getting late anyway."

"Come on now. You know that Bernard only excused himself to give us a minute to talk."

"Well talk. I'm listening."

"Just let me feel what I'm going to be working with and I'll go to the restroom. I saw you watching me while I was over there touching myself. You know that you want me to touch you the same way. It's okay. I just want to feel you. Please."

Rhonda couldn't deny that she was turned on. If Nikki felt her, she would feel how wet she had gotten. She was nervous that Bernard might come down the steps and catch them. How could she possibly explain that to him? She wondered how much longer he would be upstairs. It couldn't hurt anything for her to let Nikki feel her quickly before going to the restroom. "Okay! One time. You can feel me one time before you go to the restroom."

Nikki stuck her hand in Rhonda's shorts. She rubbed her hands over Rhonda's freshly shaved sweetness. She parted the lips and slid her fingers into sloppy wetness. "You're wet." She told Rhonda. "You feel good."

Rhonda did not respond. Instead, she stood there trying to ignore the way her sweetness was pulsating. Nikki was finger fucking her in her den and it felt so different from when Bernard touched her. It felt so good that she started moving her body. When Nikki started to take her finger out, Rhonda placed her hand on top of Nikki's. She didn't want her to stop. *Damn! This shit feels good.* Rhonda thought. *This bitch is going to make me cum. Oh my goodness, I'm about to explode.* Just as she was on the verge of one of the best orgasms she had had in a very long time, she heard Bernard coming down the steps. Nikki removed her hands and licked Rhonda's fluids off her finger before heading to the restroom. Rhonda was hot. She couldn't believe that a woman had brought her to that point but she knew that she had to release herself or she would not be able to sleep. "Bernard, it's getting late. We should call it a night."

"Sure Babe. Whatever you say."

When Nikki returned from the restroom, Rhonda didn't look at her. Bernard explained that it was getting late and he would get in touch with her about the details for Friday night. He told Rhonda that he would clean up the glasses and things out of the den while she walked Nikki out.

Once in the living room, Rhonda told Nikki that she would see her Friday.

"I'm looking forward to it. I like what I felt." She grabbed the back of Rhonda's neck and stuck her tongue down Rhonda's throat. She kissed Rhonda like she had never been kissed before. "Something to hold you until Friday night." Nikki walked out the door.

When Bernard finished putting away everything downstairs and walked into the bedroom, his wife was on the bed with her legs spread apart.

"I need you Baby. Make love to me." She was naked. Usually she wore a negligee but tonight she was in all her glory. He was only semi hard but it didn't seem to matter to Rhonda. She was in full control as she slid his magic stick into her sweetness and took his five inches. She knew that she was going to cum for him tonight. She was horny and on edge.

"Boo, let me know when you get ready to cum. I only want to please you Babe." Bernard told her.

When she got ready, she screamed "OH! Baby! I'm goanna cummm."

He pulled his magic stick out and went down on her. He ate her out as she grabbed his head and her body started to tremble. She looked at him and imagined it was Nikki.

"Whew! That was good. I love you."

Chapter Four

◇◇

Shemeka rummaged through her closet for something to wear. She had agreed to go out on a blind date with someone from work. At first she was reluctant to accept, but Rhonda helped Brandi talk her into it. Shemeka decided on a black denim skirt with the matching jacket. She chose a white tank top to wear underneath it and her leather boots.

Robert arrived at 7:00 sharp. He was tall, pecan tan, and clean-shaven. Shemeka invited him to come in while she found a vase for the dozen yellow roses he handed her. She was impressed.

"You look beautiful Shemeka. I'm glad that you agreed to go out with me. I have wanted to ask you for a while but you were always so reserved and I didn't want to feel like I was imposing. Although this is supposed to be a blind date, in many ways it is not. I asked our supervisor to set it up. I hope you don't mind."

Shemeka didn't know how to respond. She had noticed Robert and thought he was cute. She would not have dared asked him out. It was bad enough dealing with the average guy, but Robert was like a pretty boy. She assumed that he either had someone or he was a playa.

"I thought we would go out to eat and catch a movie if that's okay with you. I promise to have you in early."

Robert opened the car door for Shemeka. Once she was in, he closed the door and walked to the drivers' side. They merged onto Interstate

85. She wondered why he was taking her out of town and began to feel a bit uneasy. Her heartbeat returned to normal when he pulled up at the restaurant. The attendant opened the doors for them and parked the car.

The restaurant was nice. The lights were a little above dim and each table had a floating candle on it. A live band was playing. Robert gave the hostess his name and explained that he had reservations for two. They were seated at a table near the back. Robert pulled the chair out for Shemeka before taking his seat. Shemeka was impressed with his manners. She wanted to know more about him. They engaged in conversation and she found that he had a good sense of humor. He was thirty-one years old, had never been married and had no children. He graduated from Winston Salem State University with a degree in sports medicine. She shared with him that she was twenty-eight years old and had been out of the dating arena for a while. She lived alone and was not interested in a serious relationship. Every man that she had ever been involved with was full of game and she was not willing to step back out there. All she desired in a man was friendship.

"I can respect your honesty."

Robert took a sip of his wine. "I would never pressure you or try to force you to do anything that you didn't want to do. I just find you interesting. You are different from the other women we work with. I would like it if you would allow me to get to know you better."

"We'll see."

"Is that a yes?" He smiled at Shemeka and placed his hand on top of hers.

"It's not a yes, but then again, it's not a no. We'll see how things work out. You know how crazy things can get at work. I'd hate for us to be the latest subject of the break room gossip."

They enjoyed laughing and talking so much that they didn't notice time slipping away. Robert looked at his watch "Oh my goodness. I didn't realize it was so late. I'm sorry. I did promise to get you home early."

"It's my fault too. I didn't realize the time. Rain check on the movies?"

"Sure. That means that you'll be going out with me again after all." He laughed.

When they got to Shemeka's house, Robert let her out of the car and walked her to the door. When she put the key in the door he thanked her for a fun night and kissed her on the forehead.

"Can I call you again Shemeka?" He asked before leaving.

"Sure. I'd like that." She answered.

Once in the house, Shemeka pulled off her boots before picking up the telephone to call Brandi.

"What's up girl? How was the date?" Brand's voice was loud as it blared through the receiver.

"Hold up. Let's get Rhonda on three-way so I won't have to repeat this. Shemeka clicked over and dialed Rhonda's number.

"Hey girl!" Brandi yelled. "Shemeka's back from her date and about to fill us in on the details."

"Well, what can I say? He's a gentleman. We went out to a nice restaurant and he was very respectful. I felt special. Something I haven't felt in a long time. But it was just one date. I am not rushing into anything. You know my motto about men. *The worse you treat a man the more he loves you. Men don't appreciate a good woman.* I did tell him that I would go out with him again."

"At least that's a start. It's time for you to get out of that house and start living." Rhonda wanted to be encouraging. They both wanted Shemeka to find a nice man.

"I agree with Rhonda. It's about time."

"Okay! Enough said. I do have to get up in the morning and go to work. Good night ladies." Shemeka hung up the telephone and took a hot shower. The hot water ran down her body as she engulfed herself in lather. She thought about Robert. *He was nice. Not what I expected and he didn't even try to kiss me goodnight. Maybe, just maybe.*

Chapter Five

◇◇

Rhonda tried to focus. She and Shemeka had agreed to meet Brandi for some girl time before she took off to West Virginia again. They were to meet at 4:00 so Brandi could get on the highway by 7:00.

Shemeka didn't have anything planned for the day and Rhonda hoped that she would not want to sit around and talk about Robert. They had gone on a couple more dates and he was all that she talked about. Rhonda was happy for her but she and Brandi were tired of hearing about what a gentleman he was and how she had never met anyone like him before.

When Rhonda arrived at Olive Garden, Shemeka was already there. That was a first. She was always the last to arrive. Robert sure had made a change in her. Maybe they could get all of the conversation about Robert out of the way so Shemeka would be ready to leave when Brandi left.

Why in the hell did they have to pick today to do soul talk anyway? Rhonda asked herself. *I'm going to be pushing it to get freshened up for my ordeal with Bernard and Nikki.* She had been thinking about Nikki ever since that night at her house. She would close her eyes and see that large clit, as well as imagine that middle finger in her wet sweetness. She loved her girls but she was not about to let them stop her from experiencing her first threesome. She wanted to feel Nikki's finger in her again and she wanted to cum all over it.

It wasn't long before Brandi arrived. She was excited about her trip and anxious to see Anthony. She had planned to stay until Sunday. She bought a new dress for the visit. Shemeka wanted to see more of Robert. She felt herself letting her guard down. She was ready to take it to the bedroom. Rhonda decided that she was not ready to ask Bernard for a separation. She would try to meet him halfway and work on the marriage.

After the women talked for a hour and a half they hugged and said goodbye. Rhonda and Shemeka told Brandi to have a safe trip. Shemeka wanted to get home in case Robert called and wanted to stop by. Rhonda was anxious to get home for other reasons.

Bernard had decided on Comfort Suites. He paid for the suite during his lunch and picked up two keys. He gave one key to Nikki and he and Rhonda would use the other one. They would meet at 8:00.

Rhonda decided she would take the leopard negligee with the fishnet stockings. She threw it in an overnight bag with a few cosmetics before showering, and taking a douche. Bernard was waiting for her downstairs. He kissed her. "Are you ready Baby?"

"Yeah, I guess."

"You guess? Nah baby! I want you to be sure. If you don't want to go through with it, we can always call it off." He squeezed her hand.

"I'm sure." She answered. "Let's do it. This might be what we need. What do we have to lose?"

Bernard and Rhonda arrived at the suite before Nikki. The room was lit with twenty-five candles. Rose petals led a path to the bed. A chocolate fountain with marshmallow sat on a table. Strawberries and whipped cream sat on another table. The bar in the suite contained Grey Goose, Hennessey, Crown Royal, coke, sprite, ginger ale, and juice. There were also oysters and shrimp.

Rhonda was amazed but not surprised. Bernard knew the perfect way to set the mood. He undressed and sat on the chair naked while Rhonda went into the restroom to change. A few minutes later Nikki arrived. Bernard welcomed her with a kiss on the face and told her that Rhonda would be out shortly. She was changing.

"I'll just go in too. I need to change. We won't keep you waiting."

Rhonda had just stepped into her leopard negligee when Nikki walked into the bathroom, closing the door behind her. "Is that pussy ready for me?" Rhonda nodded. She wasn't use to her sweetness being called *pussy* but it didn't sound bad.

Nikki kissed Rhonda and Rhonda responded by giving in to her. She could feel herself getting wet. She tried to pull back but Nikki pulled her in and slid her middle finger in where Rhonda wanted it.

"Hurry up! I'm ready!" Bernard yelled from the other room.

"We're coming!" Rhonda yelled back. She whispered to Nikki, "I better get out there. We'll be waiting for you."

Bernard was sitting in the chair when Rhonda came out of the restroom. After all of the rushing he was doing, his manhood was asleep, drawn up in its skin.

"Damn! Damn! You look so damn good Baby. This is your night. Don't forget, you are in control."

The restroom door opened and Nikki came out in a red see through nightie. She wore red satin panties which were visibly crotchless. The holes in her nightie revealed her hard nipples which were sprinkled with red glitter. She wore a red satin cape and waved a wand with a feather tip. The cape fell from her shoulders as she sashayed across the room caressing her body as she blew out every other candle. She stopped in front of Bernard and took his hand to help him from the chair.

His magic stick was no longer asleep. Rhonda couldn't remember the last time she had seen it so hard. She was slightly jealous. Nikki led him to the bed and pushed him down on the rose petals. No one said a word.

Nikki left Bernard on the bed and walked over to Rhonda acting like she was a stripper and Rhonda was her pole. She licked Rhonda around her lips.

Nikki led Rhonda to the king size bed where Bernard laid jacking his magic stick, while enjoying the show. She put her hand over his to stop him. "Don't spoil it!"

She laid Rhonda next to Bernard and whispered. "Shh...be patient." Nikki reached into her bag to pull out some hot oil, which she poured over Bernard before massaging him. He moaned in pleasure while she jacked his stick. She removed her hand and replaced it with her mouth. She took him in her mouth and worked his stick like it had never been worked before. He was getting close to a climax. "Oh shitttd!" He screamed while clutching the sheets on the bed. Before he could cum, Nikki stopped. "No Bernard. Don't spoil it."

He was breathing heavily as Nikki moved to Rhonda. She licked Rhonda's face and put her tongue in Rhonda's ear. Bernard's magic stick was so hard that it looked like it was aching. He was obviously turned on. He rolled over and started touching Nikki while she was giving Rhonda a tongue bath. She put her fingers in Rhonda's sweetness. This was what Rhonda had been waiting on. It felt so good to her that she wanted to scream. Nikki started moving harder and harder inside of her.

She sucked Rhonda's clit while Bernard hit her back with his hard magic stick as if begging for permission to enter. He pushed his stick in Nikki's ass and wrapped his arms around her waist. He pumped her from behind. Nikki put her fingers in Rhonda while she ate her sweetness. When she attempted to bring her head up, Rhonda tightened the grip she had on Nikki's hair. "No!" She pleaded. "No! Don't st...oop! I'm theeerre. Yeeeeeah!"

Rhonda's body went into convulsions. She had been in such a trance that she hadn't noticed Bernard doing Nikki until Nikki pushed him back.

"I want you Baby." Bernard mumbled. "I want to fuck you."

She thought her husband was talking to her until he slid under Nikki and she proceeded to ride him. He smiled like he had just hit the lottery. She rode him while he made sounds resembling a sick animal.

"Your pussy is so tight. Give me this damn pussy. Oh yeah. Give it to me."

Rhonda couldn't believe it. This was the man who claimed he hated the word pussy but he was using it so freely.

"How much of this pussy do you want?" Nikki rubbed his chest as she rode his stick and pinched his nipples. "It's going to bite you." She rode him fast and hard as the walls of her pussy clasped his stick.

He held on to her thighs like he was giving her eight inches instead of the five inches he had. He tightened his grip on her and yelled out loud. "OH YEAH! FUCK DADDY!"

Rhonda could not believe it. She thought to herself, *This muthafucka never screamed like that for me. I thought this was supposed to be my damn night. No more. This is it. He better not cum in her. I know that shit!* Rhonda had not gotten the thought out of her mind when Bernard gave out a big "Ooooh damn! I'm coming for you. That's it! Milk that stick Baby!"

Nikki threw her body into a higher speed as Bernard's legs stiffened, his eyes rolled to the back of his head and he shot a full load of his sperm up in her hot pussy. His magic stick fell out of her and the rest of his cum dripped onto the hairs of her pussy.

Rhonda watched quietly while Nikki wiggled up to Bernard as he was catching his breath. He lay there as she straddled his face and ate her pussy like it was a fried chicken. His wife could only look, not quite knowing how to react. She wanted to curse Bernard's ass out but how could she? He had made it plain that she could stop anytime she wanted to.

Nikki climbed down after she reached her climax. Ten minutes later, Bernard was asleep. Nikki got out of the bed and took the comforter from the foot of the bed and spread it on the floor. "Lay down." She told Rhonda. "Be quiet so we don't wake your husband".

Rhonda got off the bed and lay on the comforter. Nikki massaged her with the same hot oil that had put Bernard in a trance. She stuck her fingers in Rhonda's sweetness as soft moans escaped her lips. "Um…you make me feel so good. I never knew it could feel so good. Um…oh Nikki."

"Shhh…! Be quiet! I'm going to make you cum again. Let me take care of you." Nikki went back into her treat bag and removed a strap-on. She strapped up before putting Rhonda's legs on her shoulders. She slid the head in and moved it up and down Rhonda's clit before entering her sweetness.

Rhonda bit her lip to keep from screaming as she looked up at Nikki's two hundred sixty-five-pound body. She would never have thought a strap on would feel so good. Was it her imagination or was this strap-on making her feel better than the magic stick? Why was she so turned on by Nikki? What was so special about this woman?

"Whose pussy is this?" Nikki asked her. "Who do you want to have this pussy?"

"It's yours. It's your pussy. I want you to have it." Rhonda heard the words she was saying but couldn't believe the words were coming from her lips. Why did she say that? She knew that her sweetness belonged to Bernard. "Oooh…Ooooh…Yeessssssssssss!"

"Cum for me! Give me my pussy. Didn't you say it was mine? Tell me it's mine." Nikki stroked harder bringing Rhonda to explosion.

"Um…it's yours. Damn! It's yours." She trembled as she dug her fingernails into Nikki. Rhonda was so caught up in the sex that she didn't hear Nikki mumbling under her breath. "Damn right this is my pussy and don't you ever forget it."

Chapter Six

◇◇

Shemeka was ecstatic. She and Robert had been dating for three and a half months and he had respected her decision to take things slow. There were times when she could feel that he was frustrated but he managed to control his feelings and would always end the night early.

She often cooked dinner for him and he would leave shortly after. She wondered if tonight might be a good time to invite him to stay the night. When he arrived she had just taken meat loaf out of the oven. He had dropped several hints that it was his favorite and she was a good cook. She greeted him with a passionate kiss and led him to the table.

The lights were dim and a single candle flickered on the dining room table. A bottle of wine chilled in the ice bucket. Green bean casserole, potato salad, yeast rolls and homemade peach cobbler were on the table.

Shemeka took off her apron revealing a short black dress with spaghetti straps and a deep "v" cut exposing cleavage. Robert's eyes lit up. "Whew! You look fantastic Baby. The food looks good. Everything! How did you find the time?"

"That's why I left work early. I really want tonight to be special Robert. I am starting to care about you. It has been a long time since I've been with a man. You are making me feel things that I didn't ever think I would feel again."

"I care about you too Meka. In fact, it's deeper than that. I feel myself falling in love with you. I open my eyes in the morning and I think of you. I close my eyes at night and I think of you. I want to show you that love can be fun and feel good. Love doesn't always have to hurt. I know that you have reason to be cautious but just give me chance. I'll never hurt you Meka."

"I know Robert. I want to believe you." She took a bite of her meatloaf. "Try it. Tell me what you think." Robert took a bite of meatloaf. "This is scrumptious."

After they finished eating, Robert helped Shemeka clean up the kitchen. She put in a Michael Jackson CD and they danced in the living room. "Let me lead," she told him. She led him to her bedroom where a cinnamon fragranced candle barely lit the room. She stopped in front of the bed. "I want you to hold me Robert."

He kicked off his shoes and they both lay sideways on the bed with Shemeka's back to him. Robert held her. "Meka, I want things to always be good with us. Even if you decide that I am not someone who you want as a permanent figure in your life; I want us to always have a good relationship. This time that I have spent with you has been special."

"It has been special to me too, Robert. I have enjoyed every minute that we've been together." She moved his hand to her breast and he started exploring her body.

He rubbed her shoulders. "You're tense Baby. Relax. I won't hurt you." As he felt Shemeka start to relax, he unzipped his pants. She could feel his manhood rubbing against her and prayed that he was not about to put it in the backdoor. She was ready for him to roll her over and go deep inside her.

Robert lifted her black dress and spread her legs apart. He inserted his finger into her wetness. "Only if you are ready. I don't want you to do anything you aren't ready for. I'll wait as long as you want me to."

Shemeka responded by opening her legs wider. Robert eased his penis into her from the back. After a couple of strokes, he brought Shemeka to her knees. As she positioned herself doggie style on the bed, Robert worked his penis in and out of her while she succumbed to the feeling of enjoyment. It had been a long time since she had been with a man.

"Oh Baby, this feels so good. I want you Baby," She moaned.

Robert was holding on to her tight when the doorbell rang.

"Damn! Let's ignore that Baby. They'll go away." Robert continued to please her ignoring the continuous ringing of the doorbell. He could feel from her body that she was about to cum. He whispered, "Cum with me. Ah! Ah! Baby!"

Shemeka clutched the sheets. "That's it I'm cumming with you Robert. Oh my goodness."

The doorbell stopped ringing and was replaced with loud banging on the door. Shemeka jumped off the bed and pulled her dress down. "I'm sorry Baby. I can't imagine who that is. You can clean up in the bathroom across the hall."

She quickly exited the bedroom, closing the door behind her. "Hold up! I'm coming." She yelled. Shemeka looked through the peephole, and saw Brandi. Her eyes were red and swollen. She opened the door.

"What's wrong? Come in. What happened? Did somebody die? What's going on Brandi?"

Brandi could barely hold her composure while she explained to Shemeka that Anthony was not being released in a few months. He claimed that his counselor came to him at the last minute to tell him that the dates had somehow gotten mixed up in the system. It was the second time she had thought he was coming home only to find that it was a mistake. He told her that he had to do seven more months.

She remembered one of the women who frequently visited the prison, saying something about how you could go online to the Federal Bureau of Prisons website and put in the inmates' registration number to find out the projected release date. When she put in Anthony's information, it showed that he had four more years to do.

"I can't do this." Brandi sobbed. "I just can't. I have already put my life on hold because I love him so much. I go to weddings and see the happy couple and wish it was us. I go to dances alone and watch other women with their men. I spend my spare time with you and Rhonda but y'all have lives of your own. And he just out right lied to me. Why?"

"Brandi, I can't answer that. I wish I could. It's hard as hell when someone you love deceives you. He should have been honest with you and let you decide if you wanted to ride it out with him. That's fucked up."

Robert emerged from the bedroom. Shemeka stood up to introduce them. "I'm sorry Robert. This is my friend Brandi. Brandi, Robert."

"Nice to meet you Brandi. I've heard a lot about you."

"Likewise." She looked at Shemeka. "Oh-I'm sorry. I didn't realize you had company."

"It's fine." He moved closer to Shemeka. He couldn't help but to notice how red Brandi's eyes were and the black streaks of wet mascara that ran down her face. "I can see that you two need to talk. I'll see myself out." He kissed Shemeka on the lips, and then whispered in her ear, "Thanks Baby. I enjoyed you. I'll see you at work tomorrow."

When she returned from walking him to the door, Brandi was in the kitchen gulping down a drink of vodka and juice. "I hope you don't mind. I just needed a damn drink. This shit is crazy."

"You know I don't mind. Let me take a quick shower and then we will talk."

"Take your time. I'm really sorry. I didn't mean to mess up anything. He's cute. I see why he has driven you so crazy."

Shemeka went into the bathroom to clean up. When she came out, Brandi was passed out on the couch. The empty vodka bottle was on the floor.

Chapter Seven

◇◇◇

It had been a week since the ordeal at the Comfort Suites and neither Bernard nor Rhonda had spoken about it. She didn't want to ask Bernard how he enjoyed it. From the moans, and the smile on his face, it had been obvious. The question that lay dormant in the back of her mind was whether or not he would ask for another fun night. She wouldn't have objected. The way Nikki took care of her was unforgettable. Rhonda wanted to approach the subject but decided that she would wait on Bernard. She wasn't gay or anything. Or was she? How could she have gotten so much enjoyment by being with another woman? It was different from any sexual experience she ever had. Even her orgasm. It seemed more intense. Rhonda wanted to be with Nikki again, but she feared approaching the subject. What would Bernard think?

Although he no longer satisfied her, she didn't want him to feel as if she were replacing him with Nikki. Maybe it was just something about Nikki that made people crazy. After all, she seemed to bring out the tiger in Bernard. It wouldn't hurt to wait a while. Bernard was like any other man. Once he got a taste of something good, he'd want another bite.

It was about 2:45 when Bernard called to tell Rhonda he would be late getting home. He had some paperwork to go over in order to get ready for a student's IEP meeting. It had to include transition plans because the student was going to be attending high school and somehow, Bernard found that his paperwork was out of compliance.

Twenty minutes after he hung up from Rhonda, his Benz pulled up at Nikki's house. He parked on the street, got out of the car and rang the doorbell. Nikki opened the door with a towel wrapped around her. Her daughter stood behind her. "Hey Lil Bit." Bernard said to the toddler. "How are you? Look what I have." He handed the girl a doll.

"What do you say?" Her mother asked.

"Thank you."

"You're quite welcome sugar."

"Go to your room Dean." Nikki watched as her daughter went to her room and closed the door. Once the door was shut, Nikki let the towel drop to the floor exposing her full figure body. She walked to her bedroom with Bernard right on her heels.

"What the hell happened to you last night?" She asked.

"I couldn't get away." He answered. "You know that I would have been here if I could have." He lay on the bed after removing his clothes. Bernard put his hands on his magic stick and started shaking it. It was not bone hard like it had been during the threesome.

"Get it up for me Baby."

She fell down between his legs, grabbing his magic stick in her hands. She took him in and out of her mouth. His magic stick got harder as her head bobbed up and down on it.

"Baby, you don't know how much Daddy needs you. Take care of your man. Do you like the way I fuck you in the mouth?"

"Uh Huh!" she managed to get out. Nikki continued to suck Bernard and could feel that he was nearing a climax.

"Oh! Yeah Baby!" He screeched. "Let me nut in your mouth." He grabbed her head and pushed it down as his legs straightened and became stiff. "Aww! Aww! Yeah!" He yelled as he spilled his milk into her mouth. She swallowed his fluids. When she released his magic stick, she spread the rest of his fluids around her lips and over her face. Then she got up and walked beside the bed.

"Okay. You have to leave now."

"What? What about you? Baby, I want you to get off." He looked at her not quite understanding what was going on.

"Next time Boo." She said. "Right now I want to ask a question."

"Sure! What is it."

"When are you going to leave her?"

Bernard looked away. He was speechless. This conversation was one he didn't want to have. He loved his wife. She had stuck by him and he had no plans of giving her up. Not for Nikki, not for anyone.

"I SAAAAID" She screamed. "When in the fuck are you going to leave her? Don't play with me muthafucka. I did every damn thing you asked me to do. Don't spoil it! WHEN MUTHAFUCKA?" She picked up a brush that was laying on the dresser and threw it at Bernard's head. "Ten days muthafucka. Not a day longer. Now get the hell out of my house!"

Bernard grabbed his pants. "Let me clean up and I'll leave."

"Hell no! Wash your ass when you get home!" Nikki picked up his shoes and threw them at him before taking her right arm to swoop everything off of the dresser and onto the floor. "GET OUT!" She yelled.

Bernard hurried to put on his clothes and get out the door. When Dean heard the door close, she came out of her bedroom. "I'm thirsty Mama."

Nikki poured her a half glass of cherry fruit punch from the pitcher in the refrigerator. When she handed the glass to her daughter, it slipped through her hands, spilling fruit punch on the kitchen floor.

"I'm sorry Mama." The toddler stepped back.

In an instant, Nikki backhanded the girl across the room. "Look what the hell you did! Look at this damn mess!" She yelled. "I should make you lick it up. You spoil everything!"

Dean curled up in the corner afraid to move. She hadn't forgotten about the time she put on her mama's lipstick. Nikki had put her hands in hot water to remind her not to touch things that didn't belong to her. She cringed when Nikki walked towards her.

"Mama's sorry baby. Why did you make me do that? You always make Mama do stuff. You have to be good Baby. Okay? Mama loves you." She picked Dean up and rocked her until she cried herself asleep.

Once she put Dean in bed her mind wandered back to Bernard. She mumbled to herself. "I won't let that muthafucka spoil it."

Chapter Eight

◇◇

Rhonda was on the lounge chair watching *The Young and The Restless* when the telephone rang.

"Hello."

"Hi Rhonda. It's Nikki. I want to see you. Can you meet me tonight at the Holiday Inn? Room 206?"

"Well, I don't know. I don't know what Bernard has planned."

"I've already gotten the room and I really need to see you. Please make a way."

"What time?"

"How about 7:30. My daughter is staying over at a sleepover but I have a nosey neighbor so can you make it?"

"I'll be there." Rhonda told her."

"The door will be open. Just come on in."

Rhonda went through her closet to see what she could find to wear. She decided on jeans and a tee shirt so Bernard would not be suspicious. She called in Chinese and ate dinner with Bernard. He was rather quiet as if he had something on his mind. In fact, he had not been hounding Rhonda to make love lately. It wasn't a problem because he didn't satisfy her sexually and always left her needing more.

She just wondered if it was the stress of the job. Rhonda had heard people talk about how exceptional children's teachers burned out quicker than regular education teachers and have a higher turnover rate.

After dinner, Rhonda cleaned the kitchen while Bernard sat down to read the newspaper. She thought, *I'm really blessed. Bernard is faithful and he doesn't run the streets. I live a good life. He gives me anything I want. All he wants in return is...what? He doesn't ask for anything. So why can't I be satisfied with just being his wife? Maybe I should tell Nikki that I am not coming.* The thought was only in her mind for a few seconds when she tried to justify meeting Nikki. *Well, he did bring her into our life to help keep us together. And at least I'm not fucking some man. I just want to see what it will be like one on one and this will be the last time.*

When she finished washing the dishes she told Bernard that she was stepping out for a little while. "I promised Shemeka that I would come over so we can play catch up. I haven't seen too much of her since she fell for Robert. I'll try not to be late."

"Fine Baby. Drive carefully." She kissed him before walking out the door. It was only seven miles to the Holiday Inn. She parked in the back and prayed that she would not run into anyone she knew. She walked quickly to the elevator and got off on the second floor. Rhonda went to room 206 and opened the door. She expected to find Nikki on the bed in some kind of seductive negligee but the room was empty. A note on the bed read,

Rhonda,

I forgot something and had to run back to the store. Make yourself comfortable. Can't wait to see you.

Nikki Boo

Rhonda took her clothes off and lay on the bed. She was ready to be satisfied by a warm body. Her toys were good but they could not compare to what Nikki had to offer. She rubbed her hands over her body, not realizing how complicated her life was about to become.

Nikki came in with a Food Lion bag containing strawberries and whipped cream. She also had an overnight bag. After putting the items on the table, she fell across the bed and gave Rhonda a wet tongue kiss.

Rhonda's body tingled as Nikki sucked her neck, then her breast and moved on down her body. "Take your clothes off." She murmured. "I'm ready."

Nikki did as she was told. After she undressed, she rolled over on the bed, looking up at Rhonda. "Are you going to take care of me like I took care of you? I've been dreaming about you. Have you been taking care of my pussy?"

"Yes." Rhonda whispered while she massaged Nikki.

"This feels good but I brought the strawberries for you. Get one off the table and put some cool whip on it. Make a strawberry sundae out of me and eat me up." Nikki told her.

Rhonda got a strawberry and the whipped cream. Nikki used two fingers to part her lips so Rhonda could insert the strawberry. She sprayed the whipped topping on the strawberry and on Nikki's hairs in the shape of a heart. While she ate the strawberry sundae, her hands moved to her own opening. When Nikki started to moan and squirm, Rhonda took the toy she had brought and stuck it in Nikki on a low speed. Then she increased the speed while licking Nikki.

"Damn! Shit! That's good. Oh! Oh! Rhooonda! Awww! Shit!"

Rhonda turned the Beaver to its highest speed. She stopped eating Nikki and let the toy take control. Nikki grabbed her with both hands while trembling uncontrollably. She released herself all over the Beaver. "Oh! That's it Babe. That was good. Take it out."

"I am. I just want you to let it all out." Rhonda reduced the speed from high to medium, to low and then off. Nikki was completely satisfied. Rhonda was hers and nobody was going to spoil it.

"I'm glad that I made you feel good. You made me feel good that night we were together. I needed an outlet and you provided me with one. Bernard is a good man. Don't get me wrong. I love my husband and he loves me. He's just not giving me what I need."

Let's not talk about your husband. I'm here to make you forget him. To hell with Mr. Limp Dick. Nikki said to herself. She kissed Rhonda. "I don't want to talk about your husband. Let's concentrate on us. Do you trust me?"

"Yes. I trust you."

Nikki caressed Rhonda's body finding her way to Rhonda's sweetness. She inserted two fingers in. "Damn, I love your wetness. It turns me on. Do you want me to make love to you?"

"Yes! Please! I want you to make love to me. Make me feel good again."

Nikki made love to Rhonda until Rhonda was ready to explode. "You're going to make me cum Nikki."

"No, Not yet. Let me strap up for you again. Didn't you enjoy it the last time?"

"It was good. I'm ready to cum."

Nikki strapped up while Rhonda lay with her legs open, ready to receive her. "Do you love this dick?"

"Um! Yeah, I love it. Fuck me Nikki. Harder! Harder!"

"Whose pussy is this?"

"Yours!" Rhonda screamed. "It's yours."

Nikki stopped short of letting Rhonda cum. "Oh no! Please don't stop Nikki. Why are you stopping?"

"Because I don't want you to spoil it." She rolled over on her back. "Climb up here and ride. Look into my eyes when you cum for me."

Rhonda climbed on the dick while Nikki held onto the base with one hand and used the other hand to stimulate her clit. A long awaited orgasm escaped her body like a runaway slave escaping captivity.

"Oh my goodness! I need you. Oh yes Nikki! I'm cumming!" She wet the bed like her bladder had burst. She realized that she had just gotten a g-spot orgasm with a strap-on.

"Rhonda, I want to see more of you. I want us to keep doing this."

"Likewise! I'll see when I can get away again."

"Spend the night with me. Let's just make this night last. I want to love you over and over again. Please do this for me. I have a present for you." Nikki handed her the box from the table. It contained a pair of red crotchless panties.

"Take your shower and then put them on. I'll be waiting. Or shall I join you in the shower?"

"I'm sorry. I can't stay. Bernard will be worried. I can't just stay out all night like that. I have to plan it."

As soon as Rhonda got the words out of her mouth good, Nikki slapped her hard across the face. "Damn Bernard. Didn't I tell you that I didn't want to talk about that muthafucka? Didn't I tell you to concentrate on us? Didn't I? But you want to spoil it huh?"

Rhonda was stunned. She put her hands to her face to soothe the sting. "What in the hell is wrong with you Bitch?"

"I'm sorry. I don't know what got into me. I would never hurt you. Forgive me Baby. I just want you so bad. And I guess that I am jealous of him. Do you forgive me?" She tried to pull Rhonda into a strong embrace.

Rhonda pulled away from her. "I need to shower so I can leave." She went into the bathroom to shower. When she had gotten dressed, she took her keys and walked to the door without coming close to Nikki. "I'm leaving now. Thanks."

Nikki sat on the bed after the door shut. *Twenty...nineteen...eighteen... seventeen... sixteen... fifteen...fourteen...thirteen...twelve...eleven.* Rhonda burst in the door.

"Someone has cut two of my tires. Who would do something like that? I have to get home."

"Calm down Rhonda. You have roadside assistance. They will send someone out to change your tire."

"Change my tire! Tire! I have two damn flat tires. One damn spare. What the hell am I going to do?"

"Listen! Get yourself together. Call your husband and tell him that your friend is having a crisis and you don't want to leave her tonight. Be convincing. First thing in the morning, we will get you new tires. I'm supposed to show a house in the morning but you are more important than any potential buyer. It'll be okay. And when you get home, your husband will be at work."

Rhonda hesitated. "Well, I don't guess I have much choice." She made the call to Bernard.

Chapter Nine

When Brandi woke up on Shemeka's couch, with her head pounding. She knew that she had some decisions to make about her life. It had not been her intention to impose on her friend. It was just a difficult situation and she didn't feel like she could deal with it alone.

The whole ordeal with the prison system had been challenging. She didn't need the added stress of Anthony constantly lying to her. The ride was long and tiresome. She had to walk through a metal detector and be scanned for drugs before she could visit him.

There had been times when she took the long ass ride only to get there and find that visitation had been cancelled because the prison was on lockdown. When she visited Anthony, she was allowed to embrace him at the beginning of the visit for about three minutes and then again at the end of visitation. They were not allowed to hold hands. Brandi felt that it was humiliating but she endured it because she loved Anthony so much.

Shemeka handed her a cup of coffee. "I called the hospital to let them know you would not be in today. I also called in from work. Rhonda's on the way over."

"I wish you wouldn't have called in." Brandi told her. "You should have gone to work. You said they are short staffed already."

"I know. They'll be fine. It's Robert's day off. He's going to go in and cover for me. Besides, he's the best physical therapist we have.

Rhonda stood on the porch waiting for Shemeka to answer the door. She wanted to be supportive after Shemeka called to fill her in about Anthony. She just didn't know how much of a help she could he considering the fact that she was still in a daze from her dealings with Nikki.

She felt for sure that Nikki had flattened her tires before coming to the room. Why had that bitch slapped her like that? More importantly, why did she wake up at 3:00 in the morning with Nikki standing over the bed starring at her?

Shemeka opened the door. "Come on in."

The women embraced as they always did when they got together. Brandi's eyes were still puffed but some of the redness was gone. Her hair was a complete mess. Her makeup had run over her face and dried. Everything about her appearance showed that she had spent the night with a bottle. Rhonda and Shemeka listened while Brandi told them how much she loved Anthony and wanted to ride it out with him.

"Well if that's what you want to do then why are we here? He's lied to you time and time and time again. If he loved you half as much as you love him then he wouldn't keep lying to you. That's bullshit and you know it."

"He's just scared." She defended him. "He's afraid that I won't ride with him. That's why he lied. He just wants me to be there for him and to be faithful to him."

Shemeka stood up. "Be faithful to him? What the hell have you been if not faithful? You stay in the house unless we drag you out. Anthony is always putting you through hell. He's almost turned you into an alcoholic."

"She's right Brandi. He's always disrespecting you. That bullshit he talks is not cute worth a damn. You think he loves you so much because he is jealous and always wants to know where you are. That is not love. He is insecure and you better be careful."

Before Brandi could respond, Shemeka spoke. "Well ultimately, it is your decision. We are going to stand by you no matter what you decide to do. Just remember that whatever decision you make; you are going to have to live with."

Brandi wanted them to understand where she was coming from on the matter. "Yall don't understand. I don't expect you to because unless you've been in this situation, you wouldn't understand. The prison system strips our men of everything. They don't have the privileges of making decisions for themselves. How do you think a grown man feels when he is visiting his family and has to ask for permission to go to the restroom? How do you think he feels when he can't touch his own wife? How do you think he feels when he is told when to turn out the lights at night? It's a lot to deal with. I know that he has lied to me but I also know that he loves me and doesn't want to lose me."

"I hope you're right." Shemeka sat down. "For your sake, I really hope that you know what you are talking about. But keep in mind that prison is not meant to be a vacation at the beach. Those men have committed crimes and society says that they must be held accountable."

"We're not trying to judge him." Rhonda added. "All we want is for you to be happy. I'm glad that you have faith in him. But there are men in prison who prey on women. They are lonely and they need someone to help them pass time. There are men who know what to say to women and some of them really mean well. But it's not real. It is only an illusion."

Brandi glanced at her ringing cell phone. *Unknown Caller.* She answered and heard the familiar recording; *You will not be billed for this call. This call is from...Anthony an inmate at a federal prison. Hang up to decline the call or to accept this call press 5 now. If you wish to block future calls of this nature, press 7 now.* Brandi pushed 5 to accept the call. Rhonda and Shemeka listened in silence.

"Hello... I miss you too... Yeah, I got it. That took nearly all of my money. I can't come until payday weekend... I put money on your books for commissary... Sweetheart, you have more than a few months left. I know because I was looking on the Internet and No! I'm not checking up on you... No Baby. I believe you were going to tell me. I'm sorry... I love you. Bye."

Brandi looked at her friends who had remained silent. "Anthony didn't know he had to do those extra years. He just found out. That's why he was calling me. His sorry ass counselor knew it all along but didn't tell him until the last minute. I can tell that he's scared I'm going to walk out on him but I love him too much to do him like that."

Shemeka and Rhonda looked at each other, neither saying a word. Rhonda decided to change the subject because she was afraid she might say the wrong thing. "So tell us Shemeka, how are things going with this new man in your life?"

"He's wonderful. He's everything I ever hoped for in a man. In fact, we finally took it to the next level last night."

"You mean that after all of this time, you finally got you some?" Rhonda laughed.

"Yeah, I told you that he is a gentleman. I told him that I wanted to take it slow and he respected that. But last night, I was ready."

"Oh damn! And I fucked it up. I'm sorry that I ruined your night. I don't know what got into me. It just took me by surprise. I should have known that Anthony would never deceive me. Robert seems like a really nice guy from what I could see last night. He's not bad on the eyes either."

"So when do I get to meet this gentleman?"

"How about Friday?" Shemeka answered. "He's taking over my kitchen on Friday night. Can you stop by at around 8:00?"

"Yes. I think I can manage that. Well, I hate to bounce on you girls but I need to get out of here and get some things done. It's been real." Rhonda stood.

"I need to leave too. Thanks for everything. I love you two. Shemeka, I'm sorry if I ruined anything last night." Brandi stood and walked towards the door.

"If?" Rhonda teased. "There's no if about it. You ruined the night. She just loves you too much to tell you."

They embraced again and said their goodbyes.

Chapter Ten

◇◇

B ernard took the vibrating cell phone out of his pocket and placed it in his desk drawer. It had been vibrating all morning. He knew that Nikki wouldn't stop calling and he would eventually have to answer it or she would show up at the school.

It was not like he had deceived Nikki. She knew he was married the first night she met him. He was at the bar having a few drinks after an argument with Rhonda. She brought him a drink and asked if she could join him. They talked and he told her he was married.

She claimed to have misplaced her keys and asked him if he could give her a ride home. Looking back on it later, he wondered if her keys were ever lost.

At her house; she asked him to come in. When she got the spare key from underneath the plant on the porch, he told her that he would stay for a minute. She fixed him another drink and before long she was naked and taking his tie loose while she climbed on his lap. She kissed him and his magic stick came to life. He didn't resist when she unzipped his pants and went down on him. She made him feel needed. He used the excuse of having one too many to drink but that was the first of many secret nights.

The intercom buzzed in Bernard's room. "Mr. Simpson, you have a visitor in the office."

46

"Thank you. I'm about to go on planning. You can send the visitor to my room." The students had barely exited the room when Nikki stormed in. "Is your damn cell phone broke muthafucka? I've been calling you all morning."

"No Nikki! It's not broke but I do have a job. Speaking of jobs, why aren't you somewhere showing a damn house or something? What is it? What's so important?"

"You! You are what's so important. I want you and your wife again."

"Oh hell no. She hasn't mentioned that night since we did it. I'm not about to bring that shit up to her. Do you think Rhonda would go for that again the way we ignored her and did our own thing?"

"Whoa! Hold the fuck up. Don't ever tell me no again. Do you understand that?" She screamed as she banged her fist on his desk.

"Calm down." He spoke softly. "People are teaching in the other rooms. Are you trying to get me fired?" Bernard closed the door to his classroom.

"I'm sorry. I just don't want you to spoil things. It will be different this time. I promise. I really enjoyed that night. You and I will both take care of your wife. You don't seem willing to leave her and I am not willing to let you go so we need to make this work for us. I want to see you make her cum. Let me see how you fuck your wife."

"I don't know Nikki."

"Do it for me. Do it for your Nikki Boo."

"I can't promise anything. Let me see what I can do."

"Bernard, maybe I am not making myself clear to you. I am not asking you. I am telling you so make it happen. If not, then I will blow your damn world all to hell. And you know that I can do it." Nikki sat on his desk.

"Get down from there please. I told you that I'll see what I can do." He walked to the door and placed his hand on the knob. Nikki jumped off the desk and walked to the door.

She placed her hand on top of Bernard's. "Holiday Inn, Friday night at 7:15. If you are not there by 7:30, I will make it my business to contact your wife. Understand?"

"It's not that I don't want to Nikki. It's just going to be hard going in and asking Rhonda for another threesome. You don't know the trouble I had in getting her to agree to the first one."

"Don't fool yourself. She enjoyed it. Or were you so caught up in your own pleasure that you didn't realize I was getting your wife off?"

"Okay Nikki. I'll see what l can do." He glanced at the clock. "Oops. I have a class to teach."

Nikki walked back to his desk and picked up the scissors. She jabbed them into a stack of test papers. "What the hell is wrong with you? Do you think that I don't know your schedule? You have planning for another forty minutes. Don't try to insult my intelligence."

He felt uneasy with her hands still on the scissors. "Yeah but I have to cover for Mrs. Dunlap. She asked me if I could watch her class at the end of my planning so she can drop her car off at the garage."

"Too bad." Nikki laughed. "Forty minutes is long enough for you to fuck me dizzy." Bernard thought to himself, *You're already dizzy as hell.* "Nikki you really do need to leave. I have work to do. I'll check with Rhonda and get back with you."

"Make sure you do. I am serious about this. I want to be with you and your wife." She stood close to Bernard. "Does Nikki Boo get a goodbye kiss?"

"You know that door could fly open at any time Nikki." He told her as he silently prayed that she would hurry and leave.

She moved towards the door and stood with her back against the door. "Then do it quickly Baby." He kissed her before moving her away from the door. He put his hand on the door again to open it. Nikki squeezed his magic stick hard, "Um...um...ump! I can't wait. Make sure you don't disappoint me, or you'll hate the day you met me." She opened the door and left.

Bernard stood in the doorway looking down the hall to make sure Nikki was leaving.

He didn't trust her. Sometimes she acted like a loose cannon. He knew that he needed to find a way to get Rhonda to agree to Friday night or Nikki would cause trouble. He was beginning to regret that he ever asked her to participate in the first one. Maybe he should have found another way to spice up his marriage, but at the time, it seemed like a good idea. When he first approached Nikki with the proposition, she immediately jumped at the chance to participate. She claimed that she had always been curious about it and that she would be on her best behavior.He never intended on it being a one-time thing like Rhonda had thought, but his idea was more like once every other month to keep things interesting. Now that Nikki was making demands on him, he had to find some kind of way to discourage her without making her angry. But how? That was the question.

Chapter Eleven

R honda relaxed in the Jacuzzi as she wondered what prompted Bernard to ask for another fun night. *Does she make Bernard feel that damn good that he just has to have some more of her? Maybe it just turns him on to see me with another woman. And why is she doing it? His dick isn't all that. She just wants my sweetness and she's afraid that if Bernard isn't part of the equation, I won't come. I admit that the bitch is good. She satisfies the hell out of me but that shit about putting her damn hands in my face fucked with me.*

"Sweetheart?" Bernard cracked the door open a little. "Are you almost ready? It will soon be 6:30."

"Yes Baby." She answered. "Give me a minute." Rhonda stepped out of the Jacuzzi and toweled dry. She stood in front of the full-length mirror to admire her petite body. She had always been proud of her size and managed to maintain her weight very well. She thought that people who were overweight only put themselves at risk for other complications such as diabetes, high blood pressure, high cholesterol, and early death. It seemed ironic to her that a plus size woman turned her out. And Bernard, he'd never look at a big woman twice, but he sure was all into Nikki at the hotel.

Bernard drove to the Holiday Inn not knowing what to expect. Nikki seemed to be having problems lately. She acted like she was on edge, and he prayed that she would not slip and say the wrong thing to Rhonda.

"Rhonda, I love you. No matter what happens this evening, I want you to know that I love you more than anything in this world. Thanks for agreeing to do it one more time. I just want to make sure you enjoy yourself this time."

Nikki was getting out of her car when they pulled up. Bernard had gotten room #314. Nikki stood in front of him on the elevator and squeezed his magic stick. "Are y'all ready?"

"Yes, we're straight. How about you?" Rhonda answered.

She responded by tracing her lips with her tongue.

The room was much different from the last time. There were no candles, no rose petals, and no chocolate fountain with marshmallows, no oysters and no shrimp. Not even a bar.

Upon entering the room, Nikki started to undress. She fell back on the bed with her hands immediately spreading the lips of her pussy open. She was anxious. "Hurry up. I'm ready."

Bernard hesitated as Rhonda started to undress. When she was completely naked she laid on the king sized bed next to Nikki. Bernard remained standing and watched as Nikki rolled over on his wife and started grinding on her. He could feel his magic stick getting hard while Nikki and Rhonda kissed. They were all over each other and it turned him on.

He hurried to get out of his clothes and walked to the side of the bed. "Ump...ump!" He cleared his throat loudly.

Rhonda was determined to make her husband feel better than Nikki had made him feel. She slid Nikki to the side and positioned herself on the edge of the bed taking Bernard in her mouth. Nikki got out of the bed and walked behind him, dropping to her knees. He tightened as she spread his cheeks open and stuck her tongue in his ass. He could feel himself getting weak as hell while he enjoyed pleasure from both women. It was hard to decide which one turned him on the most but he knew that they were about to make him shoot a load. He didn't want to nut that quickly. If he shot off that quickly, he'd be through for a while.

"Wait!" He exclaimed. "Let me lay down before I fall. I don't want to cum like this. I want some pussy Rhonda. I want to cum in your hot pussy." She couldn't understand why he referred to it as pussy whenever Nikki was around. But she felt a slight satisfaction that her husband wanted to cum for her. Not like the last time when he nutted all up in Nikki. "Okay Baby."

He lay on the bed and Rhonda crawled on top of him. She noticed that his magic stick was not as hard as it had been when he fucked Nikki. She rode him while rubbing his chest.

Nikki pulled a black dildo out of her treat bag. She lay beside Bernard and inserted the dildo into her own pussy, moaning while she looked up at Rhonda riding Bernard. She inserted the dildo harder and harder while yelling "Fuck her. Fuck your wife. Take care of my pussy. Make her feel good. Go ahead. Oh! Oh! Yes Baby. Fuck her! Make me cum." Nikki reached over to squeeze Rhonda's hand. "That's it Baby. I'm cuuuuummming."

Bernard continued to enjoy his wife while Nikki trembled beside him. "Yes Baby! I love you. You feel good. Ride this dick. Ride it."

Nikki got up to walk to the foot of the bed. "Turn around Rhonda. I want you to face me while you ride his dick."

"No!" Bernard told her. "I don't want to stop. I'm about to shoot. This feels good."

At that moment, Nikki dug her fingernails deep into his thigh. Bernard could feel his skin breaking as she dug deeper.

"It's okay." Nikki said. "Let her turn around. I'm going to taste her while you fuck her. She made me feel so good and I just want to repay her."

"Oh. Okay. Turn around Boo." Bernard gave in to Nikki, not wanting to feel her fingernails in him again. He wasn't sure what her angle was but he knew not to question her.

When Rhonda got up to turn around, Bernard could feel his magic stick falling. Rhonda tried to put it back but it only bent until it finally went down. He had lost it.

Bernard was disappointed that he had let Nikki mess things up for him. Rhonda was horny and he wanted to take care of her but couldn't. Damn Nikki!

"I'm fine." Rhonda lied. "Let's just lay here a minute."

"Why don't you slip on something and run to the ABC store." Nikki suggested. "A drink will loosen all of us up and we can continue to have fun."

"The ABC store is all the way across town." Bernard told her.

"Listen up Baby. I'm tense. My daughter kept me up all night. A potential buyer decided not to purchase the house I showed her today, and I just need something to help me loosen up."

"Okay. I'll go to the store. Maybe a drink will help me to get right. I'm sorry Rhonda. I'll make it up to you." He got dressed, kissed Rhonda, then left.

Rhonda was still standing by the door when Nikki whirled her around and threw her on the bed.

"Did you enjoy him? Did you like riding that dick?" Nikki asked as she strapped up.

"Yes." Rhonda answered.

"Didn't you tell me it was my damn pussy?" Nikki's facial expression changed. "Were you going to cum for him?"

"Yes, if it hadn't gone down. That's my husband."

"Well what the hell am I?" Nikki tightened the strap on. "Do you think that you can use me to make yourself feel good and then just push me aside? Do you think I am going to let you spoil it?"

"You're taking this too far. We can't continue to do this." Rhonda told her.

Nikki climbed on the bed. "Open your muthafuckin legs. I've got all the damn dick you need right here."

"No! I'm not doing that. And when Bernard gets back, we're leaving."

Nikki pressed her body against Rhonda's. "You'll leave when in the fuck I say you can leave. Give me my damn pussy. NOW BITCH!" She used her knees to squeeze in between Rhonda's legs, forcing them apart. She shoved the dick into Rhonda's opening.

"Stop! Please." Rhonda begged.

"You said I make you feel good didn't you? Tell me it's good."

"Just stop. Get the hell off of me." Rhonda screamed.

Nikki slapped her hard. "Damnit! Tell me it's good."

Rhonda's face hurt. She could not believe this was happening to her. What the fuck was Nikki's damn problem. What was she capable of? "It's good Nikki."

"Move your ass. Work that pussy." She commanded.

Rhonda tried her best to make Nikki think she was enjoying it.

"I love you Rhonda. Please don't hurt me. I won't spoil it. Please. I just don't want you to hurt me." Nikki began crying.

Rhonda was confused. Nikki had serious problems. "I'm not going to hurt you. Let me up so we can talk."

"Not until you cum. I need for you to cum for me. I won't let you spoil it. Cum for me."

Rhonda made her body tremble as if she was getting an orgasm. "Ah! That feels good. You're making me cum. That's it Nikki." Rhonda faked.

Nikki took the dick out before grabbing Rhonda's head and forcing the dick into her mouth. Rhonda sucked it while Nikki held on to her head pushing it hard back and forth. She used both hands to grab Rhonda's kinky twist in order to lead her to the corner of the room. She backed up so the dick would fall out of Rhonda's mouth.

Then she knocked Rhonda to the floor and kicked her while Rhonda curled into a knot. "You're mine. That pussy is mine. All mine. Don't ever forget that shit again." Nikki kicked her once more.

"Stop! You're hurting me Nikki." Tears streamed down Rhonda's face.

Nikki helped her off the floor. "Oh my goodness Baby, I'm sorry." She kissed Rhonda's tears. "I love you Baby. Look what you made me do. Why did you make me do that? You have to be good. I don't want to hurt my baby. Nikki Boo loves you. Can you be good?"

Rhonda nodded. Nikki stood looking at her. She placed her hand around Rhonda's throat and backed her against the wall. With one hand on her throat, she used the other hand to rub over Rhonda's body. When she got to Rhonda's sweetness, she stuck her finger in Rhonda's sweetness fast and hard. "This is my damn pussy. Give it away again and we are going to have problems."

Rhonda's heart pounded so fast that she thought it was going to jump out of her chest. She had to be hearing things because there was no way this bitch could be serious. Once she left the room there was no way that she'd ever see this psycho bitch again.

"Ah! Yeah! Your pussy feels so good. I can't share this with any damn body. It's mine."

Bernard opened the door to see Nikki fingering his wife. "I guess you couldn't wait for me huh?"

"You did take a long time." Rhonda answered. "But actually, I feel a migraine coming on. Will you take me home?"

"Sure Baby."

Rhonda remembered that she was supposed to stop by Shemeka's to meet Robert. *Not tonight.* She thought. *Brandi already messed up one night for her. I just want to go the fuck home.* "Let me slip on my clothes. I'll shower when we get home."

Nikki kissed Bernard on the face. She walked to Rhonda and tongued her. "Damn!" Bernard said. "I can see that you two enjoyed yourselves. Thanks Nikki for saving the night. Bye."

Chapter Twelve

◇◇

S hemeka glanced at her watch. It was 9:30 and Rhonda was a no show. She had hoped that her friend would stop by to meet Robert. The two had waited on dessert so they could share it with her while they got acquainted.

Robert got up and walked to the kitchen. I guess your friend is not coming huh? She might have gotten tied up. Would you like dessert?"

"Not right now." She answered. Shemeka swayed her body to the music that was playing softly on her CD player. Robert took her by the hand and danced with her in the dining room. They danced on into the kitchen.

Robert rubbed his hands over her ass and squeezed it as he enjoyed the soft texture. She stood still as he kissed her in front of the kitchen sink while taking her pants loose. She wiggled out of her pants as Robert helped her to take them down. He sucked on her neck and she tilted her head back. "Robert, I'm really feeling you."

"I'm feeling you too baby. You're everything I need in a woman. You're genuine and you're wholesome. Meka, I love you." As she was about to speak, he covered her mouth with his hands. "Don't say anything. Just let me love you. Please Meka. That's all I want is to love you."

He picked Shemeka up and sat her on the counter. He kissed her and touched her in all of the right places. He kissed her down her legs and put her foot in his mouth. He sucked her toes as the music continued to play softly in the background. He squatted as he moved his tongue from her toes up her legs to where she wanted him to be. He spread her legs and begin to eat his dessert.

She was surprised that she actually enjoyed it. Only one other man had eaten her before and she didn't get anything from it. She had come to the conclusion that oral sex was overrated. But this was different and Robert was really making her feel good. She grabbed the edge of the counter as she squirmed and moaned.

"Robert." She managed to say. "I need to tell you something." She could hear the sound of him unzipping his pants. "Robert...I've never sucked a dick before. I don't know how. I love you and I am willing to learn. Oh! Damn, you're making me feel so good."

"Don't worry about it Baby. I love you too. I'm glad that you haven't had your mouth on a nigga." He leaned her back on the counter and stood so he could put his dick in her. He stroked her long and deep, bringing her to a climax. He squeezed her legs.

"Meka...damn! That's good. Bay...bee! I'm cumming with you. Whew! I love you."

Shemeka was too weak to move. Robert took his finger to remove some of her fluids from his dick. He licked his finger. "Your milk is so sweet Baby, just lay there sweetheart. Let me clean you up. I got this." Robert went to the bedroom and returned with a wet soapy washcloth. He took great care with washing Shemeka up. He took the washcloth into the bathroom to rinse the soap off and came back to wipe her again.

"I love you Boo." She lay on the counter until Robert returned from wiping himself.

"Spend the night with me." She said. "We don't have to get up in the morning."

"Actually, I do have to get up in the morning. I promised my friend Drake that I would drop him off at the airport in the morning. He has to catch a 6:00 a.m. flight. I'm sorry Boo. Next time. I promise." He kissed her before leaving. He knew that she was not experienced but he loved her enough to be patient. He would teach her everything she needed to know. Maybe next time, they would try a sixty-nine. That would be a start.

Chapter Thirteen

◇⋈⋈⋈⋈⋈⋈⋈⋈⋈⋈⋈⋈⋈⋈⋈⋈⋈⋈⋈⋈⋈⋈⋈⋈⋈⋈⋈⋈◇

Brandi pulled her car up at the comer of Trade St. and Independence Blvd. She slowed down to check out her surroundings and see if she could spot Jody. She would have to look hard because he always wore black at night. It was 1:00 a.m. and Jody was usually never late. Two minutes later she saw Jody walking and stopped her car. Jody slid into the passenger's seat of her car and she drove off.

"Do you have it?" She asked.

"What's my damn name? Damn right I have it. Do you have my money?"

She put her hand in her bra and pulled out a wad of bills. After Jody counted the money he gave her the cocaine from his pocket. "Thanks Sexy." He squeezed her breast.

"Don't do that Jody." She hit his hand. "I've told you about that shit!"

"Damn! That nigga got you on locks like that girl? It's a damn shame cause you a fine babe and I could do things for you."

Brandi ignored him and drove two blocks before dropping him off.

He opened the car door. "Call me any time Boo. Hey! If you need somebody to keep that bed warm for you until Ant gets home, I'm putting in first bid." He closed the door and Brandi sped away.

Once she got home, Brandi went to the kitchen table. She had fixed the cocaine for Anthony so many times that she could do it with her eyes closed. No matter how many times she did it, she was just as nervous as if it were the first time. After securing the drugs in condoms, she went to bed. Looking up at the ceiling, she told herself, *This is going to have to be the last time for this. I know that Anthony is going to be mad but I'm tired of this shit and I'm tired of dealing with Jody. I'm tired of him always grabbing on me and touching me.*

"What do you see in that loser?" He had once asked her. "Big Daddy will take care of you. Don't you need some dick while that nigga is locked up? Ya better let Big Daddy knock a dent in it. Its goanna grow old."

Brandi would always reject his advances but he would sometimes grab her or touch her inappropriately. Once, he had gotten in the car and pulled his dick out. "Suck it for me Baby. You can keep your money. I have plenty of money. Put your sweet lips down here and let me see what you can do."

Brandi didn't like Jody and she didn't want to continue to deal with him or his drugs. She knew that she was playing a dangerous game by taking drugs into the prison. She was putting her career in jeopardy each time she did it.

No one at the hospital where she worked knew that she was involved with an inmate. She liked to keep her personal life separate. It was nobody's business for one thing. People had a tendency to judge men who were locked up. She didn't feel like explaining her choice. She knew that a few people would be curious to know how a registered nurse let herself get involved with a convicted felon. Brandi did not want to go through any of that. She was grown and made her own decisions.

It was difficult enough dealing with those bitches at the prison. They looked at her like she was doing something wrong by being with a black man. She loved Anthony enough to deal with the haters, rolling their eyes like they were all of that. How could a bitch think she was all of that with a head full of fake ass weave, false fingernails, and a fucked up shape to go along with it. Ghetto fabulous. Those were the women who got used.

Their men had three and four different women stringing them along. At least with Anthony, she knew that she was the only one visiting him.

Brandi closed her eyes to prepare for the long ride. It was getting to be tiresome taking that ride every other weekend. Denise was going to ride with her again but she was really only company because she didn't help with the driving. At least she had the decency to find things to do while they visited. Anthony was her cousin but she always waited until Sunday to visit with him so he and Brandi could have time alone. This was a good thing because Brandi didn't want Denise knowing what she was doing. Besides, after this time she was out of the game.

Chapter Fourteen

◇◇◇

"**M**r. Simpson?" The intercom in Bernard's room called out to him. "You have a message in the front office. Please stop by the office before you leave today."

"Okay! Thank You." He answered.

Bernard picked up his message after all of the buses had been called and the students were gone, He read, *Mr. Simpson, your wife called and wants you to stop by Chic N' Ribs to pick up the order she called in.* He loved the ribs from Chic N' Ribs. The ribs were so tender they would fall off the bones. His mouth watered just thinking about them.

He got in his car and went to pick up the ribs. As he walked across the parking lot, a green sedan coming out of the parking lot sped up and ran him down. The force of the impact knocked him in the air and he landed on the hood of another car in the parking lot. The driver of the green sedan sped away. As the alarm from the parked car sounded, pedestrians gathered around.

"Call an ambulance." Someone yelled.

"He's not breathing. I think he's dead." Another bystander screamed.

When the ambulance arrived, Bernard was still on the hood of the car. Someone had covered him with a blanket. The ambulance attendant took his pulse. "It's faint. I'm barely getting a pulse. BP is two hundred over ninety-five." Curious bystanders moved in to get a closer look. "Stand back please. We need room to work." The attendants put a brace on Bernard's neck, started him on an IV and put an oxygen mask on him. He was then slid onto a stretcher and put in the ambulance. He was rushed to Carolina's Regional Medical Center.

Rhonda was at the Beauty salon when her cell phone rang. She hesitated in answering it since she did not recognize the telephone number. If she had been home, she would have had the advantage of checking the caller ID but since she forwarded her calls to her cell phone, she had no idea who would be calling. She decided not to answer it and call the number back after she left the salon. A few seconds after the telephone stopped ringing, it beeped signaling a message had been left. She dialed one and listened to her voice mail.

Mrs. Simpson, This is Carolina's Regional Medical Center. Your husband Bernard has been in an accident. He was brought in by ambulance. Please contact the hospital as soon as possible. Thank You.

Rhonda closed her cell phone and left the salon without saying a word to anyone. She rushed to the hospital praying that Bernard was not seriously injured. She pulled into a parking space at the Emergency entrance and ran in.

"May I help you?" The receptionist at the desk asked her.

"Yes, my name is Rhonda Simpson. Someone called and said my husband Bernard was in an accident. The ambulance brought him in. Where is he? Is he okay?"

"Calm down Mrs. Simpson. Let me check on your husband's condition." She went through the charts on her nurses' station, before walking down the hall. Rhonda started to follow the nurse. "Wait here. I'll be right back."

Rhonda waited for the nurse. She looked around the crowded room. Everybody looked near death. A man held a bloody towel to his head.

She wondered if he had fallen or if someone had hit him in the head. She looked up to see the short stocky nurse walking towards her.

"Mrs. Simpson, the doctor will be with you shortly. Have a seat please."

Soon, the doctor came out and extended his hand to Rhonda. "Hello Mrs. Simpson, I'm Dr. Koontz. I'll be treating your husband. He was brought in with broken ribs and head trauma. He has swelling on his brain. He was unable to communicate with the police. We had to sedate him because he was in severe pain. He is in the Intensive Care Unit. His vital signs are stable but we have him listed in critical condition."

"What happened?"

"He was hit by a car in the parking lot of Chic N Ribs. The driver kept going."

"What? Oh my goodness. What was he even doing at Chic N Rib? I cooked pork chops today."

A uniformed police officer approached Rhonda and introduced himself.

"Who could have done something like this? What kind of a sick bastard would hit someone and leave them to die?" She asked the officer.

"Ma'am, I don't know. We're doing all we can to find the person that did this to your husband. Does Mr. Simpson have any enemies?"

"No! He's a teacher. He works in the community. He doesn't bother anyone. I don't have any idea who would do this? Why would anyone want to hurt Bernard?" She began to cry.

"Is there anyone I can call for you?" He asked.

Nikki came down the hall walking fast. "Rhonda, I just heard about Bernard. How is he?"

"Critical!" Rhonda answered.

The officer handed Rhonda his card. "If you think of anything or of anyone who might have wanted to hurt your husband, give me a call. We'll catch this person. Don't worry."

Nikki hugged Rhonda. "I'm here for you. I know that I messed things up for us but let me be here for you. I'll get us a cup of coffee."

Rhonda was hesitant. She didn't trust Nikki. *This woman has some damn issues. She thought to herself. Hell! As far as I know, she could have been the one who tried to kill Bernard. Nobody can tell me that the bitch didn't cut my tires. I just wonder how far she would go.*

Nikki returned with two cups of coffee. She was sympathetic and insisted on waiting with Rhonda. The doctor came out to inform her that there had been no change in Bernard's condition. He was slipping in and out of consciousness. The nurse advised Rhonda to go home and get some rest. She assured her that she would call if there were any changes but Rhonda refused. The two women stayed in the waiting room. Rhonda dozed off and awakened to discover that Nikki was no longer there. *Good.* She thought. *She finally left.*

Rhonda got up to go check on Bernard. She hoped he was conscious. She would ask him if he saw who hit him. More importantly, she wanted to know why he was at Chic N Ribs since he usually called home, to see if she had cooked before stopping by an eatery. When she walked into the room, Nikki was in the room walking towards his bed.

"What the hell are you doing in here?" Rhonda screamed.

Nikki was startled. "Calm down." She whispered. "I was just checking on him. What do you think I was doing? You were resting so peacefully. He seems to be doing fine. Come on. Let me take you home. There's nothing more that you can do here. He's in the best of care. Trust me. All I want to do is make sure you are all right. I have my truck parked outside."

"Thanks Nikki." She answered. "I have my car. Go home. I'll be fine."

"If you say so. I just hate to leave you here alone. Call me if you need me." Nikki told her. She hugged Rhonda before leaving the hospital. Rhonda went back to the waiting room where she called Shemeka. Brandi was out of town visiting her fiancée.

Chapter Fifteen

◇◇

B randi was twenty minutes from the prison when Shemeka called to tell her about Bernard. She wished that she could be there for her friend but Anthony was expecting her. They had run out of phone time so he couldn't call for another month. He would have a fit if he was dressed for visit and Brandi didn't show up.

She told Shemeka that she would shorten her visit to a one-day visit instead of staying the full weekend. As soon as the visit was over, she would check with Rhonda to see if there had been any changes in Bernard's condition.

Brandi was one of the first women to arrive at the prison. Two other women were already there waiting for the officers to put out the visiting forms. They would not put them out before 8:00 and sometimes they would mess around and be ten or fifteen minutes late putting them out. Others started to pile into the lobby and the women sat impatiently waiting for the officers. Once the officers put the papers out, the women took a visitation form and filled it out before being seated. After fifteen minutes the officers started to process visitors. When Brandi's name was called, she approached the counter.

She knew the routine all too well. She removed her jewelry, along with her shoes and placed them in the large container on the belt with her two rolls of quarters to be scanned. The quarters had to be secured in a clear

Ziploc bag because no purses were allowed. The prison only allowed you to bring in twenty-five dollars, which could be in the form of quarters or dollar bills. The vending machines also took five-dollar bills. Brandi often took ten or fifteen extra dollars in her bra because she wasn't sure how many trips she would have to make to the vending machine. She gave the officer at the desk her drivers' license, got her hand stamped and walked through the metal detector before being led to the next stop. She had to place her hand under the florescent light to show her stamp. A metal door opened, and the correctional officer led her to the visiting room.

Brandi had to place her hand under the light in the visiting room before walking to the desk and giving the officer her name. Once she did this, she was instructed where to sit while she waited on Anthony.

He came out a short time later and the two embraced and kissed. She explained to him that she loved the hell out of him and would never abandon him.

"Marry me Brandi. I don wan ta wait til I'm out. Dey will be performin marriages agin in October. I'll send ya da papers ta fill out and ask my counselor wat we hafta do."

"Anthony, I don't know. I love ya but I want a church wedding with all of my family and friends there." She told him. "Besides, it feels like we are already married. What would a piece of paper change?"

"It wud make ya mine Baby. Legally mine. Go head and take care of dat Boo and den we'll talk some more."

Brandi picked up the clear Ziploc bag that contained her money. She walked to the vending machines. Once she was there, she slid her hand around the band of her pants, cuffed two condoms, and slid them up the edge of her sleeve. She popped the microwavable popcorn and poured it in a paper plate to bring to Anthony. She handed him the plate while slipping him the condoms. Anthony eased his shirt loose in the back and after some careful maneuvering suit cased the condoms up his ass.

"Boo, this is going to have to be the last time. I can't keep doing this. I don't want to. And that damn Jody...shit! I hate him with his nasty ass."

Anthony sat up in his chair. "Wat did Jody do? I know damn well dat punk ass bitch ain't don disrespect me."

"Nah Baby." She lied. "I just don't like him." She didn't want to lie to Anthony but she couldn't tell him about how Jody was always feeling on her. He would find a way to blame her for it or question why she never mentioned it before. She didn't want to be stressed out any more than she already was. Brandi felt uncomfortable with the cocaine on her. The sooner she passed it off to Anthony the sooner she could relax. She felt like the correctional officers were watching her. "Anthony, I think they know something. Every time I look up at the desk, it seems like they are watching me."

"Dey ain't thinkin bout ya woman. Hell, dey always watchin ya. Dey wandar wat ya fine ass doin wit me." He laughed. "Stop actin so nervous and act natural. Ya gon brin tention to us if ya actin all jittery. Now tell me what's been goin on."

"Nothing really. I had a long ass-boring ride here. Denise slept most of the way. She's at the room. I told her that she can come the last hour of visit because I won't be able to stay the weekend. Rhonda needs me. I'll tell you about it when I get back. I'm going to get this off of me."

"Thanks. I love ya Baby. I just don wan nobody tryna play me. Ya understand dat don ya? Dere are niggas out dere who will try ya. It's really up ta ya to say no. I no dat I hav a queen and I don hav nunthin ta worry bout."

Brandi retrieved two more condoms while at the vending machine and came back to pass them to Anthony. She explained to him that Bernard had been hit by a car and his prognosis was not good so she needed to get back to check on Rhonda.

"I won't be able to come back tomorrow Boo so I know that you won't be able to get all of this." She told him.

"Nah Boo! Dat's stupid as hell. Ya got it on ya. Go back ta get anuther sandmich. Ya not takin dat back wit ya. Wat are ya gon do wit it? Ya said dis is ya las time bringin me sumthin."

"I know Anthony but I have three more condoms. Just manage with the ones you have because I don't want to keep getting up like that."

He gave her a stern look. "Woman, do wat da hell I told ya to do. Don question me. Ya know I don like dat shit. Hurry up Boo. I love ya."

Brandi went back to the vending machine and purchased a chicken sandwich. She came back with three condoms and passed them to him. One... two...then three. "Is dat it? Is dat all of it?" He asked. "Cuz you ain't leavin wit none of dat Babe"

"Yes Baby. That's it."

"Good cuz I am uncomfortable as hell. I'm having a hard time gettin dis last one in. All dem da same size ain't dey?"

"Yes Baby. I made them all the same size." She answered him.

"Don worry bout it. I'll get it in. I don hav a choice cuz dey will do a strip search when I go to da back. And yes, dat includes a cavity check. Ah! It's in. Whew! We can relax now."

"Anthony. I love you so much. I will be glad when you get out of here! It's been hard not having you with me. I know that you are worth the wait though. Don't ever think that I will leave you because I am with you 100%. We are in this together. Let me run to the bathroom and I'll be back in a minute."

"Okay. Hurry back Baby." He told her.

Brandi was getting ready to go to the restroom when she heard keys. The Duty Officer and the Lieutenant came in the door on the right. Two more officers came from the door on the left and one came from the back. They all walked towards where she and Anthony were seated. Brandi froze. She felt her heart pounding as she prayed to God that the officers would walk past her. The men stopped in front of them.

"Woodruff!" The Duty Officer said. "We need for you to come with us." Anthony got up quietly as the men surrounded him and led him to the back.

Brandi sat in the visitation room waiting to see what would happen. After Anthony was gone for over twenty minutes, she was beginning to panic. She wanted to leave but how could she? She would have to get permission to leave and she would look guilty of something if she asked to leave before Anthony returned.

Soon, two men came out of the back and escorted her to a room. They informed her that they caught her on camera passing contraband to Anthony. They asked her what she had given him. She denied the allegations. They told her that she could be charged but they were giving her a chance to cooperate. She continued to deny everything. She was grilled for forty-five minutes until the Duty Officer came in and said she was free to leave.

Brandi was escorted to the door and put her hand under the light to be checked. The door soon opened and she was escorted to the lobby. She looked at all of the razor wire above the fence. No one could escape the prison without being cut to death. She was thankful that she was allowed to leave. Those inmates were like caged animals, and she had come close to a life of incarceration. For what? Nothing was worth losing even a day of freedom. When she got to the lobby, she was given her driver's license back after she took her personal belongings from the lockbox and turned the key in to the officer at the desk.

Her mind was a ball of confusion. *What happened to Anthony? Did he tell them anything? What are they going to do to him? Are they going to charge him later? When will I be able to see him again? Shit! Are they going to charge me later?* She asked herself. She remembered Anthony telling her about another guy who was suspected of smuggling in contraband. He was put in a dry cell and had to have three clean shits before he could leave. She knew that if they put Anthony in a dry cell that his shit would not come out clean. It would be a month before he would even be able to make a telephone call. It would be six more days before the first. There was nothing she could do but wait. The tears rolled down her cheeks as she cranked up her car and pulled out of the parking lot.

Chapter Sixteen

◇◇

N ikki called the hospital to check on Bernard's condition. She wondered if he would pull through. "Hello, I'm calling to check on Bernard Simpson. He was brought in yesterday and is in the ICU unit. Can you tell me his condition please?"

"Ma'am. I'm sorry but we are not allowed to give out that information over the telephone. He has a family member in the waiting room. I will be glad to transfer your call."

"Yeah! Go ahead." Nikki told her.

"Hello. Intensive Care waiting room. May I help you?"

"Sure." Nikki answered. "I' was calling to check on the condition of Bernard Simpson. May I speak with someone from the Simpson family please?"

Nikki was placed on hold until she heard another voice on the other end of the phone.

"Hello. This is Shemeka, may I help you?"

"I want to speak to Rhonda Simpson." Nikki was beginning to get agitated.

"I'm sorry. She is resting at the moment. This is her friend Shemeka. May I ask whose calling?"

"Hell no!" Nikki screamed. "You can't ask me shit. Who the hell are you? I never heard her talk about a damn Shemeka. You better watch yourself Bitch!" Nikki slammed the telephone down on the receiver. She clutched her fist together and started talking to herself. *What the hell is going on? I'm not having this damn shit. Not having it at all.* She paced around the living room stopping to hit her fist on the table.

Dean came out of her bedroom. "Mommy, I'm hungry."

"Hungry?" Nikki yelled. "Didn't I give you a bowl of cereal? You eat too damn fast. Take your time and chew your food. I'm trying to think. Get the hell out of here so I can think."

Dean stood there looking at Nikki. When Nikki drew her hand back, the child ran to her room. She picked up the half eaten peanut butter sandwich she had left over from the night before. Dean crawled behind her nightstand and took small bites. The doorbell rang and startled her.

"Who the hell is it?" Nikki yelled.

"Who are you expecting?" The voice answered back.

She ran to the door and quickly opened it. "Oh my goodness. Where have you been? I've missed you. I thought you were mad at me. I know that my attitude was fucked up the last time I saw you but I'm trying to get things together." Nikki burst into tears. "I'm trying Robert."

He put his arms around her. "What's wrong? I can tell that something's wrong. I almost didn't stop because your car wasn't out there."

"I know. It's in the shop. I'm driving my truck. I don't know how much more of this shit I can take."

"What's wrong? Tell me." He begged.

"Muthafucka's trying to play me. I don't like for nobody to fuck with what is mine."

"Sweetheart, is it Dean? Are you having a hard time with Dean? Where is she?" He asked wanting to make sure Dean was all right.

"She's in her room. I'll go get her." Nikki walked down the hall and returned with Dean who smiled when she saw Robert.

"Hey!" She said and ran into his arms.

"Hello there pretty girl." He said to Dean. "What happened to your arm?"

"She fell!" Nikki blurted out. "She's clumsy as hell. She fell and broke her arm in two places. My baby is going to have to be more careful. Mama doesn't like to see her baby hurt."

"I don't like to see her hurt neither." Robert responded. "When she hurts, I hurt. Children can't help themselves. It's up to us to protect them. I came by to see if Dean wanted to go to the fair." He turned to look at Dean. "How does that sound to you Lil Bit? Would you like to go to the fair and see what they have to ride? I haven't had a candy apple in a mighty long time."

Dean smiled and looked first at Robert, then at Nikki. "Can I? Please. I'll be good."

"Yes Dean. You can go. Put your shoes on. You know that you can always go with Robert."

Dean came out of the room with her shoes on and anxious to leave with Robert. He always treated her nice and any time he took her out, they would always stop for ice cream before he brought her back.

"Can I get a hot dog at the fair?" She asked. "I'm hungry."

Robert looked at Nikki and shook his head. "Yes Baby. You can have all of the hotdogs you want. Get in the car and wait for me. I'll be right out Sweetie."

"Okay." Dean walked out the door.

Robert stood directly in Nikki's face. "You better get your act together. Don't let me come here again and find Dean hungry. It doesn't take much for you to fix her something to eat. And what's up with these accidents? She is never clumsy when I have her. Whatever personal problems you are dealing with, I won't let you take it out on her. If I have to bring her to live with me, then I will."

Nikki was speechless. When Robert closed the door, the telephone rang. Nikki walked to the table and snatched the telephone out of the wall before slinging it across the room. "Damn you Robert!" She screamed. "Since when are you a damn expert? You didn't take care of me. I was the one who came through for us."

Minutes later, the doorbell rang. Nikki ran to the door. "What you want now?"

She asked as she swung the door open. On the other side of the door stood an elderly white woman with thick glasses; she was dressed in a suit and carried a briefcase.

"I don't want any." Nikki told her.

"I beg your pardon." The woman replied.

"I don't want any. Whatever the hell you are selling, I don't want any." Nikki tried to close the door. The woman put her hand up to keep the door from closing.

"I'm sorry. I'm Mrs. Cutshaw with Children's Protective Services. Are you Nicole Harris?"

"Yeah why?" Nikki asked her. "What do you want?"

"May I come in please?" She asked.

"Yeah. Might as well. If I don't, you are only going to come back with some more white people. Make it quick. I was on the way out. As I asked you before, what do you want? I'm tired of you damn people bugging me."

"Miss Harris, I've been assigned to your case."

"What case? I don't have a damn case." Nikki interrupted her.

"As you know there have been some concerns about the injuries that your daughter has had. I am not accusing you or anyone else of hurting her but anytime there is a suspicious injury of a child, we have to look into it. Your daughter's safety is our number one concern. During the course of my investigation, I will conduct home visits to make sure that everything is going well, and the living conditions are suitable. During my unannounced visits, I will also do a body check of your daughter. At the end of my investigation, I will report my findings to the Department of Social Services. Do you have any questions, Miss Harris?"

"No, I don't have any questions." Nikki said in a disgusted tone of voice. "Yall are always messing with black people, looking for something to criticize. My house is spotless, I have a fridge full of food, my daughter has a room full of toys, and I love my daughter. What more do you want from me? No! I don't have any questions. Now if you are finished, BYE!" She walked to the door and opened it.

Mrs. Cutshaw walked to the door. She took a card from her purse and handed the card to Nikki. "If you have any questions, concerns, or even feel yourself becoming overwhelmed, please don't hesitate to call."

When she left, Nikki walked over to the window with tears streaming down her face She tore the card into small pieces. "Why do they keep fuckin with me? Why does every damn body want to fuckin make me do shit? That damn bitch Shemeka is trying to take my woman from me. Robert won't come out and say it but he wants to take my daughter from me. Rhonda is acting like I have some kind of a disease or something. Bernard has his stupid ass laid up in the hospital getting sympathy. His ass should have died. FUCK!! Everybody is trying to spoil it." She shouted.

Nikki dried her eyes and splashed her face. She decided that crying would not help and she had to make something happen. She thought to herself, *Nobody gives you a damn thing. You have to go out and take what you want. And that's what I'm going to do.* She picked up her keys and walked out the door.

Chapter Seventeen

◇◇

B randi knew that she looked bad. She had not slept since her incident at the prison. Anthony had not been able to call her so she didn't know what was going on. *Maybe he was able to call and decided not to call her. Maybe he was calling some other woman. Maybe he blamed her for them getting caught. Maybe he didn't need her anymore and therefore he no longer wanted her. Maybe the prison was on lockdown and he couldn't use the telephone.* She didn't know what to think.

Brandi pulled her red Toyota Camry into the parking deck of the hospital. She wondered if she should tell Rhonda what had gone down. Would Rhonda criticize her and tell her how stupid she was? Would Rhonda tell her that Anthony is no good and had only used her? She didn't need to hear any of that. She felt bad enough without being lectured. Anthony had not used her. She was a grown woman and she made the decision to go along with his plan knowing full well that there were risks. Yes! It was a stupid ass decision but she was not the first to make a stupid decision. Brandi decided that her friend had enough to deal with. She would not add to it.

The hallways on the Intensive Care Unit floor were cold. A bulb had blown in the waiting room, which made it resemble a funeral parlor. Shemeka and Rhonda were having a cup of coffee when Brandi walked in. It was ten minutes before the next scheduled visiting time. Rhonda explained to Brandi that Bernard was now conscious but unresponsive due to being heavily sedated. There was no apparent brain damage and they had stopped the internal bleeding. Each time Rhonda had gone in to visit, he opened his mouth in an attempt to try to speak. Although he was struggling to talk, she was unable to make out his words.

When it was time for visit, Nikki stepped into the room. Rhonda introduced her to Brandi and Shemeka. She looked Shemeka over from head to toe before putting her arms around Rhonda.

"How is he?" She asked.

"I'm about to go in and see. You can all visit him but they only allow two people in at a time."

"I'll go in with you and your other friends can visit afterwards." Nikki stood up. "I have an appointment to show a house in half an hour."

"Yeah. Go ahead." Brandi responded. "We're fine. We'll go in after you check on him."

Bernard was still hooked to the machines with several tubes attached to him. When they entered the room, his eyes were closed. Rhonda lifted his hand and placed it in hers. She rubbed his hand. "Bernard, Honey, I'm here."

His eyes fluttered as they adjusted to the light. He looked at Rhonda and his lips formed into a slight smile. As his eyes roamed around the room, he saw Nikki standing quietly in the corner. Suddenly Bernard's body started to jerk and alarms on machines blared. A nurse rushed into the room. "He's coding!" She yelled. "Code Blue! Get a crash cart in here!"

A team of doctors and nurses ran into the room. "I'm sorry. I need for you women to step outside please." A doctor told Rhonda and Nikki.

"What's happening?" Rhonda asked. Is he going to be okay?"

"We're doing our best to help your husband ma'am but we need for you to step outside and let us work. Please!" The doctor placed his hands on Rhonda's back and edged her towards the door. Nikki had already stepped out.

Brandi and Shemeka had run out into the hall following the commotion. Shemeka held Rhonda with Rhonda's head resting on her chest. "It's going to be alright Rhonda. Just pray. He's in God's hands. I'll stay right here as long as you need me."

Nikki looked at them and thought to herself, *I'm going to have to fuck that bitch up. I see that right now. She must not know whom the fuck she's messing with.*

Brandi and Shemeka led Rhonda to a couch in the waiting room. Nikki walked behind them. "I'm sorry to leave like this but I need to show that house. I'll check with you later Rhonda."

"She'll be fine." Brandi answered.

"Nice meeting you." Shemeka added.

"Sure! Nice meeting you also." Nikki answered as she walked towards the elevator. She mumbled under her breath, "And even nicer when I get rid of your ass."

Nikki drove to her appointment wondering what she could do to get Rhonda alone. She had not expected Shemeka and Brandi to be at the hospital. Rhonda had never mentioned them before. She needed for Rhonda to be solely dependent on her. How were they going to be a family if people interfered? Hopefully Bernard would not recover and Rhonda would discover that Nikki was the best person for her.

She turned the radio off in her car so she could think. *Why in the hell is Rhonda hovering all over his ass anyway. She knows that he doesn't make her feel anything like I make her feel. She should just be herself. Yeah, I might have been her first woman and it might have started out as an experiment but hell... she loved what I put on her. She better not cross me. I know that. The pussy is MINE!* Nikki began to feel frustrated. She beat her fist on the steering wheel.

When Nikki pulled up in front of the two story house she was scheduled to show, the couple was already there waiting for her. She had to put on her pleasant face even though she was upset that she had to leave

Rhonda. If anything went wrong because she had to leave the hospital…if this gave Shemeka a chance to move in on Rhonda…if Rhonda was gone when she got back to the hospital…the couple would have to pay. Nikki would have no choice but to go to their residence and burn the house down with them in it. They would simply have to pay if they spoiled it.

Chapter Eighteen

◇◇

Shemeka was tired when she got home from the hospital. She had missed three calls from Robert. His messages left on the answering machine were sweet and understanding.

I miss you Baby but I know that your friend needs you. Meka, you make me feel things that I never felt before. I can't wait to see you Sweetheart, Boo I'm going to try to get up with you later on tonight. I want to see you.

She pressed replay after the last message. It sounded like there was a child in the background but she couldn't be sure. After pressing the replay three times, she decided to leave it alone.

A hot bath seemed like a better idea than a shower. Shemeka wanted to relax and soak in a hot tub of oils and bubbles. She lay back in the tub and closed her eyes while thinking about Robert. He was a dream come true. He had given her life meaning and it was because of him that she felt like waking up in the morning. Until he came into her life, there was no life. She would listen to Brandi and Rhonda talk about exciting things that happened in their lives. She thought it was ironic that the tables had turned.

Her life was together now. She had found her soul mate and was happy. Rhonda's husband was in the hospital and no one knew what the outcome would be. Brandi was tied to Anthony who had lied to her repeatedly and who may end up being incarcerated indefinitely.

We should all be happy. This is just not fair. Shemeka thought. *Rhonda having to deal with Bernard being hospitalized. Brandi having to deal with Anthony doing more time. Why can't everybody be as happy as I am? I love Robert so much I never thought I would love a man the way I love him.*

She finished her bath and felt between her legs. She was hairy and knew she needed to shave. Her hairs grew fast and had become long enough to plait. Just as she stepped out of the tub, the doorbell rang. She put on her bathrobe before going to the door.

"Who is it?" She asked through the door.

"It's Robert." He answered. "I was out riding and thought I would take a chance on you being home."

"Just a minute." She told him as she hurried to get the deadbolt unlocked. She didn't mind her naked body which was dripping wet. Come on in. I just got out of the bathtub." She stepped to the side to allow Robert to enter.

"Um...um...umph!" He muttered. "Lawd, have mercy." Robert gave Shemeka a nice wet tongue kiss.

"Let me get a towel and dry off. Have a seat Boo. I'll be right back. I wasn't expecting to see you tonight." She turned to walk towards the bathroom. Robert stopped her.

"No! Lie on the couch and let me dry you off. I can't stay long but I took a chance that you would be home. I miss you and I want to see you. Actually I'm supposed to be at the bowling alley with the guys but I missed you so much that I wanted to see you."

The room was dimly lit by the light in the hallway. "Let me get some light in here and a towel from the linen closet and I might just take you up on that offer to towel dry me."

"Boo, the lighting is perfect, and I don't need a towel. Did I say towel dry you? I'm going to tongue dry you. I'm already late so what the hell. I have to take out time for my woman. Just relax Sexy."

Robert kissed Shemeka on the forehead before dropping down on his knees in front of the couch. "Damn. You are gorgeous. I love you Meka. Just be patient with me Baby. You'll see how much I love you."

He lifted her foot and started licking it. Then he sucked her toes. Afterwards he licked her leg and up her thigh. He got off the floor and moved to the end of the couch. With a soft and gentle touch, he parted her legs. *What a beautiful, hairy pussy.* He thought. She sometimes kept it platted but tonight it was loose and inviting. He moved the hairs to reveal a luscious pink clitoris. He licked his finger and stuck it in her opening. After he tasted her sweetness, he licked her clit, slowly at first and then picked up speed. He fingered her as she swayed her body and moans of pleasure escaped her lips.

Shemeka wanted him badly. "Robert, put it in. Please! That feels so good. I want you in me." She was barely whispering as she begged him to make love to her.

"Not tonight Sweetheart. I can't stay." He continued to finger her. "This is for you. Give me that nut. I want you to cum before I leave."

Shemeka moaned. "Please. Don't you want me?"

"More than I have ever wanted anyone. My dick is hard as hell. Yes, I want you." He unzipped his pants and pulled out his manhood. He entered her with force. "I want this pussy bad as hell. Oh my goodness, you feel good Meka."

He made love to her while she lay back on the couch and enjoyed. No one had ever made her feel so good. Robert was incredible. He brought her to a climax and her body trembled while she released herself. "Oh YEEEES! That's it." She screamed.

"Yeah Baby. Me too. I'm cummming. Ohhh! Ohhhh! Yes." He collapsed on her and kissed her. "I love you Boo. That was sweet. More than sweet. It was fantastic. But damn! I'm late!"

Robert jumped up from the couch and ran to the bathroom. "I need to wash up and get out of here Boo. I hate to hit and run but I'm extremely late. I'll make it up to you."

Shemeka hated that Robert jumped up so fast. She wanted to touch him, hold it in her hands and possibly even kiss it. She knew that she would eventually go down on him and she wondered if she would be able to take all of him in her mouth. From the way he felt inside her, she could tell that he was well endowed. Since he was already late, she would be patient. She appreciated that he took the time to make love to her because she needed it. Robert was nothing short of a dream come true.

"It's okay Baby. I understand. Damn! You took something out of me. Whew!" Shemeka didn't move from the couch. "I might end up crashing right here tonight If you want to come back after bowling for a second round, I'll be here."

Robert came out of the bathroom and kissed her. "I love you. Gotta go. Don't get up. I'll lock the door." He left.

Shemeka managed to get up from the couch and make it to the bathroom. She enjoyed Robert and wanted to ask him to move in with her. She had never lived with a man before but she was not against it. They could share the expenses and ride to work together. She decided that she would wait for another month before asking him. If things kept going the way they were currently going, she wouldn't have to ask him. He'd be asking her a question.

Next week I'm going to ask Robert to spend the night. I'm going to pamper him and show him a preview of what it would be like to be with me all the time. She thought.

Shemeka would also use that time to go down on him. She wished that she were a little more experienced in that area. When she asked Rhonda and Brandi about it, they had laughed. They told her that practice makes perfect "You'll know from his reactions if you're pleasing him or not. Don't worry." Brandi had told her. "He'll just be happy to have it in your mouth."

Rhonda had nodded in agreement. "There's a first time for everything. You said that you feel comfortable with him and he's comfortable with you. Ask him. He'll tell you what he likes."

Shemeka finished cleaning up and climbed into bed. *My life is just beginning.* She thought.

Chapter Nineteen

Rhonda woke up to the aroma of country ham. She looked around the very neat bedroom. Nikki's house was well kept. She had to admit that she was glad Nikki had come back to the hospital last night. She was a nervous wreck when Bernard suddenly went into cardiac arrest. The doctors were able to revive him and told Rhonda she should go home for some much needed rest. She didn't want to leave but they assured her that she would be notified of any changes. She agreed since he was in stable condition and Nikki offered to bring her home with her so she wouldn't be alone. They gave the hospital Nikki's phone number as well as Rhonda's cell phone number in case they needed to reach her.

It didn't take Rhonda long to fall asleep. She took a long hot shower and Nikki had a nightgown laid across the bed for her. She had one drink of Hennessy and sprite before retiring for the night. Nikki had been very sweet and attentive. Nothing like the monster she had encountered in the hotel room. Rhonda wondered what Nikki's story was? Did she have a split personality, was she bipolar or what?

She sat on the side of the bed and looked around the room, which was decorated in pink and white. The pink and white curtains were tailor made to match the lace bedspread. She had almost forgotten that Nikki mentioned having a daughter. This was clearly a child's room. Stuffed animals were arranged neatly in the corner. Dolls were on the dresser and a pair of bunny ears slippers was on the floor.

The door opened and a small chocolate girl entered the bedroom. She was pretty, with big cheeks and big smile to match. Although the child was smiling, Rhonda noticed that her eyes had a look of sadness. Rhonda had never met the child before but there was something familiar about her.

"Hey Mrs. Rhonda."

"Hello there. What's your name Sweetie?" She asked the child.

"My name is Dean. My mama said to tell you that breakfast is ready. Here is a clean washcloth." She handed the washcloth to Rhonda and dashed out of the room in her sponge bob pajamas.

Rhonda got up and found her way to the bathroom. She washed her face and went into the kitchen. Dean was seated at the table and Rhonda sat next to her. Nikki was pulling hot biscuits out of the oven.

"You're very pretty." Rhonda told Dean.

"Thank you." The child appeared to be shy. She looked at her arm, which was in a sling.

"How old are you?" Rhonda tried to engage Dean in conversation.

"Three." She answered and put up three fingers to show Rhonda how many three was.

"What happened to your arm?" Rhonda asked her.

Dean didn't answer. Instead she shrugged her shoulders. Nikki had placed the hot biscuits in a bowl and was putting them on the table. "She fell. I've told her about being so clumsy. She has to be more careful and learn not to jump on the bed. She could get seriously hurt. Help yourself."

Nikki fixed Dean's plate and Rhonda enjoyed a breakfast of country ham, red-eyed gravy, grits, scrambled eggs, biscuits, jam, and coffee.

"Well no one called from the hospital so that's a good sign. I checked before you woke up and the nurse told me that Bernard had a restful night with no problems." Nikki spread jam on her biscuit. "Dean is going to be leaving shortly and I will take you back to the hospital."

"Thanks Nikki. Thanks for everything."

When they finished eating, Rhonda volunteered to put everything away and clean the kitchen. "It's the least I can do."

"Come on Dean. Let's get you cleaned up so you'll be ready to go when"-Her sentence was interrupted by the doorbell. "Damn! What time is it? Come on Dean. Let's hurry. Rhonda, do you mind getting the door please?"

"No! Sure, I'll get it. Go on and get your daughter ready." Rhonda opened the door and saw a man standing there with a beautiful smile and dimples. He was dressed casual and stood there waiting to be invited in.

"Oh. I'm sorry. Come in. I'm Rhonda, a friend of Nikki's." She waited for him to enter before closing the door. He extended his hand to hers. "Hi, I'm Robert. Nice to meet you."

She noticed that he didn't divulge any other information other than his name. He didn't say if he was Nikki's man, Dean's dad, or a relative. "Have a seat please. She will be out in a minute. She's getting Dean dressed."

"No thank you. I'll stand. She shouldn't be too much longer. Nikki is usually very punctual."

"Would you like a cup of coffee or something while you wait?" Rhonda asked him.

"No, I'll pass. Thank you though. I had a cup on my way over." At that moment, Dean burst out of the bedroom and ran to Robert. He scooped her up in his arms and tossed her midway in the air. He brought her back down with a kiss on the cheeks.

"How's my favorite girl doing this morning?"

"I'm good." She answered.

"Are you ready to go have some fun?" He asked the child.

"Yep! I'm ready." Her big pretty eyes had gotten even bigger with the anticipation of leaving and having some fun. Excitement was in her voice as Robert led her to the door.

He kissed Nikki. "I promise to have her home early."

"And not too much junk food either. She had a stomach ache the last time you took her out. I don't feel like staying up all night with a sick child because you don't have sense enough to say no." She kissed Dean and Robert kissed her on the cheek before they left.

"I'll get dressed now. I need for you to take me by my house before we return to the hospital. I need to get a change of clothes."

"I might have something in the closet that you can wear." Nikki told her.

That shit would swallow me. Do you not realize how big your ass is? Rhonda thought. "Nah! You've done enough already. Besides, I have this outfit that Bernard loves to see me in. It might make him feel a little better and lift his spirits if I wear it."

"In that case, I will be glad to run you home. Give me a minute." Nikki went into her bedroom.

Rhonda made the bed she had slept in and sat on the side of the bed while she waited for Nikki. She wondered what the relationship was between Nikki and Robert. It hadn't seemed that he and Nikki were in a relationship. He only kissed her on the cheeks. He didn't show her any kind of affection. Dean was certainly happy to leave with him.

Although Rhonda was curious, she decided that she wouldn't ask Nikki about him. If Nikki wanted her to know, then Nikki would tell her. One question that lingered in her mind was if Robert had been the man to hurt Nikki. She felt that Nikki must have been hurt really badly by some man to cause her to turn to women. Even though she had sex with Bernard during their threesome, Rhonda had the feeling that Nikki was not really into men. She was only going through the motions. Rhonda doubted very seriously if she was actually the first woman that Nikki had been with. All of those questions would have to wait until later. She needed to get home and change so she could visit her husband.

Chapter Twenty

B randi ran to the house tearing the envelope open as she went in the door. She had finally gotten a letter from Anthony. She pulled the letter from the envelope and hesitated for a brief moment before unfolding it. She was not sure what to expect. She had been waiting to hear from Anthony but now that she had finally gotten a letter, she wasn't sure that she would be able to handle what it said. There was always the possibility that he would blame her for them getting caught and not want to deal with her anymore. She was not ready to let go of that relationship. If he decided that he didn't want her any more, what was she going to do? She would never know what was up unless she read the letter. Brandi unfolded the letter and read:

Wifey,

> *I'm sorry for all of da problems dat I hav cause ya. I put ya in a very bad situation dat ya did not deserb ta be in. I was totally wrong. All dat ya hav done is love me and be good ta me and look how I paid ya back. I put ya freedom on da line. I shud neva hav asked ya to do wat I asked ya. I am already locked up and dis place is pure hell. I wud neva wan ya or anyone else ta go thru da bullshit dat I hav gon thru. Please*

forgiv me Boo. Bein confine ta da Special Housing Unit and only bein allowed out fer one hour a day is torture. The one good thin dat has come out of dis is dat it has allowed me ta think. I now realize more dan eva how much I love ya and how I neva wan ta loose ya. I can't do dis without ya. Ya are truly my soul mate.I need fer ya ta be mo patient now dan ever before. Now dat I am in SHU, I only get one fifteen-minute phone call a month. Dey hav also suspin our visits fer a year. Afta a year is up, we will hafta do six months of non-contact visits. Dat means dat we will hafta visit from behind a glass and won be allowed to hug or touch in any way. As soon as dey brin da phone round for dis month, I will call ya. No tellin wen dat will be. Dese sorry ass C.O's do wat da hell dey want to do. I think they get a nut by makin us miserable. Baby, I love ya and I hope that ya will forgive me for all of dis. I am so sorry Brandi. I love ya.

Love Ant

Brandi held the letter to her breast while tears rolled down her face. She tried to absorb what she had read. An entire year without seeing Anthony? Eighteen months without being able to touch him or kiss him? Only one fifteen-minute telephone call a month? That was crazy as hell. She was used to them having three hundred minutes a month and four hundred minutes during the months of November and December.

She balled the letter up and threw it across the room. It just didn't seem right to her. Brandi wasn't sure quite what to think. *He could be playing me. Am I the only one who can't visit with him? What other damn bitch is going to be sliding up in there to visit him while I am not able to visit his ass? And what the hell does he expect me to do for a whole damn year? I'm just not strong enough for this bullshit. It's his damn fault. Not mine.*

This was more than Brandi could handle alone. She walked over to the telephone and dialed Erik's number. He had been a close friend of Brandi's for many years. In fact, if Erik had not been white, she once told him, *I could see myself in relationship with you. But you know I don't do white guys. Besides we are too close for that, and it wouldn't work. We know each other too well.*

They used to hang out frequently until Brandi got in a relationship with Anthony. For some reason, Anthony was jealous of the relationship and asked her to stop hanging out with Erik so much. He used the excuse that he didn't trust Erik but Brandi knew he was only jealous and insecure because of Erik's status.

The telephone rang until it rolled over into voice mail. Brandi knew that he was probably with a patient and would not answer his cell phone. He was the one person, she felt like she could confide in and look to for guidance. Shemeka and Rhonda were her girls and the three of them had shared a lot but she didn't want them to know what she was doing. She most definitely didn't want them to ever find out that she had smuggled drugs into the prison. It was foolish as hell for her to have put her freedom in jeopardy. Brandi left a message.

Hi Erik. It's Brandi. Surprised to hear from me huh? I know that it has been a long time.

If you don't mind Erik, how about giving me a call whenever you have a minute. I need to talk to you about something and I was hoping you would be able to drop by the house. She hung up the telephone and prayed that Erik would get her message and call her soon.

In less than an hour, her prayers were answered when the telephone rang.

"Hello Brandi, what's up? Long time, no hear from."

"I know Erik. You don't have to rub it in. We have both been very busy. I was wondering if you would have time to stop by later on.'"

"For a friend. I'll make the time. It's going to be around 6:00 before I get things wrapped up here but after that, I can stop by."

"Thanks. I'll see you later." She hung up the telephone and went into the room to change her clothes. She wanted to be comfortable and she wanted to make up her face. It looked bad with the dried tears. She slipped into a tee shirt and some sweat pants to wait on Erik.

Brandi walked over to the letter she had thrown on the floor. She uncrumbled it and looked over it again. Anthony seemed very apologetic but how could he possibly expect her to wait on him under the circumstances. It was difficult enough to deal with the fact that he was going to be doing more time. She was an affectionate person. She needed those visits and the connection with him. Brandi not only needed those visits but she lived for them. To hear that she may have to settle for anything less was almost unthinkable.

Chapter Twenty-One

◇◇

Nikki turned her truck into the parking deck of the hospital. Shemeka was getting out of her car. Rhonda let her window down and waved her arm as she called to her friend.

"There's Shemeka." She told Nikki. "Go ahead and park so we can catch up with her."

When Nikki parked the car, Rhonda quickly opened the door and ran to embrace Shemeka.

Nikki took her time getting out of the car. She could feel herself getting agitated at the situation. She was the one who had been there for Rhonda last night when Bernard went into cardiac arrest, not Shemeka. She was determined to find out what was going on with Shemeka. Why wasn't she somewhere doing some therapy on a patient if that was her damn job? Why was she at the hospital trying to spoil things? She didn't know who the hell Shemeka thought she was but one thing she did know; Rhonda belonged solely to her and anyone who tried to get in the way of that was going to have hell to pay.

Rhonda and Shemeka waited for Nikki to catch up with them before entering the elevator. The women got off on the ICU floor and went to the waiting room.

"It will be time to visit again in about five minutes." Rhonda told her friends. "I'm going to check with the nurse before visit begins to get an update on his condition. I'll be right back."

Shemeka sat down and picked up a pamphlet that one of the local churches had left on the table. She had just started reading it when Nikki approached her. "So tell me, how long have you known Rhonda?"

"Oh girl! We've been friends since childhood. We go way back. That's my gal. She has helped me through a lot of problems. How about you? She never mentioned you until I met you here at the hospital. How long have you known her?"

"We haven't known each other for long. I met her through her husband. We hit it off right away. Rhonda's a good person."

"Yes she is." Shemeka agreed and as she lay the track back on the table. "I hope they find the low life that did this to her husband. What kind of a person would run a man down and leave him to die like that? It had to be a sick bastard."

"You're right. There are a lot of dangerous people out there. And it's hard to tell who they are. You could be sitting in the room with one and not even know it." Nikki answered.

"Sickos." Shemeka answered. "It's a damn shame."

"Shemeka." Nikki looked her square in the face. "Please don't misunderstand me. I see that you are a good friend to Rhonda and you have her best interest at heart. I know that she appreciates your support, but I think she needs some space."

"Some space?" Shemeka raised her voice to be sure she got Nikki's attention. "What are you talking about some space? Anytime I have had to deal with a crisis in my life, Rhonda has been right there for me. I'm going to do the same thing for her. I don't know who the hell you think you are or what your agenda is but I suggest you mind your damn business."

Nikki took a step towards Shemeka who sprang to her feet in preparation for whatever might go down.

"I knew it!" Nikki spoke above a whisper. "I knew it all along. You didn't have me fooled for one damn minute bitch."

"Who the fuck you calling a bitch? BITCH!" Shemeka kept her voice to a low tone with Nikki, remembering that she was in the hospital and they were on the ICU floor with very sick people.

"Let's take this shit outside. I gotcha bitch alright."

"You didn't have me fooled for one damn minute. I see the way you look at Rhonda. How stupid do you think I am? I tell you one damn thing. You better back the fuck up. You don't know who the hell you are messing with."

"Let me tell your psychotic ass one muthafuckin thing." Shemeka walked up to Nikki and was directly in her face.

"Bernard's doing better." Rhonda walked into the room before she could finish her response. "He's alert. He had a good night and his condition is stable. Although his breathing is a little shallow, he can breathe on his own. They are going to have to keep him on the respirator a little longer. He keeps trying to talk but it's hard to understand what he is saying. I guess that's because of the sedative."

Nikki walked towards Rhonda. "That's great news. I know you must be relieved. This has been a stressful time for you." She looked at Shemeka.

Rhonda also looked at Shemeka. "What's wrong Shemeka? Do you feel okay? You look like you don't feel well?"

"I'm fine." She answered. It hurt her like hell not to blast Nikki right there in front of Rhonda but she knew that her friend had enough to deal with. "I have a slight headache."

"Those headaches can be hell." Nikki smiled. "Why don't you go home and take some medicine and get you some rest. Rhonda will be fine. I'll take care of her."

"Well no. It's probably stress related. I have a lot on my mind. In fact, if you don't mind, I'd like to talk with Rhonda in private." Shemeka looked at Rhonda. "Since Bernard is doing well, would you like to accompany me to the coffee shop down the street? Its two more hours until you can visit again anyway. I just need to talk."

Nikki stood straight with her arms by her side. She dug her fingernails into her own thighs without realizing it. Looking at Shemeka, she struggled to maintain calmness and not lose control. The last thing she wanted to do was snap in the hospital.

"Can't this wait? Rhonda has her hands full right now with her husband. She doesn't need the added burden of having to deal with your problems. You are being insensitive."

Rhonda responded. "It's fine. Bernard had a restful night and the doctors are optimistic. Let me get my things and I'll be ready." She got her purse from the table and looked at Nikki.

"Thanks for everything Nikki. You don't have to wait around. I'll let you know if anything changes with Bernard."

"You're very welcome." Nikki wanted to scream. This is not how things were supposed to go down. Shemeka had crossed the damn line. "Just let me know if you need anything Rhonda."

"I will. Come on. We can all walk out together." The three women headed for the elevator. When they got to the ground floor, Nikki headed to her truck. She paused as she watched the women walk down the street until they were out of sight. After they were gone. Nikki walked to the parking lot. She saw Shemeka's car.

I'll go to the passenger's side and see if I can't get the door open. Imagine that bitches surprise when she gets in and I jump up from the back seat. If that whore wants to battle with me then it's on.

Nikki searched her purse to see what she could find to get the door unlocked. She placed her hand on the door and the car alarm sounded. "Damn!" She screamed as she backed away from the car and walked to her truck. "Next time Bitch!"

Shemeka sat down at the Coffee House unaware that her car alarm was sounding. She had changed her mind and decided not to tell Rhonda about Nikki's accusations. When the waitress brought their mocha, she could tell that Rhonda was still worried about Bernard.

"So what's up Mek?" She asked.

"Rhonda, I don't want to burden you right now. Let's just have our mocha and table this conversation until later."

"No! You've got me here and you have my attention. Is this about Robert?'

"Robert! Damn! I had completely forgotten. Robert and I have a date. Rain check?"

"Yeah, if you're sure that you're okay." Rhonda answered.

"I'm good. I'll check with you later. By the way, we're going to have to arrange for you to meet Robert. Gotta go. I hate to leave you like this."

"Girl, go on to that man." The women stood and embraced before departing.

Chapter Twenty-Two

◇◇

E rik pulled his Lexus up in front of Brandi's house. He used to be attracted to Brandi but she treated him like a brother, a friend and a confidante. Anytime she was going through a crisis or had a major decision to deal with, Erik was there. Whenever something good happened with her or to her and she had a reason to celebrate, Erik was there. He had never tried to cross the line with her for fear of messing up the friendship. He wanted to always have her in his life; if not as his woman, as his friend. She had been equally as supportive of him. He could tell her anything. Well, almost anything.

When Erik learned of Brandi's relationship with Anthony, he was concerned. He had warned her to be careful. Sometimes, he felt like Brandi was naive and a man could take advantage of her if she were not careful.

She had argued that Erik was only judging Anthony because he was black and because he was a convict. "Erik." She had said to him. "Would you be so willing and ready to warn me if Anthony was white? Or if he were a free man?"

"Come on now Brandi, you know better than that. What do I care about him being black? What does that have to do with anything? Now about him being in prison, well you may have a point on that. I don't want to see you hurt. Those men in prison are looking for a sugar mama. I just want you to take things slow and not feed into all of that shit Anthony tells you. It is probably just prison talk. Trust me."

"Please! Let's not talk about Anthony because you and I are not going to agree on the subject. I can't change your mind and you sho-nuff can't change mine. So we will agree to disagree. How's that?"

After four and a half months in the relationship, Brandi slacked up on seeing or calling Erik. He would call her and leave her messages on her answering machine. Sometimes she would return his call and other times, she would ignore the call.

Although his medical practice kept him busy, he would call occasionally to see how Brandi was doing. He worried about her. One of his patients came into the office one day and tested positive for HIV. The woman said she had gotten it from her boyfriend who was incarcerated. They had sex in the visitation room.

"I thought those visits were monitored." Erik had said to her.

"They monitor as well as they can. If you really want to do it then you'll find a way. Other people took the attention away from us. It's more restricted now, with cameras, and C.O.'s walking around. But there are still people who are willing to take that chance. I wish that I hadn't." She cried and went on to tell Erik how her man was on the down low and she had no idea.

When Erik had mentioned it to Brandi without calling his patient's name, she didn't believe him and thought he was coming up with something else to discourage her from being with Anthony. Now he was sitting in his car in front of her house praying that she had not fallen fate to the same thing his patient had. He couldn't imagine what she had to talk to him about and a strange feeling in his gut told him that it was about Anthony.

He knew that some of the men in prison led women on. There were men in there who had women visiting them and kissing them knowing they were going to be with their male lover as soon as visit was over. Erik did not judge those men. He only felt like there should be some kind of way for them to have protection. Condoms would at least protect the innocent ones who loved these men and who would be with them when they got out. It was okay if they chose that lifestyle but protection was the key. Erik had rescheduled his appointments for the day. He prayed that Brandi was all right and healthy.

She watched out of her window as Erik got out of his car and walked up the sidewalk to her porch. She slung the door open before he could ring the bell.

"Come in."

Erik came in the house, hugged Brandi and sat down on the Lazy Boy recliner. Usually he would wait for her to ask him to have a seat but he was anxious to find out what was going on with her. Brandi didn't look too bad and he could not tell anything from the greeting. However, he could smell the alcohol on her breath when they embraced. There was also a glass on the coffee table, which he was sure contained alcohol.

Brandi remained standing. "I appreciate you coming over Erik. I didn't know whom else to call. Rhonda's husband is in the hospital and Shemeka is finally in love for the first time in a very long time. I just don't know what to do." She paced back and forth across the floor. Her tears begin to flow.

Erik got up from the recliner and took Brandi in his arms. He rubbed her back. She still had not told him anything. She began to cry louder and held on to him.

"What's wrong Brandi? Talk to me." He walked her over to the loveseat and sat beside her. He was quiet as Brandi told him about Anthony not getting out anytime soon. His facial expression changed and he shook his head as she told him about how she had been taking drugs into the prison and got caught, thus causing them to lose visits for a year. Tears began to stain her face. Erik pulled a few Kleenex from the box on the table and wiped her face.

"Brandi." He placed a hand on each of her shoulders as if he were about to shake some sense into her. "Listen to me Honey. You don't need this. What has Anthony ever done for you except hurt you? What was he thinking? Asking you to smuggle his ass some drugs in the prison? Oh yeah. He wasn't thinking. At least not about you. Do you understand that you could have been locked up?" He waited for a response from Brandi.

"I know Erik. It's not entirely his fault. I could have said no. But I just love him so much."

"You think you love him Brandi. Just like you think he loves you. If the man loved you, he never would have put you in such a compromising situation. When a man loves a woman, he will do anything in his power to protect her. He won't jeopardize her freedom and her career." Erik looked at her. "Damn! Wake up woman. You are a nurse. Don't you know that if you had been charged with smuggling drugs in the prison, you would never work again? Not as a nurse. Some people might even think that you would steal medicine from the hospital. If Anthony is not going to look out for your best interest, then you better look out for yourself."

"I know that he loves me. He just doesn't think at times. He's sorry." She handed him the letter from Anthony,

Erik looked at Brandi. Her bloodshot eyes were begging him to understand. Her voice trembled. Her soul sought comfort. He put his arms around her and she sobbed in his chest. "It's going to work out Brandi."

Brandi felt safe in the arms of her friend. She wondered why she had even allowed Anthony to make her distance herself from him. He had always been there for her. Erik was a friend who she could depend on. It was Erik who had encouraged her to go into the field of nursing. There were times when she wanted to give up, but he wouldn't let her. It was because of him that she had a career.

"I'm sorry Erik. I'm sorry for putting my career on the line. You spent many long hours coaching me and tutoring me for finals and I don't want you to think I don't appreciate it because I do."

He lifted her chin. "Brandi, I think you know what you need to do. You don't need for me to spell it out for you. Anthony doesn't love you and you have put your life on hold for long enough."

"But you don't understand Erik. Nobody seems to understand. I know that Anthony has his faults. We all do. I can't see myself bailing on him right now. I owe it to him to stick it out with him."

"You don't owe him shit. If that's how you feel, then why did you did call me? I'll tell you why. Because you want me to talk you out of making a stupid ass mistake. One that you will regret."

Erik gave Brandi the letter back. "So he claims to be sorry. Don't they all claim to be sorry when they are caught?" Erik gently moved her body from him. A wet spot stained his shirt from her tears.

"Well since you have your mind made up, it appears that you don't need me after all." He proceeded towards the door.

"Wait Erik. Please don't leave." She begged. "I just don't know what to do. I want to stick with Anthony. It's not about the drugs I took in there. I am as much to blame as he is. It's about this extra time he has to do. It's about not being able to see him for a whole year. It's about not being able to talk to him but once a month. How can that be considered a relationship? How can I limit myself like that? I won't even have a life. I just want to do the right thing for both of us."

"I'm not going to tell you what to do Brandi. Give it some thought and I am sure you will come up with the solution to your problem on your own. If you need me, I am only a telephone call away." He kissed her and walked out the door.

Chapter Twenty-Three

<<<<<<<<<<<<<<<<<<<<<<<<<<<<<<<<<<<<<<>>>>>>>>>>>>>>>>>>>>>>>>>>

Shemeka pulled Robert by the hand as she dragged him into Olan Mills Studio. "Come on Boo. Don't act like that. You said we could take pictures since we didn't get out to the fair to take any. Look at the bright side of it. At least I'm not asking you to go somewhere and find me some cotton candy."

"Okay! Okay! We'll take the pictures." Robert stopped resisting and entered the Studio willingly. Shemeka put their name on the list. When they were called, they took several pictures. Shemeka ordered two of the five poses.

It was seldom that they had the same day off and Shemeka wanted to take advantage of it. Robert had invited her to spend some time at his house. She had never been to his house before; she considered this a special treat. She loved him and wanted a future with him but until he invited her over, there was a small nagging doubt in her mind. She wondered if it were possible for her to be so happy? Why had he never invited her over? Why did, he always hit it and run? And most importantly of all, did he have a wife hidden away? Now that he was bringing her into his home, all those doubts vanished and she wanted to concentrate solely on pleasing him.

She decided that this would be the day for her to go down on Robert. How much more perfect could the timing be? Other questions clouded her mind now. Will I be able to please him? What if I do it wrong? How big is his dick? What if I can't get the whole thing in my mouth? After going over the questions repeatedly in her mind and not coming up with any answers, she decided that she would just wait until the mood was right and take him in her mouth. If he didn't act like he was enjoying it, she would ask him to coach her.

Shemeka was lost in her own thoughts when they left Olan Mills. Robert stopped across the street from the drug store. "I'll be right back Boo. I'm going to run in and pick up some condoms." He kissed her before getting out of the car.

She watched him as he walked across the street. She noticed a woman approach him. From the look on Robert's face, Shemeka gathered that it was not a pleasant conversation. She continued to watch, wondering what was going on. When the woman turned around, Shemeka recognized the woman. *What?* She asked herself. *Why in the hell is he talking to that nut? Who the hell is Nikki to Robert? And who in the hell is that child he just lifted in his arms and kissed? Is that his daughter? Okay. Let me calm down and not jump to any conclusions. I'm sure there is a logical explanation. Don't tell me that psycho bitch is his ex.*

Nikki and Robert talked for about five minutes before he headed back to the car. He didn't go into the store to pick up condoms. Shemeka didn't know how to approach the subject without seeming like a jealous insecure woman. If she were going to be in a relationship with Robert, she would have to trust him. She decided that she would wait to see what he told her. Nothing was going to ruin today. After all, no matter who Nikki was to him, she was not his woman. Shemeka already occupied that title.

"I'm sorry Boo." Robert told her as he slid into the car. "I didn't mean to take so long. I love you." He kissed her and cranked up the car.

Shitttttt! I'm sorry? How about a damn explanation? How about I ran into my muthafuckin ex, into a friend, into a sister, into any damn body?" She said to herself. She waited but Robert offered no explanation. *Stay calm. He loves you. Don't mess this up. Robert is everything you ever dreamed of. It was nothing. Don't make too much out of it. Enjoy this man and work your stuff. Show him what you're made of.*

When they pulled up in front of Robert's house, he got out and opened the car door for Shemeka. When they went inside, she was impressed. His house was immaculate. Everything was in place. The color scheme was black and gold. Shemeka remembered that Robert once told her black was his favorite color.

"Have a seat Baby." Robert said to her as if nothing had happened. "Let me fix you a drink."

He walked into the kitchen. After he fixed Shemeka a drink of vodka, and then one for himself he joined her on the couch and kissed her. She couldn't help but to give in to him. She loved Robert. He was a dream and she would not ruin the relationship by being insecure. Shemeka gave him one of the most powerful kisses he had ever had.

"Damn!" Robert told her while grabbing his crotch. "My dick is hard as hell."

"And I'm wet as hell Boo." She told him although it was hard for her to push Nikki out of her mind. She wondered why Robert had not said anything to her about Nikki yet.

Robert continued to kiss her while sticking his hands down in her pants. She grabbed him and felt the thickness of his manhood. He moved his hands from her pants to her breast. He lifted her blouse and took out a breast from her bra.

She had made up her mind that after he finished sucking her breast, it would be a good time for her to go down on him. She would slide down on her knees in front of him, unzip his pants, and take out his dick and put as much of it as she could in her mouth. Her plans were spoiled when Robert didn't suck her breast. He kissed her breast and put it back in her bra.

"I love you Shemeka. It wouldn't be fair for me to start a fire that I can't put out."

"What the hell are you talking about Robert?" She looked at him and waited for an answer.

"Boo, somehow I forgot to mark my calendar about an appointment. I can't miss this appointment. I'm so sorry. I really wanted to spend this time with you. Maybe we can do it later but I seriously can't change or cancel this appointment at the last minute. I hope that you are not too upset with me."

"Not too upset with you? Why the hell would I be upset? You stop by the store to pick up condoms, you bring me to your house, you get me all wet and ready, and then you spring this shit on me about you having a damn appointment. What's there to be upset about? It's all good. Take me home. I wouldn't want you to miss your appointment."

"Come on now Boo. It's not that I don't want to be with you. You know that. I love you sexy. I've fallen in love with you. I'll make it up to you. I promise." He tried to put his arms around her, and she pushed them away.

"Just take me home Robert. I'm ready to go. That's what you could have done in the first place. What was the purpose in bringing me to your house to tell me that you are canceling?" She stood up.

"Shemeka, listen. I'm sorry. We can hook up later. It's just that I have..." She walked out of the front door before he could finish his sentence.

They traveled to Shemeka's house in silence. When they got to her house, she opened the door and got out before he could assist her. With her keys in her hand, she stuck her head back inside the car. "Go ahead. I'll be fine. I need to check on Rhonda anyway."

"Boo, are we okay?" Robert asked her.

"Why wouldn't we be okay?" She asked him. Shemeka closed the car door and watched Robert pull away from the curb and down the street. When she saw his car round the corner, she jumped in her car and sped down the road. She didn't want him to get too far ahead of her. *Let's see what kind of a damn appointment he has.*

Robert was at least five cars ahead of Shemeka when he put on his left turn signal and veered off to the left. She slowed her car down when she saw him put on his right turn signal, slow down and pull in front of a house. *What kind of a damn appointment would be at a house? There are no offices on this street.* She was starting to get a sick feeling in her stomach. Instead of making that left turn, she continued straight and turned at the next street. After circling the block, she parked her car down and across the street so she would not be noticed. When she looked up, Robert was already out of his car and at the door. Tears rolled down her face when she saw Nikki come out of the door and hug Robert before walking to his car. Robert opened the car door for Nikki then got in on the driver's side and pulled away. Shemeka had seen all that she could stomach. Instead of following them, she decided to go to the hospital. She didn't want to burden Rhonda but she needed to know what Rhonda could tell her about Nikki.

Chapter Twenty-Four

Rhonda sat in the chair next to her husband's bed. He was stable and his vital signs were good. Although his condition had been upgraded, he remained unresponsive. The police had not been able to question him concerning the hit and run. Rhonda held his hand in hers. "I love you Baby. I'm here." She felt someone's presence in the room behind her. When Rhonda turned around, Shemeka was standing in the door with swollen red eyes. She slid her chair back and went quickly to her friend. She wrapped her arms around her and whispered, "What's wrong?"

They stepped out of the room and into the hall. "Rhonda. I'm sorry to come here like this. I just need to talk to you. I'm sorry. I don't mean to be insensitive. How's Bernard?"

"He's in and out of consciousness but his vital signs are good. He will be moved to a regular room soon. They are going to keep him in ICU one more night to monitor him. But what's up with you? Let's walk to the Coffee House so we can talk."

Shemeka wiped her eyes and walked with Rhonda to the elevator. "I'm glad that Bernard is doing better. Maybe he will be able to tell you who did this awful thing to him."

"I know. That's what I am praying for. The whole thing just doesn't make any sense to me. Bernard never should have even been at Chic-n-Ribs. I don't understand why he was there. I had cooked."

"Who knows? Maybe he wanted to surprise you. I know that you have a lot going on Rhonda. I never would have bothered you if it weren't important. I hope you know that." Shemeka told her.

They walked in the Coffee House and chose a table in the back corner. Rhonda ordered sweet tea and BLT's for both women. "So tell me what's going on girl." Rhonda looked at Shemeka. "What has gotten you so upset?"

"There's just so much going on that I don't really know where to start. That friend of yours. Nikki. What do you know about her?"

Rhonda was confused. She wondered if Nikki had tried to come on to Shemeka. "Not much. She has a daughter. I met her through Bernard. Why? Did she do something to you?"

Shemeka hesitated for a moment before speaking. "When I was at the hospital earlier and you went in to see Bernard, she accused me of being gay."

"What?" Rhonda knew that Nikki might be capable of anything. Even though she seemed stunned at what Meka said, she knew that her friend was not lying on Nikki.

"She acted like I was not at the hospital as a friend but as your lover." Shemeka continued. "And that's not the half of it. When I left to go meet Robert, I saw him outside the store talking to a woman. It was Nikki."

"Well maybe he knows her. That's nothing to get upset about. But this shit about her accusing you of being gay; I'm going to have to say something to her about that. She must be crazy to come out of her mouth with some shit like that."

"No! You don't understand." Shemeka started to cry. "I thought Robert and I were about to make love and-"

"Here you are ladies." The waitress put the BLT's on the table and a basket of chips in the center of the table. "May I refill your tea?"

"Later." Rhonda answered. "We're straight for right now."

Shemeka took a napkin from the table to dry her eyes. "As I was saying, I thought we were about to make love and then he told me that he had forgotten about an appointment. I followed him...and...he...he...he went to that...bitches house and picked...her up."

Rhonda didn't know how to respond. She remembered being over Nikki's house when a man named Robert stopped by and picked Dean up. She wondered if it was the same man. It had to be. But what was the connection? She was feeling sorry that she never got around to meeting Robert because she would have been able to blow him out of the water right there on the spot. Maybe Nikki really was crazy as hell. Why had she accused Shemeka of wanting Rhonda?

"Nikki does seem to have some issues Shemeka. I'm not sure what is going on with her. As I said, I don't know her that well. I met a guy named Robert at her house one day but I can't swear that it was your man because I've never met your man."

"It was him." Shemeka answered. "What are the chances of her knowing two different Robert's?"

"Regardless, if he is messing around with Nikki, you don't need him." She wanted to keep Shemeka as far away from Nikki as possible. If Nikki accused her of wanting Rhonda, there was no certainty that Nikki wouldn't let it slip about the threesome. Rhonda loved her friend but she didn't want anyone to ever know that she had let Bernard talk her into doing something so stupid. Being with Nikki was the biggest mistake of her life.

"But you should have seen her." Shemeka interrupted her thoughts. "She was almost threatening. She acted like you were her property and I was trespassing. That bitch is sick. Has she said anything to you? I bet that she is bisexual. She probably wants you and Robert."

Rhonda ignored her. "What are you going to do about Robert? Are you going to let him know that you followed him? You can't still want him. He lied to you."

"No! Yeah! I don't know. I don't know what to do. I have to talk to him I guess. But what can he possibly say to explain this? I thought he was different from the rest of the guys I had dated. He's not, is he?"

"I can't answer that. I don't have enough information and to be honest, neither do you. After you talk to him, you'll know more. Just put it out there to him." She answered.

"Give him a chance to explain. You say that you love him."

"My grandma told me a long time ago that men ain't shit. She said to never be surprised at anything a man does unless he does right. Then you are surprised. I lived by that motto for a long time, until Robert came into my life. Now I don't know what to think."

"Meka, I can't tell you what to do. The ultimate decision has to be yours. Just know that I'm here for you." Rhonda waved for the waitress.

"What can I get for you?" She asked.

"We're ready for those refills now." Rhonda looked at Shemeka. "So what's it going to be?"

"I'm not goanna let a muthafucka play me. That's out. If there is something going on with Robert and Nikki, she can have him because I don't want him anymore. Thanks for letting me vent."

The women finished their tea and Shemeka picked up the ticket from the table. "This one is on me. Thanks for being such a good friend. I'm going to handle my business now."

Chapter Twenty-Five

◇◇◇

B randi picked up the telephone and called the V.A. Medical Center to tell them she was sick and would not be in to work. She didn't want to try working on only a few hours of sleep. She had spent the night tossing and turning in bed while thinking about her situation.

Although Erik had not come out and said it, she knew that he was sexually attracted to her. They were good friends and he was her confidante. Neither one of them dared to cross that line. If they took things to another level and it didn't work out, they stood the risk of losing a valuable friendship.

She wondered if she were fooling herself. Could she really hang in there with Anthony? Did he really appreciate all that she had sacrificed for him or was he using her? Did he have someone else helping him to pass the time away? She would never know. It was not like she was allowed to visit. She was not even allowed on the premises. What would her co-workers at the V.A. say if they knew she was involved with an inmate? That would probably be the talk of the hospital. It upset her that society looked down on men who were incarcerated. It would not be socially acceptable for her to be a nurse and be in love with Anthony but if she were in love with Erik, it would be looked at as a match made in Heaven.

Why didn't people understand that sometimes things happen to people and they find themselves in a situation that they never imagined they would be in? Should Anthony pay for his mistake the rest of his life? Yes, he sold drugs and yes he was wrong for doing so. In no way did Brandi condone what he had done. He was tried and found guilty but he was paying his debt to society. He was separated from everyone he loved. He was stripped of his freedom. He was stripped of his manhood. If the judicial system had attempted to teach him a lesson, he had learned it very well. Didn't he deserve for someone to forgive him? Didn't he deserve for someone to understand and hang in there with him?

Brandi tried to rationalize staying with Anthony and riding it out with him. The conversation with Erik lingered back and forth in her mind. He had said it was time for her to start living. She had to admit to herself that she wasn't living. It had been so long since she had been with a man. The toys were nothing compared to a real man. She needed someone to hold on to her at night and to be there when she was lonely. It would be great to wake up in the morning and roll over into the arms of the man she loved. Now Anthony had killed that dream by telling her that he had more time to do. It may have been a little more acceptable if she was able to see him but since their visits were cancelled, she didn't know if she could handle it or not.

She loved Anthony but did he love her? Erik had said that if he loved her, he would not want her to be out here alone. Maybe Erik was right. Maybe she should live her life and not wait on Anthony. Maybe she should go ahead and step back into the dating arena. If she and Anthony were meant to be together, then it would happen when he got out. If not, then maybe it was not meant to be.

Brandi got out of bed and walked into the kitchen. After pouring herself a glass of orange juice, she walked into the living room and turned on the television. She flipped through several channels before settling on *The Montel Williams Show*. The episode was about women behind the wall. It featured women who were locked up. 95% of them had gotten involved with the wrong man. The men had involved them in crimes ranging from burglary, to breaking and entering, to drugs, and even murder.

Brandi thought to herself. *Is there anything a woman wouldn't do to find love? Hell, I could have been one of those women. I took drugs into the prison. I jeopardized my freedom. And for what? The love of a man. Erik was right. Anthony was not looking out for me. I'm sure that he didn't want to get me into any trouble but he wasn't thinking. Erik would never put me in a situation like that.*

When the talk show went off, Brandi turned the television off and stepped into the shower. As the hot water ran down her body, the tears ran down her face. She realized that she did not have a man to wash her back. She was not only alone but she was lonely.

Anthony was in the hole and had already used his one telephone call for the month. It would be another month before she could hear him tell her that he loves her more than life. She couldn't have phone sex with him. She needed that. Anthony made love to her mind. Although they only had fifteen minutes, he made her feel like he was in the room with her. It turned her on to have him in her ear telling her how much he loved her while she touched her body. He would tell her to insert her finger into his pussy and give it to him. Brandi didn't mind him calling it his pussy because it was his. She enjoyed having him with her when she got her orgasm. It made it so much more intense than when she was at home with her toys.

Now she wasn't going to have that. With only one phone call a month, they had things to talk about. They wouldn't have enough minutes for phone sex. Their only other form of communication was letters. That didn't console her any since Anthony had only written her one letter since the incident. Brandi lathered her body and washed herself as she wondered what was going on with Anthony. Before he got put in the hole, he wrote her three times a week. Maybe he was writing that whore he had the baby by. That bitch opened her legs and started giving up the pussy as soon as he was sentenced. He could very well be writing that whore. Men were stupid like that. They seemed to always go back and fuck with the ex no matter how badly she treated them. Shit! The bitch was fucking other men while she was in the relationship with Anthony and he didn't have sense enough to know it. Some men want to feel like their dick is so damn good that a woman won't cheat. Nah! A real woman won't cheat but a whore will.

Brandi rinsed her body off and stepped out of the shower. She wrapped the towel around her and walked into the bedroom. After drying her body she put on body oil to smooth her skin. She slipped into a pair of shorts and a tank top before picking up the telephone to call Erik. The receptionist informed her that Erik was with a patient. She left a message for him to call her. Forty minutes later her telephone rang.

"Hello."

"Hello Brandi. It's Erik. I just got your message. Is everything okay?

"Yeah." She answered. "Everything is fine. I was wondering if you have time to stop by. I really need to see you."

"Well, I have a break for about an hour and fifteen minutes. It's time for my lunch. If you need more time than that, I'll stop by when I get off." He told her.

"No. That's good. In fact, I will fix lunch for us and we can talk." She responded.

"Brandi is this about Anthony again? I've told you that I can't make that decision for you. Don't waste my time if you are expecting me to tell you what to do. You already know what you have to do."

"No Erik. I don't need for you to tell me what to do. I am simply asking my friend to come over. Is there anything wrong with that?"

"I'll be there shortly." He answered and hung up the telephone.

Chapter Twenty-Six

◇◇◇

Nikki picked up the pair of pants that Dean had left on the floor. She walked to the dirty clothes basket and tossed the pants inside before slinging the basket and all of its contents across the room. *Ugh! When in the hell is Robert coming to get that damn child? I need some time to wind the fuck down. I'm sick of this shit. I have stuff to take care of. I don't have time to clean up after a damn messy ass chap.* She said to herself.

She went to the telephone to call Robert and see how much longer he was going to be. She dialed his number and it went over to voice mail. "Damn!" She yelled as she slammed the telephone on the receiver.

The doorbell rang. She opened the door and Robert stood there. "You're late. I just called your ass. Why didn't you answer the damn phone?"

"There was no need in answering it. I was walking up the sidewalk when you called."

He walked into the house. "Where's Dean?"

"In her room." Nikki answered. "Deeeeeeean! Robert's here."

Dean emerged from the room and ran to Robert. He gave her a kiss. "Are you ready to go Princess?"

"I'm not Princess. I'm Dean." She smiled at Robert.

"Well you are my Princess. Are you ready?"

"Yes. I'm ready. Let's go." She ran to the door to wait for Robert.

"Her things are right here." Nikki handed him a rolling tote bag. "The fee has already been paid. The camp is only for four days. I'll pick her up on Thursday."

Robert took the tote from Nikki. "Give your mom a hug and kiss before we leave."

He looked at Nikki. "I am going to give them my telephone number as an emergency contact. If she gets homesick or decides she does not like it, I'm picking her up."

"Whateva." Nikki gave Dean a kiss and a squeeze. The child flinched like she was in pain when Nikki put her arms around her. "Bye Baby. You be a good girl."

"I will." Dean walked to Robert and took his hand in hers. They walked to his car while Nikki stood in the door waiting for them to leave. Once they were gone, she closed the door and went to the telephone.

I need Rhonda to get her ass over here. Nikki thought. *Um! What can I say to her?*

She acts like she has to be at the hospital every damn minute. I can't pull this off unless I have her here with me. Why do I have to ask her to come over here? Why can't she come on her own? Doesn't she know that I need my pussy? She's going to have to stop playing with me. I'm not feeling that shit at all.

Nikki dialed Rhonda's home phone and got no answer. She figured that Rhonda had to be at the hospital all stuck under Bernard like he was something good to eat. Why was she acting like such a faithful wife when she knew all along that Nikki was the one who made her feel good? Nikki couldn't understand why Rhonda didn't just face the facts. She had sent Dean off to camp for four days and she needed all four of those days to convince Rhonda to leave Bernard as soon as he got well. Why couldn't he have died? That would have made it so much easier.

Well, if need be, that can be arranged. If Bernard gets in my way, then I will kill that motherfucka before I let him spoil things. She said to herself.

She called Rhonda's cell phone and got voice mail again. "Fuck!" Nikki screamed.

"What's going on?" She picked up the telephone book and found the number for the hospital. She called the waiting room.

"Hello. ICU waiting room." A voice on the other end said.

"Hi, I'm trying to get in touch with Rhonda Simpson. Her husband is in ICU and l was wondering if she was in the waiting room."

"Hold on and let me check." Nikki could hear the woman talking in a low voice. "Is there a Rhonda Simpson here? Oh! Well you have a telephone call."

"Hello, this is Rhonda."

"Rhonda, its Nikki. How are you? How's Bernard?"

"He's good." She answered. "What's up?"

"Rhonda, I need to see you. It's really important. Can you come over?"

"What's wrong?" She asked Nikki.

"I'd rather not get into it on the telephone but it's important or I wouldn't have called. I know what you are going through with Bernard and him not being able to communicate with you. I never would have called you if it were not urgent. Please say that you will come."

"Look Nikki, I'm on the hospital phone and in the waiting room. I can't really talk right now. Hang by your telephone and let me call you back in about three minutes. I'm going to get my cell phone and step outside." She hung the telephone up. Nikki answered the phone on the first ring. "Okay, I can talk now. I didn't want to talk in front of those people in the hospital. Shemeka told me what happened at the hospital with you and those false accusations. That was fucked up and you know it."

"I know, I'm sorry. I don't know what I was thinking about. I owe her an apology and I will apologize to her the next time I see her. I was totally wrong for that. I'm just going through something that no one would understand. I was trying to hold it in but I can't. I need to talk to somebody and you are the only person I feel like I can confide in." Nikki sounded desperate.

"Maybe I can stop by for a little while but can it wait until later?" Rhonda asked her.

"No Rhonda. Please come. It's urgent. It can't wait until later. Trust me. If you come, I promise you that I won't ever bother you again."

Rhonda thought about it for a minute. Shemeka needed answers about Robert and maybe that is what Nikki wanted to talk about. Maybe she could get some answers and tell Shemeka what was going on.

"Okay Nikki. I'll be there in about thirty minutes."

Nikki hung up the telephone and danced around her living room. She was excited that Rhonda had agreed to come over. It had been too long and she was tired of waiting for Bernard to recuperate so Rhonda could breathe again. He had nurses and doctors taking care of him. He didn't need to occupy his wife's time like he was doing with his selfish ass. She was the one who needed Rhonda worst. Bernard, Brandi, Shemeka, nor Dean was going to spoil it for her. She danced into the bedroom, singing as she pulled the linen off the bed. She waltzed to the linen closet and decided on the red satin sheets. After she changed the bed she sprayed some perfume on the pillows and went into the living room to wait on Rhonda.

When Rhonda arrived, she greeted her with a hug. "Come in and have a seat. Can I get you something to drink? I have fresh lemonade in the fridge."

"Sure, Lemonade sounds great. So tell me Nikki. What's going on? What are you so upset about that you needed to talk to me right away?" Rhonda sat on the loveseat and waited for a response.

"Hold on. I'll tell you about it. Let me get us something to drink." Nikki walked into the kitchen. "It's just so much Rhonda. I needed someone to confide in and I know you will keep it real with me." Nikki removed two glasses from the cabinet and filled them with ice. After she poured the lemonade over the glasses of ice, she eased the drawer open and took out a Rohynol. As the pill dissolved in the lemonade, she shook the glass before sticking her finger in it to mix it up. She was glad that the old roofies were still available because she had heard that the new pills turn blue when added to liquid. She handed Rhonda a glass and watched while she took a sip.

"Thanks." Rhonda said. "This is good. Nothing beats a nice cold glass of lemonade."

She drank the lemonade unaware that Nikki had spiked it with the tasteless, colorless, and odorless drug. "Nikki, you didn't sound quite like yourself on the telephone but you sound fine now. I don't understand."

"Let me show you." Nikki got up from the chair and started undressing. Rhonda sat there not knowing what to expect. When Nikki was fully undressed she walked over to Rhonda and stood in front of her. Rhonda looked her body over expecting to see some bruises or marks from abuse. She wondered if Robert had abused her in some kind of way. She saw nothing to be alarmed about.

"What?" Rhonda asked. "I don't see anything. Did somebody do something to you?"

If he had abused Nikki, it was all the more reason for Shemeka to steer clear of him. Besides, what did Shemeka really know about him or his past? He was somebody she had met at work. He could be a serial killer for all Rhonda knew.

Nikki turned in two full circles. "What do I look like?" She asked Rhonda.

"Huh? What do you look like?" Rhonda was lost. She didn't know what was going on with Nikki. "Certainly, you didn't call me over here to ask me what you look like. What's going on Nikki? I need to get back to the hospital."

"Do you think I look good? Do you find me desirable?" Nikki stood in the middle of the room with her hands on her hips. "Keep it real with me. Is this a body that you can love?"

Rhonda was starting to feel uncomfortable. "You look nice Nikki. There is nothing wrong with your body. Did somebody say something about your body? Is this about that Robert guy who I met over here?"

"Fuck no!" Nikki screamed. "It's not about him. It's about you. You and that bitch. Is her pussy better than mine? I'm not stupid. I know what the hell is going on. Do you think I am fuckin blind? Shemeka. Do you think she looks better than me? Is her pussy better than mine?"

"No Nikki. I don't think you are blind. I think you are fuckin crazy as hell. I'm not going to listen to this shit. Stay the hell away from me and my friend." Rhonda was feeling lightheaded.

"Damn your muthafuckin friends." Nikki screamed. "I don't give a damn about those bitches. If they know what the hell is good for them, they'll stay the hell away from my woman."

Rhonda wondered why she had been stupid enough to let Nikki talk her into coming over. She should have learned a lesson by now. Nikki was nothing short of being unstable. "Shemeka is my friend. I used to consider you as being a friend but I can't do this. I won't do this. I'm leaving." Her legs wobbled as she held on to the loveseat to get up. After gaining her balance she headed to the door walking slowly. Feeling dizzy and disoriented, she took a step backwards before Nikki caught her.

Nikki put her arm under Rhonda's arm and around her waist. She led the physically helpless Rhonda to her bedroom where the covers were already turned back. She assisted Rhonda in getting into bed. She tried to raise her arms but experienced a loss of muscle control. "Nikki, what-?" Her speech was slurred before she lost consciousness.

"Don't worry Baby. I gotcha. Mama's right here. Mama's goanna take care of you."

Chapter Twenty-Seven

Robert walked over to Shemeka while she was working with a patient recovering from knee replacement surgery. "What's good for tonight Sexy?" He asked her. Shemeka had been distant and had not seemed herself. Robert wondered if she was still upset with him because he had to cancel on her for the appointment. He knew that he had not spent much time with her and he wanted to make it up to her if possible. How could she not know how much he loved her? She looked away from him.

"You tell me. You mean that you don't have to meet the guys tonight? No appointments tonight?" She said sarcastically.

"Come on now silly woman. You know that I love you and I am not about to argue with you up in here. It will be time for us to bounce from this place in about forty-five minutes so let me just run home, shower, change and stop by your place."

"Are you sure you have time?" She asked him. "I mean like I wouldn't want to interfere with anything."

"Where is all of this coming from?" Robert turned her face towards him so he could look her in the eyes.

Shemeka didn't want him to touch her. She didn't know what was going on with him. All she knew was that he had bailed on her to be with Nikki. She knew that she had to calm down if she was going to get the answers she wanted. They had not broken up officially but she felt like he was no longer hers. So why did she feel like he was a magnet drawing her in? She could not let herself be a fool.

"Robert, we need to talk. You don't have to go home. You can shower at my house and we can talk."

He shook his head. "And put back on the same clothes? I don't think so. Besides, I have something that I need to stop and pick up. I'll be there at 6:00."

"Well 6:00 it is. I'll be waiting." She turned and continued working with her patient.

He was going to have to come clean or she would cut him off completely. She would be professional with him on the job but if he was trying to be a playa, he had played out.

After work, Shemeka checked her voice mail. *You have one new message. First message received at 12:00 a.m. Message from 406-661-9742. Shemeka, I'm on my way to Nikki's house. She called me sounding desperate and wanting to talk. It might be about Robert. I'm on my way over there. I'll let you know what happens. End of new messages.*

Shemeka appreciated all that Rhonda was willing to do for her but it was not necessary. She was going to find out what Robert was up to on her own. Nikki would never tell the truth about it. She dialed Rhonda's number and got her voice mail on each phone. She hung up without leaving a message.

When she got home, she said a silent prayer. *Lord, I'm so in love with this man. Please don't let me fall for any lies. I know that you placed him in my life for a reason. I just don't want to be a fool for him or any man. I thought he was my soul-mate but if he is not, let me bow out gracefully. If he has any secrets Lord, please let them be revealed. Thank you Lord. And oh yeah! I'm coming back to church soon.*

She kicked off her shoes, undressed and jumped in the shower. When she finished her shower, she brushed her teeth, put on deodorant, and body powder, and sprayed on some perfume. She put on a pull over shirt, and casual pants.

When Shemeka heard Robert's car door slam shut, she headed to the door and opened it. She watched as he climbed the three steps to the porch. He tried to kiss her and she pulled back.

"Come in."

"What's wrong Boo? Don't you think that you have treated me cold for long enough? Are you still upset with me?"

"Upset?" She answered. "Let's see now. What the hell would I have to be upset about? Would I be upset because the man who claims to love me is barely here with me? Would I be upset because every damn time you have made love to me, it has been a hit and run? We've never cuddled together, we've never showered together, and we've never spent a motherfuckin weekend together. Forget the weekend. We've never spent the motherfuckin night together. Or...wait a minute. Hold up. Would I be upset because I followed you, and saw you with that crazy ass bitch Nikki? Yeah! I know about Nikki. You son-of-a-bitch."

"Oh! That's what this is about. You're wrong Boo. I promise. It's not what you think."

"Then what the hell is it? You're a damn liar. Get the hell out of my house. I thought that we were going to talk but I see that you want to lie. Are you going to tell me that I did not see you with that bitch? Just go Robert!" She walked over to the door and opened it.

Robert walked to her and placed his hand on top of hers. "I love you. Please give me a chance to explain. You can at least do that much. Or are you willing to throw away what we've built. Five minutes. That's all I ask and then if you still want me to leave, I'll leave." Shemeka closed the door.

"Sweetheart, I'm sorry. I see that I have hurt you." He looked at her, wanting to touch her but afraid of being rejected. "I promise you that there is nothing going on between Nikki and me. It's a long story Boo. She does have some problems and I've tried to help her."

"Yeah. I bet you did try to help her. You tried to help me too didn't you?"

He continued to look at her. She honestly didn't realize how much she meant to him.

"Shemeka, I love you. I never thought I would find a woman like you. You are everything to me. I'd never jeopardize our relationship by running around on you. Nikki is my cousin. Honest Boo. If you don't believe me, you can call her. Or better still, we can ride over there." He took her hand. She could hear the sincerity in his voice. Nikki had to be his cousin. He didn't have to prove it to her. She knew that he was telling the truth.

"No Robert. We don't have to go over there. I believe you. But why didn't you just say so? You never mentioned her. I didn't know what to think. I never should have doubted you."

"Baby, my cousin is dealing with some personal problems. She is in therapy and I forgot that I was supposed to go with her. I couldn't ask her to cancel her appointment at the last minute. I should have told you. I'm sorry. Please forgive me."

Shemeka hugged him. "I forgive you. I hope that you will forgive me for being so stupid." With her arms around him, Robert stuck his hands into his pocket and pulled out a small box. He handed the box to Shemeka. "This is for you. I hope you like it."

She opened the box and removed the most beautiful ruby ring she had ever seen. One large ruby was in the middle and it was circled by diamonds. "I love it. Oh my goodness. Ruby is my birthstone."

She and Robert kissed long and hard. "I love you Baby." She told him. I will never doubt you again". She whispered to herself. *Thank you Lord.*

"I want you so bad Baby. Can I have you?" Robert asked her.

"I'm all yours Robert. You can have me any time you want me." She took his hand and led him to her bedroom. He lifted her shirt without pulling it off and took her bra off. He took one breast in the palm of his hand and sucked it while he used the other hand to finger her.

"Baby, today belongs to you. Let me take you places that you have never been. Do you trust me?" He asked her.

"Yes, I trust you." She answered as he slipped her pants off her and positioned her on all fours. She remembered telling him once that doggie style was her favorite position. She welcomed it. He unzipped his pants and went to the foot of the bed where he let them drop to the floor. Robert then climbed on the bed behind her. The next thing she felt was Robert's tongue while he was licking her ass. "Baby, I won't do anything you don't want me to do but there is so much I want to experiment with you. Can I?"

Shemeka knew what he was talking about. "Just be careful Baby. Don't hurt me. I've never done this before."

"I won't hurt you Boo. In fact, let me get a little bit of this Vaseline from the dresser."

She stayed in her position while Robert got the small jar of Vaseline. He greased himself down to prepare to enter her anally. She tightened up when he pushed the head of his dick in her. "Relax Baby. Don't tense up on me. Once you get used to this, you are going to love it. Trust me."

He went deeper into her while she gritted her teeth. She had expected a little pain but this was almost unbearable. "Nah! Stop Robert. I'm sorry. I can't take it. It hurts."

"Just relax Meka."

"No! Take it out. I can't." She begged.

"Okay." He told her as he gently eased his dick out of her "Let me try something else.

Just lay there. I'll be right back. I think I have some lubricant in the car."

Robert got off the bed and picked up his pants from the floor. He had pulled them midway to his waist when Shemeka turned over. "Noooooooooooo! Fuck no!" She screamed to the top of her voice. "A motherfuckin dildo? Oh my goodness. You fuckin freak!"

She sprung to her feet screaming. "Dyke! You're a dyke! Nasty bitch ass dyke!"

Chapter Twenty-Eight

◇◇

E rik had not expected Brandi to call but he knew that she had been struggling with making a decision about her future. He hoped that she had made a decision concerning Anthony. He cruised down Martin Luther King Jr. Blvd. as Tank blared from the speakers of his sound system singing, *Please Don't Go*. Erik imagined what it must be like to lose the person you love, knowing it's your own fault for fucking up. And even worse, begging her to please not go. He always felt like there were men out there who didn't appreciate a good partner. They claimed to love them but the love was to a certain degree. Could that be called love? True love? Wasn't true love unconditional? And if it was, then why did society force people to wear masks?

Erik got out at Brandi's house and rang the doorbell. She opened the door and let him in. Once he was inside the door, she closed it and fell into his arms. She held to him like she was holding on for life. "Hey there ladybug. You alright?" Erik held Brandi out at arm's length so he could look her in the face.

"Yes. I'm fine. I'm just glad you came. Let me get lunch because I know that your time is limited. I'm not going to keep you from your patients."

"Well actually, I'm through for the day, my P.A. is going to handle the rest of my patients. I didn't know how long I would be out and I didn't want to keep anyone waiting. He's a good guy. He'll take good care of them."

Brandi went to the kitchen and placed the sandwiches on plates. She had made turkey on wheat with lettuce, tomato, and mayonnaise. She added a dill strip and boiled egg on the side. Erik was not into fried foods. He believed in eating healthy. When Brandi called him to the table, he sat down and blessed the food. Brandi poured Ginger Ale for them to drink.

"How are things going with you Brandi? You look good."

"Thanks. I feel good." She told him. "I've been thinking a lot about my situation. I know that you wanted me to make up my own mind and I appreciate it. I appreciate you. There is no way that I can continue to hang in there with Anthony. I am only depriving myself and it's not fair to me. It's just too much."

"You already know how I feel about it Brandi. There are too many men walking around here that are free. Why should you have to settle for one who is locked up? You don't have to sell yourself short. You are too beautiful for that." He looked at Brandi and admired her beauty. If his life had turned out differently, maybe Brandi would have been his wife. Nah! Who was he trying to kid? They never would have worked out.

"Erik, I hear what you are saying and I know that you are right. Anthony has put me through some things that I didn't deserve but he really is not a bad person. Most people have not been exposed to the side of him that I have seen. That's because he keeps it hidden. He doesn't want to appear weak."

"Brandi, I'm not going to argue that." He told her. "What you are saying may very well be true. But love yourself first and foremost. Don't depend on a man for your happiness. Give yourself, but don't give all of yourself. Save some for you."

When they finished eating, Brandi put the dishes in the sink and suggested they take the conversation in the den. They sat on the couch together and he took her hand into his.

"You know that I support you Brandi. You've been my dearest friend." He kissed her on the forehead. "I'm here for you girl. I'm going to always be right here whenever you need me."

"You'll never change." She laughed. "Why hasn't some lucky woman snagged you? You're the perfect man. Who wouldn't want perfection?"

"Maybe I'm not as perfect as you think I am. Besides, you're supposed to say that. You're my friend." He teased Brandi, "On a more serious note; you just need to relax. I know that it has been stressful dealing with the Anthony situation but now that you've decided to move on, things will be better."

"Remember that time we played doctor and you pretended to examine me?" She asked him.

"Yes Brandi. How could I forget? I was touching you all over your body and then when I told you to take off your clothes; you looked at me like I was crazy. I told you that all doctors make you take off your clothes. But when I took off mine, you jumped up and put your clothes on." He laughed. "You must have been scared of what you saw."

"It wasn't that I was scared. It was that I had never seen anything that big before. Who would have thought that you would actually grow up to be a doctor?"

They laughed. Erik put his arms under Brandi's legs and lifted them onto his lap. After he slipped off her bedroom shoes, he rubbed her feet. "How does that feel?" He asked her.

"That feels good. It has been so long since I have had a man attending to me that I had almost forgotten how relaxing it could be." She closed her eyes and enjoyed his touch.

She wanted to be careful not to move too fast. Even though Erik had made it clear that he didn't have a woman in his life, she didn't want to seem desperate. But she was desperate. She wanted to be loved. She took Erik's hand and put it on her legs, not letting go, but sliding his hand up her leg until it was where she wanted it.

"Make me forget." She whispered. "Make me forget everything and everybody."

"Brandi, it's not that I don't want to. You know how much I would love to make you forget. But I don't want this to be some rebound shit. I'm not down with that. You still love Anthony."

"I never said that I don't still love Anthony. Sure I love him. But it's time to move on.

If you don't want me then say so." She said in a defensive tone. "Am I supposed to wait until Anthony is completely out of my system?"

"If we do this Brandi, how will you feel afterwards?" He asked her.

"I think I will feel damn good." She laughed. "You're not scared of this pussy are you? I know it has been a while since I have had some dick but I promise to take it easy on you. Loosen up."

"Damn, you're tempting me. I've been after this pussy forever and now you finally want to give it to me. But what are you expecting Brandi? I don't want to mess up our friendship. What if it doesn't work?"

"Why wouldn't it work? We know each other up and down. You know all of my secrets and everything about me. I know all of yours. It can only make us closer." She was pleading her case as if she was in front of Judge Mathis. "What could possibly go wrong? And even if it doesn't work out, you will have done me the biggest favor in the world by helping me get over Anthony. Besides, no matter what happens, we are always going to maintain our friendship."

"You promise?" He asked her.

Brandi raised her right hand. "I promise." Then she planted a kiss on Erik. He was hesitant at first but he soon gave in to her. She unzipped his pants and assisted him in getting undressed. "This time, I'll be the doctor."

Brandi slid down on her knees and took Erik in her mouth. She could feel him growing with every bob of her head. He moaned with pleasure. She wanted him to feel good. Erik pushed her head back and helped her to her feet.

"This is not about me Brandi. This is about you. About making you forget, and I am determined to do just that."

They walked into the bedroom and Erik pounded her pussy. She had not been with a man in so long that she wanted to cry. It felt so good to feel him inside of her.

"Ah...ah...yeah...mmm...mmm. "That's it." She could not help it. The words escaped her lips while the fluids escaped her body. Erik had not cum yet but she needed that release.

She wanted to make sure he got his. Her mouth was magical. In a few minutes he was exploding and trembling.

They ignored the ringing telephone and let the answering machine in the living room pick it up. The hospital was trying to get in touch with Rhonda. Bernard had regained consciousness. The police had been notified and were in route to the hospital to question him.

Chapter Twenty-Nine

Rhonda lay stretched out on Nikki's bed unaware that she was in the world. Nikki undressed her comatose body before massaging her. She ran her hands over Rhonda's and told her, "You're going to have to behave. You can't have things your way Bitch. I've tried to work with you but you won't let me. You're mine. When in the hell are you going to understand that?" Nikki got herself undressed. "Don't I take good care of you? Don't I take care of my pussy?"

She lifted Rhonda by her shoulders and shook her as if she expected a response. "I love you. Nobody will ever love you like I do. I'm going to take care of your every need. Now open your legs so I can get to my pussy."

She spread Rhonda's legs apart and licked her clitoris. "Damn! You taste good." She continued to taste Rhonda, lifting her head often to speak. "How does that feel to you Baby? Does that feel good? Yeah! I know it does." She licked her finger before sticking it in Rhonda. "Go ahead Baby. That's it. Cum for Mama."

Nikki got up from the bed and licked her fingers. "Now, it's time for you to take care of Mama. You have to make me cum. This is not a one-way street. I want to feel good too." She walked over to her dresser and opened the bottom drawer. Underneath, her gowns and negligee, she found her sex toy. "I'm coming Rhonda. Be patient. I know you want me."

She lay on the bed next to Rhonda and inserted the toy inside her. With the other hand, she rubbed Rhonda's body. "Oh yes Baby. That's so good. Uh! Yeah! Give it to Mama. Fuck me Baby. Ooooh! Rhonda don't stop. Fuck me harder." She inserted the toy harder inside her. She dug her fingernails in Rhonda.

"I'm getting ready to cum." She had barely gotten it out when the toy fell out of her pussy. She started hitting Rhonda. "Why did you take it out?" Put it back." Nikki put the toy back in and worked it until she reached a climax.

Rhonda was still knocked out from the drug-induced lemonade. Nikki put her head on Rhonda's breast area. "Now this is the way it should be all of the time. You should be by my side with me loving you and you loving me. Your breasts are so firm." She leaned over to put one in her mouth. "Am I turning you on? Why can't you act right?" What the hell do you want from me? Oh yeah. Do you want me to fuck you?"

Nikki got off her bed and went to get her oils. She rubbed oil all over Rhonda. Then she took the tube of k-y jelly and squeezed some on two of her fingers. She stuck her fingers in Rhonda and saturated her pussy. Afterwards, she put on the strap-on and tried to put Rhonda's legs over her shoulder. Because her muscles were relaxed from the roofies, Nikki was not able to keep Rhonda's legs up. She was getting frustrated She slapped Rhonda across her face. She spread her legs apart again and shoved the dick in her.

"Give me this damn pussy. Don't you resist me Bitch. What I tell you about not cooperating with me?" Tears started to form in Nikki's eyes. "I can't let you go. I won't. Please don't ever take this pussy from me. Please Rhonda. It would kill me." Nikki climbed down from the bed. She took off the strap-on and let it drop to the floor. "You've got the best pussy I ever put my dick in. Let me get something to clean you up." She was walking towards the bathroom when she heard Rhonda mumbling.

Rhonda slowly lifted her head. "What happened?" She asked. "How did I get in your bedroom?" She looked around the room while trying to get herself together.

"Don't you remember? You said that you were feeling dizzy and thought you were about to pass out. I guess that you have been under too much stress. I let you lay down for a while so you could rest." Rhonda couldn't remember anything.

"But I'm naked Nikki. Where are my clothes?"

"Calm down. You really must not remember anything. You were breaking out in balls of sweat so I took your clothes off you. They should be dry now." Nikki lied.

"You're naked too Nikki. What's going on? Where are your clothes?"

"I was getting ready to step into the shower Rhonda. That's why I don't have any clothes on. But I'm glad that you are awake and feeling better. I need you so badly. I need you to help me cum."

"Nikki, you know that I am not with that any more. Please get my clothes so I can leave. I need to get to the hospital." She wanted to get out of Nikki's house. She didn't trust Nikki. Rhonda could feel the wet k-y jelly between her legs and felt like she had woken up in time to keep Nikki from sexually abusing her. She couldn't understand why her body ached but she knew that the sooner she got away from Nikki the better. There is no way that she should have let Nikki talk her into coming over. She had planned to get information on Robert and didn't know any more than she did when she walked through the door.

"I can't fuckin let you leave. I need you!" Nikki screamed. "Please Rhonda. Don't do me like this. I love you and I'm so horny. I want to fuck you. Cum for me before you leave."

Damn! I knew it. The bitch was about to rape me. Rhonda told herself. She felt sorry for Nikki but she was scared of her. She watched while Nikki picked up the strap-on and put it on. She was adamant about having Rhonda and would not let her leave until she had her way. "Come on

Nikki. Let's go ahead and do this because I honestly need to leave. How long have I been out anyway?"

She ignored Rhonda's question and climbed on the bed. The dick went in with ease. While Rhonda lay on the bed motionless, she pounded away at her pussy.

"Yes Baby. Give it to me. Mama needs this. I'm gonna fuck your ass. Oooh yes. Oh, that feels so good Baby."

Rhonda wondered how Nikki could seemingly get such pleasure out of it. She acted like she really had a dick and was throwing down on some pussy. Suddenly she stopped and dug her fingernails in Rhonda again. "Please don't make me fuckin flip. Give me my damn pussy. Who the hell are you saving it for Bitch?"

At Nikki's request, she moved her body. She wanted the whole ordeal to be over with as soon as possible. She was ready to get out of there. Nikki slapped her. "Tell me you want me. Tell me to fuck you."

"Fuck me Nikki. I want you Baby. You should know how much I want you. Give it to me. I want you to make me cum." Rhonda faked.

"Yes Baby. That's it. Mama's going to take care of you." She put Rhonda's legs over her shoulders again. They stayed this time. She went deep in Rhonda and enjoyed the screams that escaped Rhonda's lips. The more Rhonda screamed the more pleasure Nikki got. "Aww! That's it. Mama's cummming!"

"Me too. I'm cumming too Mama." Rhonda was glad when Nikki collapsed beside her. "Nikki, that was great. I didn't realize how badly I needed you." She stood. "Can I come back tomorrow?"

"Yes. Any time. You are always welcome. I'm glad you are seeing things for what they are."

Rhonda picked her clothes up from the chair. "Don't!" Nikki told her.

"Don't what?" She asked, afraid that she was going to be trapped there.

"Don't ever take this pussy from me. I'm begging you Rhonda Don't spoil it." Rhonda glanced at the clock. "Damn I didn't know it was this late. I've been here for hours. May I take a quick shower before I leave?"

"Yeah. Do you want me to join you?" Nikki asked her.

"Next time. I promise." Rhonda answered her.

"Okay. I love you." She blew Rhonda a kiss before Rhonda went into the bathroom.

If there is ever a next time, I'll kick my own ass. Rhonda told herself. She turned on the shower.

Chapter Thirty

Brandi felt excited as she recalled her love making session with Erik. It was good to feel like a woman again. She couldn't seem to get him off her mind. She regretted that she had cum so fast but it had been such a long time since she felt a man's touch. She was faithful to Anthony throughout their relationship until this fling with Erik. She put herself on lockdown with him. She didn't talk to other men or let other men visit her because it would only cause problems.

Brandi was determined not to do anything that Anthony would consider disrespectful.

For some reason, it always seemed to be a respect thing with the guys who were incarcerated. When she visited him, Anthony didn't want her to speak to any of the other inmates. She remembered an argument that they once had at visit because a man said hello to her on her way to the snack machine. Anthony saw her speak back to the man. When she got back to her seat he was livid.

Wat da fuck ya doin talkin to dat son-of-a-bitch? I saw ya. Make dat ya last damn time disrespectin me like dat again. He had raised his voice and the couple seated next to them had turned to look at them. She didn't understand what the big deal was.

Ant, I only said hello and kept walking. What are you talking about? And lower your voice. People are looking at us.

I don giv a fuck! He gritted through his teeth.

Anthony, I'm not going to let you embarrass me in here. Please! I don't even know the man.

Damn right ya don no him. All da more reason fer ya not to speak ta him. I no him and I don like him. It's disrespectful as hell ta me fer ya ta speak ta a muthafucka up in here who I am beefin wit. Den he gon go back ta da compound talkin bout Ant's woman tryna holla at him. Don do dat shit no mo.

Brandi's mind went back to Erik. Having his hands on her had put her in a trance. Would she say that he had her hypnotized? Nah, more like dicknotized if there was such a word. It didn't faze her that Erik was white. All that mattered to her was that she needed him and he was there for her. If it had not been for the 911 his mom had put in his pager, Erik would probably still be there with her. She wasn't complaining because he had served his purpose very well. He and his mom were close so it was understandable that he would jet as soon as he called her back and found out she was sick. She was having chest pains and Erik left to meet her at the hospital. Brandi offered to go along with him but he insisted she stay. There was no need in her coming along because he would probably be at the hospital for hours. He promised to keep her updated on his mom. She gave him a washcloth and towel. After a quick shower he kissed her and left.

The ringing of the telephone interrupted Brandi's sweet memories. She leaned over and grabbed it without checking the Caller ID. "Hello."

You have a prepaid call. You will not be billed for this call. This call is from...Anthony...an inmate at a federal prison. Hang up to decline the call or to accept the call press 5 now, if you wish to block future calls of this nature press 7 now.

Brandi listened to the recording play out before hanging up the telephone. She was ready to talk to Anthony but she wasn't sure how to tell him that it was over. There was no way to tell a man in prison that you couldn't take any more. How could she tell him that she had decided to move on and hoped that she could continue to be in his life as a friend? Nobody wanted to hear those words from someone they loved and had planned on spending the rest of their life with.

The telephone rang again. Brandi looked at it and decided to let it ring. She knew that she was going to have some explaining to do. Anthony was not going to give up until he got in touch with her. After the fourth time he called, she answered the telephone and pushed 5 to accept the call.

"Why ya playin wit the da damn phone Brandi? I told ya I don get but fifteen minutes a month. Wat da hell are ya doin?"

"I'm sorry." Brandi said. "I had just stepped out of the shower and I wanted to get dry before I answered the phone. How was I supposed to know that you were going to call? You told me that you would only be allowed one fifteen-minute telephone call a month?"

"Yeah, dey gave me a phone call. I just wanned to holla at my Baby. I din't mean to go off on ya baby, but I'm frustrated as hell in dis hole. I miss ya and I can't call ya and dis shit is killin me. As soon as we get our visits back Baby, we're gon hafta go head and get married."

Brandi felt bad for Anthony. He was not a bad person at all. He used to be such a strong man, but prison had worn him. He had to take on the persona of a tough guy or he would not have been able to survive as long as he had. He could not appear weak or they would think he was a punk. He had gotten in trouble before because he had to prove that he was a man. When another inmate took his food and talked shit to him, Anthony had to go to his ass. If he hadn't then the other guys would not have respected him and he couldn't have that.

Not only had prison worn him, but also it had worn Brandi. She was being punished for his crime right along with him. She had tried to be a strong woman and stick with her man but when she found out he had more time to do; she knew deep down in her heart that she would never be able to do the additional time.

"Anthony, we can't get married Boo. I love you but we can't do that. I wish that you could arrange for a special visit. I want to talk to you about something and I swear that I don't want to tell you over the telephone."

"Look Brandi. I don like da way dis shit is soundin. Did ya hear that beep? I dint have any money to put on da phone. It's bout to cut off. So wat is it? Spit it the fuck out befor da phone cuts off."

"Anthony I will always love you and I will always do watever I can do for you. I hope you know that…" She wanted to tell him in a way that he might understand.

"But what? Ya bout to jet on a muthafucka?" He asked her. "Damn! Is dat wat ya tryna say?" Before she could answer, the phone went dead.

Brandi held the telephone in her hand and gently tapped her forehead with it. She wished that she had told Anthony and gotten it over with. The sooner she made things right with Anthony; the sooner she could get on with her life with Erik. Next month, when he got his telephone minutes, she would have to tell him.

She hung up the telephone and noticed the flashing light on the answering machine. When she hit the button to listen to the message, it was from the hospital trying to get in touch with Rhonda. She called both numbers and was unable to reach her friend. She hung up and dialed Shemeka's telephone number next but there was no answer on her phone either. She figured that the two were probably out together. She would catch up with them later.

Chapter Thirty-One

⬦⬦

S hemeka was hysterical as she grabbed Robert by the arm and swung him around. He had pulled his pants up over his waist and was zipping them up. "Baby, hold up." He said and tried to restrain her.

"Why? Why Bitch?" She screamed to the top of her voice. "I know what the hell I saw. It's a damn dildo or strap on or whatever the hell you call that gadget." As soon as he loosened his grip on her, Shemeka pulled his pants down. Her eyes had not deceived her. She pounded on his chest with her fist. "Oh my goodness. How could you? What did I ever do to you? Get the fuck out of my house Bitch!" She slid to the floor crying uncontrollably. "GET OUT! You've made me look like a fool. I can't believe this shit."

Robert got on the floor beside her. He started to put his arms around her but decided against it. "Just hear me out. Please Shemeka. I love you so much. I was going to tell you. In fact, I was going to tell you tonight." He took her hand.

"Don't touch me, you motherfuckin freak. I hate you. It's a little late for explanations now, don't you think? Leave Robert or I swear that I won't be responsible for what I might do." She got off the floor and sat up on her bed, crying into her hands.

"No Shemeka. I'm sorry but I can't leave you like this. I was wrong. I should never have waited this long to tell you but I didn't know that we would click like we did. I didn't know I would fall in love with you."

Robert got on the bed beside her. "Please don't touch me." She sobbed, "Say what you have to say and then leave."

"It's hard to know where to begin. I love you and I never meant to deceive you. I would never do anything to hurt you intentionally." He told her.

She pushed him backwards on the bed and climbed on top of him. Before he had a chance to wonder what she was doing, she had her hands around his throat applying as much pressure as she could. He lay there with his head bobbing back and forth while she cried, "I hate you! I should kill you!" He started to gasp for air.

Shemeka removed her hands from his throat. "Go Robert. Just leave. Oh yeah, you are not Robert are you? Who the hell are you anyway?'

"My government name is Roberta Holloway. I was born in Atlanta, Ga. When I was eleven years old, my mom died and my dad raised Nikki and me.'"

"I thought you said that Nikki is your cousin, not your sister." She said.

"She is my cousin. My parents took her when she was two years old. Her mom and my mom were sisters. Nikki's mom died from cancer and we never knew who her dad was." He wanted to hold Shemeka and make everything right again but he knew that she would never accept him for who he was. Not the way she had freaked out.

"I feel so damn stupid. How could I not have known? Why couldn't I see that there was something wrong with your ass? Am I that damn gullible? Do I want a man that bad?" She asked him.

"No Meka. It's not your fault. The last thing in the world that you need to do is blame yourself. You didn't see it because I didn't allow you to see it. Think about it. We always made love in the dark before today. When you told me that your favorite position was getting it from the back;

I felt elated. When I did get you from the front, you were on the counter top. But I promise you that I had planned to tell you everything tonight."

Shemeka started crying again. "I just can't believe it. That's crazy. I don't understand.

You don't even have breast."

"I know." Robert answered her. "I had a mastectomy. The surgeons did a complete removal of my breast tissue, including my nipples but not the muscles of my chest wall. I never meant to hurt you Baby. If you don't believe anything else, you have to believe that."

"Why didn't you just tell me? You should have let me make the decision. I should have had the choice of deciding if I could deal with this dyke shit or not." She screamed.

"And tell me Shemeka. What would you have said? What would your reaction have been?"

"I would have said no. I would have said that I am not like that but at least we could have maintained a friendship. At least you would not have deceived me into falling in love with you."

"Please calm down. I know that you are hurt and confused. I promise you that I was working it out. When I realized that my feelings had gotten to that point, I called the surgeon. We talked about Gender Reassignment Surgery. I'm willing to do that for you Baby. I'm willing to do that for us. Even though after my examination, he told me that there might be problems with the flaps such as necrosis or contracture; I was not deterred. He said there is the possibility of a malfunction of the prosthesis. Urinary fistulae may occur. But I'm willing to do that Meka. I'm willing to do whatever it takes to make things right for you. I just want you to feel comfortable."

Shemeka couldn't believe it. He was talking like they could still be in a relationship.

How? How could she possibly stoop so low as to be with his weird ass? Didn't Robert understand that she was sick to her stomach? She had let him touch her, and make love to her, and she had enjoyed it. Ugh! She had even kissed him, or her. She wasn't sure which gender to use. She didn't understand how he could act as if it was something they could get pass. She felt violated.

"Make things right for me? Do whatever it takes to make me comfortable? Are you crazy? I want to be left the hell alone. There is nothing you can do to make this right. You've destroyed me. What happened to you? What made you like this?"

"I couldn't escape." He answered her. "Nikki and I had twin beds. When she was eight years old, and I was thirteen years old, my dad crept into our bedroom. It was the night after my thirteenth birthday. Mama had died from a heart attack. He kept telling me all day long that I was not a child any more. He said that l would be able to have more freedom and do things that teen-agers do. It made me feel good because I thought that I would be able to go to some dances and be with my friends more. That's not what he meant." Robert stood up and walked to the bedroom window. Shemeka was quiet as she listened to him.

"I heard the door when he came into our bedroom. Nikki was sleep. I pretended to be sleep when he pulled my panties down. I was hoping that Nikki would not wake up and see him. He rubbed my clit. I wanted him to stop and go away but I dared not say anything. When I heard the zipper on his pants, my heart started to race. He continued rubbing my clit and stuck his finger in. I could hear him moaning but he wasn't in me. He used only his finger. When I squeezed my eyes open he was jacking his dick with the hand that wasn't in me. When he released his nasty sperm, he took his finger out of me and shot his fluids in his hand. Then he left the room. He didn't even bother to pull my panties back up."

Shemeka didn't know how to respond. This was the last thing she had expected to hear when she asked Robert what happened to him. She was expecting him to tell her some shit like how he was born like that and was always a trapped in a male's body. It was a sad situation and something that no one should have to go through but that still did not minimize what he had done to Shemeka. She had never done anything to hurt him and it was not her fault that his dad had hurt him. She let him continue.

"It was two days later when he came back into our room. He did the same thing and I felt dirty and nasty. I wanted to jump up and shower but then he would have known I was awake. I waited until the next morning and ran the shower as hot as I could stand it. I scrubbed and I scrubbed but I was not able to get his filth off of me. After that night, he started finding excuses to punish me. Nikki could go outside and play but I had to stay in the house with him.

The first time he kept me in; he locked the door and told me to take off my panties. I was scared to do it, but I was even more scared not to. He unzipped his pants and rubbed his dick against my pussy. He didn't penetrate me though. He made me lay there while he jacked his dick and he shot his sperm all over me. Then he laughed and told me not to spoil it.

Girl that felt good. You know that your mama is dead and your old man has needs. You better not tell anybody because they will take me away and put you and Nikki in separate group homes. If you go to a group home, they will really hurt you. The men that work there will rape you every day. Daddy just needs a little maintenance from time to time. Do you hear me girl? You better not spoil it. Then he would tell me to clean up while he unlocked the door."

Robert was pitiful as he recalled the painful childhood memories. "I hated him. One day he kept me home from school telling me that I had a fever. I told him that I felt good and wanted to go to school but he said that he couldn't let me go infect other students. After Nikki got on the bus, he came into my room with his pants off and his hard dick wagging back and forth in his hands. I begged him not to do it. I told him that I didn't feel good.

Shut the hell up and take off your panties. Do you want your daddy to get sick? If I get sick, who will take care of you and Nikki? Don't spoil it for us.

When I hesitated, he tore my panties off of me. He rubbed his hard dick up and down my clit. I wanted him to hurry up and stop so he could jack his dick and leave. But he was no longer satisfied with rubbing my clit and jacking his dick. He spread my legs open and pushed his dick hard in me while I screamed. I told him that he was hurting me, but he didn't stop. He only laughed. *Daddy needs to be the one to bust that cherry for you. Cut out all of that damn screaming.* When he got up, I was in blood mixed with his filth. My body ached. I wanted to cry but nothing came out."

Shemeka truly felt sorry for Robert. He had gone through things that no child should have to go through. He needed counseling. She didn't want to hear any more. She wanted to wake up from this nightmare. She could imagine how Robert felt during those traumatic years. It was probably similar to the way he had made her feel. She felt as if she too, had been abused.

"Robert, let's not talk about it anymore. I'm sorry for what your dad did to you. I can see that you were a victim. Right now, I feel like I am a victim. It's been a lot to absorb. I don't want to hate you Robert, but I need for you to go ahead and leave."

There was a brief silence, which was broken by Robert. "I know that I messed up Meka. I messed up big time. But I love you and I was honestly going to tell you everything tonight. I was trying to give you enough time to be able to deal with it. When I left Atlanta, I moved to Cartersville, Ga. and became involved with a woman who I thought was cool. I thought she loved me as a person and could handle my situation. I was straight up with her and explained to her whom I was. She couldn't handle it. She wanted to make me out to be bi-sexual. But I'm not bi-sexual. That's not who I am. Bi-sexual means that I would have enjoyed being with both sexes. I don't want anything to do with a man. Not ever. I don't want one to touch me and to be honest with you; I don't want a man to even look at me. Men think they can do any damn thing they feel like doing and it should be acceptable. They walk all over women; fuck em, get em pregnant, and then move on to the next woman."

"Robert, you have been through a lot but I can't help you. You need to talk to someone professionally. I'm sorry. Don't you understand what you have done to me though? I can't take this. I've heard enough." Tears ran down the front of Shemeka's face. Robert ignored her and continued.

"When I was fifteen years old and Nikki was ten, I came home in time to see him coming out of our bedroom. He stuck his head back in the bedroom door and I heard him tell her, *Remember, don't spoil it.* You can't imagine how I felt as I raced to our bedroom. I found Nikki balled up naked on the bed. Her clothes were on the floor. It was my fault Meka." He cried.

"No Robert. It wasn't your fault. You can't blame yourself for what your dad did."

"But I should have protected her. I knew how he was. They were having basketball tryouts and I stayed after school. I was good so I knew that I would make the team. I thought that if I were on the team and out of the house, I wouldn't have to be bothered with that bastard as much. But I never thought about Nikki. I let her down."

Shemeka didn't know how to respond to Robert. He was in a mood to talk. It was like he wanted to get this heavy load off his chest. She was still in shock from finding out that he was a woman. Robert felt responsible for Nikki. That was why he went with her to counseling. Maybe his dad was the reason she had turned out crazy as hell.

"Why didn't you tell somebody what was going on Robert? Surely a group home would have been better than what you went through." Shemeka asked. Before he could answer, there was a loud knock at the front door.

"Police! Open up!"

Chapter Thirty-Two

◇◇◇

Soon after Rhonda got in her car, she powered her cell phone on. There were several missed calls and messages. When she heard the message from the hospital that Bernard had regained consciousness, she headed in that direction. She didn't know how she would be able to explain her absence. She should have been there when he regained consciousness but instead she was with that crazy ass Nikki. Why in the hell did he choose to bring Nikki into their lives? Of all the people in the world, why Nikki? She was unstable and unpredictable. She had to stay away from that lunatic.

Rhonda tried to recall the events prior to her waking up in Nikki's bed. She couldn't remember a thing. She knew that waking up naked and sore was no accident. She didn't believe that shit about feeling dizzy and breaking out in sweat. The whole thing didn't make sense to her. Nikki had done something but she didn't know what. She didn't have time to figure it out because she needed to get to her husband.

When she got to Bernard's room, the nurse had him sitting up in bed. He looked good except for the fact that he could have used a shave. The color had come back to his face. Before, he had looked pale and his skin was chalky. She walked fast towards his bed.

"Baby, you look good. How are you?" She asked, kissing him on the forehead.

"I'm fine. Where have you been? The nurses tried calling you on both phones." He looked at her waiting for her response.

"Bernard, I was tired. I went home to get some rest and turned the ringer off on the telephones. I'm sorry I wasn't here when you woke up. Isn't that the way things go? I was here around the clock praying and waiting for you to regain consciousness. Then, the very minute I decide to get me some rest, you wake up. What are the chances of that?"

"Yeah. I'm sure that the phone has been ringing nonstop." He said.

"Nonstop is an understatement. My friends, your friends, church members, your colleagues and even your students have been concerned. It's good that I will be able to give them some positive news."

"The doctors said I am doing great. They are going to move me to a regular room and monitor me, but I should be released tomorrow." He smiled. Rhonda was a trooper. The best decision he ever made was to make her his wife. She would be with him through thick and thin. Bernard was proud to claim her as his.

"Boo." Rhonda looked at him with concern. "Why were you at Chic and Ribs? I had cooked Babe."

"I got a message at work. The receptionist said you wanted me to stop by Chic and Ribs to get the order you had called in. I never made it to the door."

Rhonda thought to herself. *Didn't nobody do that shit but psycho ass Nikki. I knew that Bitch was crazy. She thinks that if she kills Bernard she can have me. What's to stop her from trying again?* "Damn! I'm sitting here trying to figure out who could have done this terrible thing and..."

"I know who did it. I saw his face as clear as day before he ran me down." Bernard turned to the side of the bed and let his legs hang over the side.

"Who?" She asked.

"His name is Robert Holloway. I don't really know him. I met him over Nikki's house a couple of times. He's good friends with her. That son-of-a-bitch ran me down intentionally." Bernard saw from the look on Rhonda's face that he had spoken too quickly and said too much.

"When were you over Nikki's house? You said that you saw him over there a couple of times. I didn't know you were visiting her like that. And what reason would he have to run your ass down?" She knew that he was the man she had also met at Nikki's house. There was still the question of his relationship to Nikki.

"Baby, I went there a couple of times with one of my dawgs. I told you that she was seeing one of my co-workers. I would sometimes drop him off there so his car wouldn't be in front of her house." He knew that he had put his foot in mouth. He didn't want to talk about Nikki anymore or Robert.

"Oh! If he were single, he wouldn't have to worry about anybody seeing his car. And since he was married, he should have had his ass home with his wife." Rhonda knew that Bernard was lying. His whoring ass had been sleeping with that bitch. Not only had he been sleeping with her but he had the nerve to bring that tramp into a threesome. She had always given him his props for being a faithful husband but she was only deceiving herself. She wanted to curse his ass out but how could she? She had been sexing Nikki herself so she decided to leave it alone.

"Well it doesn't make any sense that he would want to hurt you but maybe he is crazy or something."

"I don't know what his problem is. He might be crazy for real because he ran me down like I was a dog. I will never forget the look in his eyes as he ran me down. He seemed to be in some kind of trance or something."

"Hello there sleepyhead. So you decided to wake up huh?" Brandi stuck her head in the door before entering Bernard's room. She walked over to Rhonda and hugged her. "I thought that I would find you here. The hospital called looking for you and said that this handsome young man was woke and wanting some company. I tried to reach you myself and couldn't. I even called Shemeka and couldn't get her."

"Oh damn! Shemeka! How could I forget?" She said out loud. Robert was dangerous. What if Shemeka tried to confront him about Nikki? What if it got ugly? He had already tried to kill Bernard. Shemeka might be in grave danger. There was no telling what Robert was capable of.

"Boo, since you are going to be moving to a room, you can get out of that hospital gown. I'm going to run to the store and get you a pair of pajamas." Rhonda told her husband.

"Ah Baby, I'm probably coming home tomorrow. Don't go through any trouble on my account." He said.

"It's no trouble. We are not sure if you will come home tomorrow or not. You know that people will be stopping by to see you. You need a shave and everything. I'm going to pick up a few things. Come on Brandi, you can ride with me." She kissed Bernard. "I won't be long Sweetheart." She followed Brandi out of the room.

When they got down the hall and out of earshot Brandi asked, "What's going on Rhonda? I know you better than that. You were in a hurry to get out of there all of a sudden for some reason." Rhonda was walking fast. Brandi had to almost run to keep up with her. "Slow down. What's up?"

Rhonda stopped at the elevator and pushed the down button. "Brandi, it's a long story but I will try to make it short. We need to get to Shemeka. There is a possibility that she might be in danger. Do you remember that guy Robert who she is dating and so in love with?"

"How could I forget? He's her whole conversation. I've met him a couple of times. He seems nice enough. Why?" Brandi asked as she stepped into the elevator.

"Well..." She continued. "He's the bastard that ran Bernard down and left him for dead. He tried to kill my husband."

"Damn!" Brandi responded while dialing Shemeka's telephone number. "Who would have thought?" She closed her cell phone. "I'm not getting an answer. I hope that she's not out somewhere with him. We need to let her know what is going on."

"Dial it again. She may be in the bathroom." Rhonda was desperate to get in touch with Shemeka. If Robert was half as unstable as his friend Nikki, then Meka was in trouble. Serious trouble. Who knows? He may have been playing Shemeka all along. She looked at Brandi for some kind of reassurance but got none.

"Still no answer." Brandi closed the telephone again and looked at the speedometer.

Rhonda was going 50mph in a 35mph zone. "Slow your ass down or we won't get there."

"I know. I'm sorry but I don't want anything to happen to her." She slowed the car down to 40mph.

"I'm sure she's fine. Just take your time." Brandi told her. "We'll be there soon. She's probably taking a nap and not answering the phone."

Brandi looked out the window. She was concerned also. She didn't want her friend to get hurt.

Rhonda gradually resumed her speed. *We're coming Meka. Just hold on,* she said to herself and sped down the road.

Chapter Thirty-Three

◇◇

R *obert Holloway, you are under arrest for vehicular hit and run; and the attempted murder of Bernard Simpson. You have the right to remain silent. If you give up that right, anything you say can and will be held against you in a court of law. You have the right to an attorney. If you cannot afford an attorney, one will be appointed to you. Do you understand your rights?*

Shemeka replayed the scene in her head. Robert had looked at her without saying a word. His hands cuffed behind his back, his shirt still unbuttoned and his shoes untied. He was silent and cooperative with the officers. He didn't deny hitting Bernard and offered no explanation. The two officers led him away while she looked on.

Shemeka didn't understand any of it. What reason would Robert have to run Bernard down? As far as she knew, the two men didn't know each other. She didn't know what to do. This day had been a roller coaster ride and she wanted to get off. If it were not devastating enough to find out that Robert was Roberta, she had the added stress of him being arrested for running down the husband of one of her very best friends. How could she face Rhonda? How could she face herself? Robert had spent months deceiving her and had turned out to be someone totally different from who she thought he was. She was startled by the ringing doorbell. Shemeka looked through the peephole to see Rhonda and Brandi. Rhonda must not know yet about Robert. She opened the door and the women practically ran inside.

"Sit down Shemeka. We need to talk." Rhonda said. "Bernard has regained consciousness and named the person who ran him down."

Shemeka burst into tears. "I know. The police just arrested Robert. I'm so very sorry. Rhonda. I didn't know."

Rhonda put her arms around Shemeka "It's not your fault Honey. You didn't do anything. We were just worried about you when we found out. We didn't know what else he was capable of."

She walked over to the end table where the picture of her and Robert was. "You don't understand." She picked the picture up. "See this? See this fake shit?" She threw the picture across the room. Rhonda and Brandi watched as the picture hit the wall before shattering into hundreds of pieces of glass on the floor. They looked at each other and said nothing.

"He's a fuckin' bitch." She screamed.

"You're right," Brandi answered. "Only a straight up bitch would leave a man to die like that. But it'll be fine. You'll get through this. The main thing is that he didn't hurt you."

"No!" Shemeka sat down on the couch. "Robert's a fuckin woman."

"WHAT?" Brandi and Rhonda shouted in unison.

Shemeka slid from the couch to the floor. Tears flooded her cheeks. "I've been with a woman all this time. A damn bitch. I trusted that bitch. How could he do this to me?"

Rhonda didn't know what to say. She thought about her episodes with Nikki. She was definitely in no position to judge anyone. A part of her wanted to tell the girls about her episode with Nikki and how Nikki had transformed from an angel to a demon but she decided not to. This wasn't about her right now. It was about Shemeka.

Brandi broke the silence. "Meka, how could you not know? I thought you said that you had finally gotten the dick. She doesn't have a dick does she?"

It sounded strange to hear Robert being referred to as a *she*. "No!" Shemeka whimpered through sniffles and sobs. "It's strapped on him. I never saw it until today. We did have sex but not like that. He was careful to keep me from seeing it. We were always in the dark or by candlelight. We had sex from the back and I didn't think anything about it because that was my favorite position. We had it from the front once while I was on the countertop and once on the couch. After we finished, he went in the bathroom and cleaned up because he had to leave. I feel so damn stupid.

"Stop beating yourself up about it girl." Rhonda told her. "We have all done stupid things at one time or another that we regret. Shit happens. You're naturally hurt and anybody would be but you can't be so hard on yourself."

"I'm just so ashamed of myself. I told him how good it felt. Oh my goodness. Lord please help me." Shemeka got off the floor and stood in the middle of the room.

Rhonda didn't want to comment on that. She knew all too well how good it could feel a woman using a strap-on to fuck you if they knew what they were doing. She knew how real it could be and she understood how Shemeka could have been fooled.

"Damn Girl!" Brandi responded. "You always look at the dick Meka. I make it my business to see what a brother is working with. He might have a sore or something on that thang. Shit! I have to see what's going up in this pussy."

Rhonda stood up beside Shemeka. "Come on now Brandi. It could easily happen and you know it. The first time you were with Erik, if ya'll had gotten all caught up and in the mood and Erik started playing with you, and was standing behind you and lifted your dress up and stuck his dick in, then what? You know damn well that you wouldn't say *Hold up Baby. Let me examine that dick.* Now would you? Hell no."

"Well I guess you are right but that is some weird ass shit. Meka we love you and we're here for you." Brandi joined her two friends and they engaged in a group hug.

"We've all been through some things and trying to deal with them on our own. We're going to have to do better. Our lives should never get so busy that we are not there for each other when we are needed. That's what friends do." Rhonda said.

Shemeka agreed. "You're right. Friends not only have your back but they have your front and your sides as well. I just feel so let down though. I can't even hate Robert. I don't know how I feel. I don't know what to do."

Brandi wanted to be supportive of her friend but she didn't understand Shemeka talked like she still had feelings for that woman. She didn't want to talk about Robert. She wanted to talk about them being closer as friends but she knew that Robert was part of the equation. Being a good friend meant being a good listener at times. She would do whatever she needed to do to help Shemeka get through this, whether she agreed with her or not.

"We are all going to be just fine. God knows that I have been dealing with issues. This thing with Anthony and Erik has been almost unbearable. We need to start back with our girls' night out. We'll have to schedule one for soon."

Tears continued to run down Shemeka's face. She knew that Rhonda and Brandi loved her but they didn't understand how she felt. It was something that you had to go through to understand. And how many women could say they had gone through being in love with a man, only to find out that he was a woman? She had anticipated a future with Robert and now that would never happen. Everything she had hoped for and dreamed of was out of her reach because he had fabricated a lie.

Shemeka wanted to hate Robert for everything he had done to her and everything he had put her through but she couldn't. She still felt something for him. What? She didn't know. She wasn't sure if she loved him or if she felt sorry for him and all that his dad had put him through. His story was a sad one. Neither Rhonda nor Brandi would understand if she told them that she wanted to bail him out of jail. There had to be an explanation for why he ran down Bernard. Maybe that crazy cousin of his would come to his rescue. If she bailed out the man who tried to kill Rhonda's husband; it would be like a slap in the face to Rhonda. She would wait. After all, he hadn't used his one telephone call to contact her.

Shemeka looked at Rhonda. "Go to your husband. I'm sure that he's wondering where you are. I'll be fine."

"Actually, I was supposed to be picking up a few things for him. I hate to leave you like this. Are you sure?" Rhonda asked her.

"Yes. I'll be fine." She looked at Brandi. "You too. Get out of here. I'm sure that you have something else you can be doing besides baby-sitting me."

"I can't think of a thing, and who said that I'll be the one baby-sitting you? You might be the one baby-sitting me." Brandi laughed and sat down. "Go ahead and handle your business Rhonda. I'll hang out with Meka for a while." Brandi wanted to ask Meka again, how she let herself be fooled like that. She wasn't feeling it. There was no way she wouldn't be able to tell a false dick from the real thing. She knew that Shemeka had been out of the dating arena for a while but DAMN!

"I'll check back on you girls later. I love ya'll." Rhonda kissed her friends and left. Brandi decided not to question Shemeka about Robert. Whenever she decided to talk, she would. They talked about Erik instead and Shemeka was in a state of awe that Brandi had decided to give it up to a white man. She could see that Meka was exhausted. After about an hour, she fell asleep on the couch. Brandi found a throw in the linen closet and covered Meka up. "Sweet dreams. Tomorrow will be better." She curled up on the loveseat and went to sleep herself.

Chapter Thirty-Four

◇◇◇

N ikki pulled up in front of the police station to pick Robert up. "What the hell?" She asked as he climbed into her truck.

"I know." He replied. "It's a long story Nikki. I wasn't trying to kill Bernard. That's not what happened. I did intend to hit him but I was only trying to teach him a lesson. He hurt you and I am sick of him thinking he can walk all over you. Enough is enough. I swore to myself that I would never stand by and watch another man hurt you."

"Robert, that son-of-a-bitch hasn't hurt me. I don't want his sorry ass. Fuck him. I could care less about Bernard Simpson."

"But it's his entire fault. The way you talk to people and curse people out for nothing, the way you treat Dean, the way you talk to your clients. I thought it was all because of the way Bernard does you. He pops in whenever the fuck he gets ready, he tells you that he's leaving his wife and all he does is use you. I was just trying to protect you Nikki. I know that I didn't do a good job of protecting you from my dad, but I'm grown now. I won't let anybody else hurt you."

Nikki slammed on brakes missing the car in front of her by only a few inches. "I told you to stop blaming yourself for that bullshit. I'm good. You're fucked up worse than I am. Let the lowlife continue to rot in hell." She held the palms of her hand on the car horn and yelled to the driver in front of her, "Keep moving Bitch. What the hell you waiting on? Christmas?"

Robert placed his hand on top of hers, "Nikki, have you taken your medicine today?"

"No! I'm out. I told you that I don't need that shit anyway. I'm good. It's just that these no driving bitches get on my damn nerves."

"Well just calm down Nikki. Do you need money for your meds?" He asked her.

"No Robert. I told you, I don't need that shit. All it does is make me sleep. How did you get out anyway? I know they didn't let you post your own bail. So what's up? Not enough evidence? What?"

"Nah. They have enough evidence. Eyewitness. Bernard looked straight at me when I hit him. I was surprised that it took them so long to pick me up but he had not regained consciousness."

"If only I had known. To think Robert, I was right there in the hospital with him. If I had known he was going to point the finger at you, I would have finished him off in the hospital." She said.

"I'm glad you didn't. What if you would have gotten caught? I am the one who should be protecting my younger cousin and you are the one who has taken all of the risk. I could never let you do that again Nikki."

"Let's not talk about that. How did you get out?" She asked.

"They are going to issue another warrant for my arrest. It's only a matter of time. They couldn't keep me legally. The arrest warrant was for Robert Holloway. I'm not legally Robert. I'm Roberta Holloway. You should have seen those men when they got me undressed. One tried to hurry up and cover me up. I think he was scared that I would do something like holla rape."

"Oh snap." Nikki laughed. "Ain't that a bitch? Out on a technicality. Well I'll just be damned."

Robert looked at Nikki who was laughing uncontrollably. "That's not funny."

"Yes it is." She continued to laugh while weaving in and out of traffic. "I wish I could have seen the look on their faces when they strip searched your ass. Ha...ha...ha! Damn! I know they freaked out."

"Speaking of being freaked out, I need for you to drop me by Shemeka's house. She didn't take the news too well and I need to make sure that she is okay."

"Hell to the fuckin no!" Nikki protested. "I'm not taking you by that bitch's house. Ain't nothing wrong with her. She's fine. Every time I turn around she is all up in Rhonda's face. Leave that bitch alone. She's not worth your time Robert."

"Nikki, I need to talk to her. She knows about my past and what I've gone through. I just didn't have enough time to answer all of her questions before the police came to pick me up. I would like to check on her." He explained to Nikki.

"Fool! You told her about your daddy?" Nikki asked.

"Yes I told her. I love her." He answered.

"Everything? You didn't tell her everything did you?" Nikki continued to question Robert. She wanted to know how much he had told Shemeka. She didn't trust that woman. Robert shouldn't trust her neither. Shemeka wouldn't hesitate to use the information against Nikki.

"Nikki, you were protecting me sweetheart. That is our secret. I promise you that I will carry that secret to my grave. No one will ever know that you killed my daddy. We swore not to ever talk about that again. Like you said, let him continue to rot in hell."

"I know that you wouldn't say anything Robert. I don't know what I was thinking. It's just that the bitch seems to have you wrapped around her finger. I still see that muthafucka sometimes in my dreams. I hate him. He's dead and I still hate his ass." Nikki said.

"That's our secret Nikki. You were twelve years old. No one ever questioned our story. My dad had so many enemies that they wouldn't have known where to begin looking for his murderer anyway. You saved me and I would die before I let anyone know what happened that night. Trust me Nikki. I love Shemeka but the bond that you and I share can never be broken."

"Thanks Robert but I still don't trust that bitch. Now she's trying to act like she's all freaked out about you being a woman. She is no stranger to pussy. You can't tell me that she and Rhonda haven't been kicking it. And if they haven't then she wants to. I hate her. I'm not taking you over there." She told him.

"Well just let me out Nikki. I'll catch a taxi. I'm not going to argue with you about a woman who means everything to me. I love Shemeka. She didn't deserve for me to treat her like that. I need to make things right. Pull over right her and let me out if you are not going to take me." Robert put his hand on the steering wheel and Nikki took the next exit.

"I'll let you off right here. Don't go over there Robert. Can't you see that she is trying to spoil things for us? She wants to come between us. I'm not going to let her do that."

Robert got out of the car and stuck his head back in before closing the door.

"Please take your medicine Nikki. You know what the doctor said. Every time you start feeling well, you think you don't need to take your medicine, but you do. I love you." He blew her a kiss before closing the car door.

Chapter Thirty-Five

◇◇◇

E rik waited for Brandi at the restaurant. He was a little early for the
reservation so he sat at the bar.

"Whatcha having?" The bartender asked.

"Crown and coke." He answered.

"Coming right up." The bartender prepared the drink and sat it down
in front of Erik. He took a sip of the drink. His mind wandered to Brandi.
Things hadn't happened exactly the way he thought they would. He had
desired to be with Brandi for years but never anticipated it happening. She
always looked to him as if he were her brother. Now that they had crossed
the line and slept together, he knew that she expected more. He had made
a mistake. He never should have given in to her and slept with her knowing
that he could not be what she wanted. They could never have a meaningful
relationship. He should have told her that he was involved with someone
but she was hurting. All Erik wanted to do was ease her pain and make
her feel better. His thoughts were interrupted by the hostess.

"Sir, your party has arrived." The hostess told him.

Standing at the entrance, Brandi looked beautiful. Her hair was up in
pin curls. Her black and silver strapless dress exposed her shoulders. The
silver necklace that adorned her neck matched perfect with the earrings
that dangled from her small ears. The two toned black and silver heels
looked like they were made exactly for her dress. Erik admired her poise

as she stood there watching him walk towards her. He had not seen that sparkling glimmer her eyes in quite a while. He kissed her on the cheek.

"Hi Sexy. You look absolutely stunning." He said to her.

"You don't look so bad yourself." She said with a smile.

The hostess grabbed two menus. "Your table is ready. Follow me please." They followed the hostess to a table in the far corner of the restaurant. Erik had requested the table and the restaurant to lessen his chances of being seen. The band played while a woman sang one of Gladys Knight's songs, *A Letter Full of Tears*. Brandi's mind briefly flashed back to the letter she had received from Anthony. He loved her in his own way. She was the only one he had that he could depend on. But he was there and Erik was here. She wanted to live in the moment.

Erik pulled out the chair for Brandi and took his seat. After ordering a bottle of wine, he looked at Brandi. "Brandi, I don't want us to rush into anything. I know that you are still hung up on Anthony and I know that you are looking for someone who can make you feel alive again. I don't want this to be a rebound thing."

Brandi didn't know how to respond. She didn't want Erik to feel like she was using him. He made her feel special and she needed a warm body. It was time for her to start living her life. She was young and she couldn't stop living her life while Anthony was locked up. Why should she let life pass her by? She hadn't committed a crime. He had. She was going to always do what she could do for him but the system had taken its toll on her.

"Erik, before we get into us, tell me how your mom is doing. You didn't say anything about what was wrong with her." She said to him.

"Oh yeah. Mom's doing fine. It was a false alarm. She worries about her heart because heart failure runs in the family. She's resting."

"Good. I was worried about her. I've been praying for her. Listen Erik, I am not trying to rush things or make you feel like this is a rebound thing. I want us to explore all possibilities and see where this leads. We were friends before we were lovers so that gives us a better chance than most. No, we are not in love with each other but we care about each other and have a lot in common. I think we can make this work. If I didn't believe that I wouldn't waste your time nor mine."

Erik didn't want to hurt Brandi. She had been hurt enough by Anthony. He wanted her to be happy but he knew that her happiness did not lie with him. "Brandi, let's just take things slow. If it happens, it will happen. No expectations and no strings. Can you live with that?" He asked her.

"I can live with that. I need to make a clean break with Anthony the first chance I get. As long as you and I keep it real with each other, we shouldn't have a problem." She answered.

Erik took another drink of wine. He didn't look at Brandi. How could he agree to be in an honest relationship when he was starting the relationship out based on a lie?

"Let's dance. I think they're playing our song." He said and led her to the dance floor.

When Erik walked Brandi to her car after a wonderful meal and dancing, she felt a little tipsy. Her head was spinning with emotions. She was really feeling Erik and was disappointed when he had not offered to follow her home. He kissed her and told her what an enjoyable time he had. He opened the car door for her and helped her into the car before watching her drive away.

Brandi walked into the house and kicked off her shoes. She fell back on the bed and smiled as she looked at the ceiling. Erik was wonderful. He was romantic and he was free. Her smile quickly vanished when thoughts of Anthony flashed through her mind. How could she tell him that she had moved on? She needed to let him know. It was not fair to him for her to let him sit up in prison thinking she was faithful and devoted to him when all the while she was seeing Erik. Knowing that she would not be able to talk to him for a couple of weeks, she decided not to put things off.

She walked over to her chest and took out a pen and some stationary. No matter how delicate she tried to be, she knew that it would hurt Anthony. But in the end, wouldn't he want her to be happy? If he truly loved her, wouldn't he want her to go on with her life? She sat at the table and wrote:

My Dearest Anthony,

How are you? I hope that my letter finds you doing well despite your present circumstances. It has to be difficult being in SHU and having the added limitations placed on you.

I really don't know where to begin. There is so much that I need to say to you and it's not easy. I love you very much Anthony and if love alone could get us through this, then we wouldn't have a problem. Now, I'm starting to ramble. Let me get to the point.

Baby, there is nothing I wouldn't do for you. Four years is a long time out of my life. I know that it doesn't seem like a long time to you but to me it seems like eternity. I am lonely here without you. There is a void and it's not being filled with us unable to communicate. I'm sorry Baby. I need so much more than you are able to give me. I've found someone to fill that void Anthony. I have the utmost respect for you and I wouldn't want you to find out from anyone besides me. I was not looking for it and I was not out there disrespecting you. It just somehow happened and I really need to explore the possibility and see where it leads.

The last thing I ever want to do is hurt you. Please know that I will always cherish what we shared. I love you and if

there is ever anything I can do for you, let me know. Take
care of yourself Ant. I wish you all the best.

Brandi

With tears in-her eyes, she folded the letter and placed it in an envelope. Brandi knew that Anthony would be hurt but he had to know the truth. She couldn't make a fool out of him like some of the others girls did inmates. She had seen it so many times. Girls would come to visit their so called man but once they left the prison they returned to the man they had on the outside. Men who had longer sentences were the ones who usually got messed over but occasionally those with shorter sentences happened to be attached to a whore.

She once heard a woman saying, *My husband knows I have needs. These men don't expect us to sit around and twiddle our thumbs. They just don't want to know about it. I do what I do but don't let any man get attached to me because I don't want any problems when my ole man gets out. It's not what you do; it's how you do it.*

Brandi found that a lot of the women had that same mentality but she wasn't going along with that. Anthony was a rare breed. He would never accept a woman of his being with another man. Some men didn't care because all they wanted the woman for was to put money on their books and come visit them. Anthony didn't give a damn about the money or the visits if he didn't have complete loyalty.

Brandi prayed that he would not overreact when he received her letter. It was bad to have to tell him that in a letter but she was not able to visit him and the longer she waited, the more chance there was of someone seeing her with Erik and getting the word back to Anthony. Hopefully, by her explaining things to him, he would not do something stupid to get himself into trouble. She said a silent prayer before licking the envelope and putting a stamp on it. She needed a drink.

Chapter Thirty-Six

❖❖

Shemeka stood in front of the window and watched the raindrops fall; she had taken a leave of absence from her job. She figured that word of Robert's arrest had gotten out and her coworkers would be full of questions. Questions that she didn't wish to deal with. She felt stupid enough on her own without anyone else making her feel like a fool.

Shemeka wondered how Robert was doing. She had heard that he got out and was re-arrested about forty-five minutes later while trying to hail a taxi. The Sheriff's office had to issue another warrant using his legal name. He had been informed of the process and knew that a warrant was pending. They could not hold him there because the federal and state statues dealing with legal mechanisms would not allow it.

If only she could get her feelings in check. How could she still have feelings for Robert after he had manipulated her and betrayed her trust? He had to know that his secret would come out sooner or later. What was he going to do when it was time for them to shower together? Why did he let her fall in love with him?

As the rain continued to fall, so did her tears. She ignored the ringing telephone. It was probably Rhonda or Brandi. She knew that her friends were concerned but she needed to deal with this on her own. There was nothing anyone could say to make things better. Nothing could erase the past. Maybe she was meant to be alone. Not every woman was meant to have a man by her side.

Shemeka had been so careful not to let her guard down. After all these years of protecting herself from letting any other man hurt her like Darnell did; she slipped up. No matter what Robert was, she could not consider him as anything but a man. It was too devastating to admit that he was actually a woman. She couldn't wrap her mind around the concept of thinking that she had fallen in love with a woman and had allowed that woman to hurt her.

Darnell was handsome and every girls' dream. He was the star quarterback for her high school's football team. When he walked into the room everybody noticed. It was no wonder that Shemeka thought she had died and gone to Heaven when he asked her to be his date for the prom.

Others envied her and spread lies about her. She would hear girls in the halls asking things like, *What's so special about her? You know that she's giving it up. Oh, she thinks she's something since she's dating Darnell.* Shemeka ignored the haters. It was not important what anybody thought. All that was important was the fact that Darnell was her man and she was happy. She even ignored the rumors that he was messing around with Tiffany Davis. How could he be messing around with that slut when he spent most of his spare time with her? No, she was not giving it up to him like people thought but he understood. He told her that he would wait until she was ready. Another similarity to Robert.

When Rhonda approached her with the insinuation that Darnell was being unfaithful she listened. "Girl, that muthafucka ain't shit. Darnell is messing around with Tiffany."

"How? He's with me most of the time when he is not at practice. He doesn't have time to mess around. You know how jealous Tiffany is. She would start any kind of rumor to get us to break up. I admit that I was a little bit concerned at first. I asked him about it and he explained how the rumor started. She came over his house, one night a couple of months ago to study for a biology test. The rumor started from there. He doesn't want Tiffany." Shemeka remembered how naive she had been back then.

"Well, I think it is a little more than a rumor." Rhonda told her. "I heard Tiffany tell Darnell that she is pregnant."

Shemeka had not wanted to believe that but she knew Rhonda would never lie to her about something like that. Upon confronting Darnell about Rhonda's accusations, he admitted that Tiffany was indeed pregnant and that the baby might be his. If it was, he was determined to be there for his child.

She was crushed and retreated into her shell. Everybody in school talked about how Darnell had used her and made a fool out of her. She considered dropping out of school but Rhonda and Brandi persuaded her to stay. They convinced her that if she dropped out, she would only be doing herself an injustice and that the best way to get back at Darnell was to get her education. "Knowledge is power." Brandi told her. "His grades are not worth a damn. All he has going for him is football. It's not going to carry him through life."

Sure enough, she was right. Darnell injured his left knee during the summer and was unable to play football again. Shemeka vowed not to ever get involved in another serious relationship. Until…Robert. She let her guard down and he snuck in. He invaded her heart and then he burst it wide open. This was worse than any experience with Darnell.

She had beaten herself up for being too stupid to realize that Darnell was cheating. There had to be signs. Had she just ignored them or was she so desperate to have him that she settled? And what about Robert? There had to be signs. Had she ignored them or was she so desperate to have a man that she just settled? Hell no! She wasn't that desperate. If she had known Robert was a woman, there is no way that she would have allowed herself to fall in love with him.

Shemeka was confused. *I still love him. Am I gay? Am I attracted to women? Why did he do this to me?* She thought to herself.

The doorbell startled her. Although she was standing in the window, Shemeka was lost in her thoughts and didn't see a car pull up.

"Who is it?" She asked.

"Robert! May I come in? We need to talk Shemeka. I promise not to stay long but I can't leave things like this. Please let me in." Robert pleaded.

"I don't have anything to say Robert." She answered from the other side of the door. "Just go away. There is nothing left to talk about."

His continual dancing on the doorbell was a strong indication that he was not going anywhere without talking to her. Slowly, Shemeka twisted the doorknob and opened the door. Robert walked in without looking at her. He stood next to the loveseat and motioned for Shemeka to sit down.

"I'll stand. What is it Robert? Say whatever you feel like you need to say."

"I'd rather you have a seat Meka. I won't be long. I just want to say that I'm sorry. I know that you must hate me. I need for you to understand that I never meant to hurt you. I'm in love with you. I swear that I love you."

"Robert. Excuse me but I can't get use to calling you Roberta. I don't know Roberta. I only know Robert. But you should not have come. What do you expect from me? What do you want? Am I supposed to run into your arms? Am I supposed to open my legs and let you eat me out? Or better yet, am I supposed to lie down so you can strap up and fuck me? I can't Robert. I can't deal with the betrayal. I'm sorry."

"Do you love me Shemeka?" He asked her.

She looked away. "How can I love you when I don't know you? Can I love a stranger?

You are not who I thought you were."

"You thought I was a man who loves you very much and who wants to be with you for life. That's who I am. I am the man you thought I was. I want us to put all of this behind us. What can I do to make it right?" He asked.

"You want what?" She cried. "You are not a damn man. I don't know what you are. All I know is that you've ruined my life."

"Baby, please let me fix this." He walked towards Shemeka. "I want to..." The doorbell rang. Shemeka walked to open the door. Before she reached the entrance, the door flew open. She froze in her tracks not knowing what to expect. Robert was in complete shock.

Nikki burst in with blood red eyes. A scarf was tied around her head like she was the pancake lady. She wore sweat pants and a tee shirt, which showed years of wear and tear. The thin places in the tee shirt revealed that she was not wearing a bra. Her breast stood firm and her nipples left indentions on the shirt.

"I asked you to stay away from this bitch. You can't do it can you? She asked Robert.

"Nikki, you need to leave. Shemeka and I have things to discuss. Did you do what I asked you? Have you gotten your meds Nikki? You don't look good." He remained by Shemeka's side.

"How the hell are you going to bust up in my house like this? Get out of here. You are not welcome." She told Nikki.

"Bitch, I know what you are trying to do. Rhonda is not answering my calls. Now you have my cousin over here asking me to leave. You think that you can turn everybody against me don't you? Well I won't let you spoil it."

Nikki looked at Shemeka while retrieving a 38 Smith & Wesson from the back of her sweat pants.

"Oh my God! No Nikki. Please don't. Come on. I'll leave with you. Let's go. Put the gun away." Robert begged.

Instead, Nikki pointed the gun at Shemeka's heart. A loud noise filled the room as she pulled the trigger.

Chapter Thirty-Seven

◇◇

R honda was filled with anticipation. Bernard was being released from the hospital. They had not been in each other's arms for quite a while now. She was anxious to get him home so she could pamper him.

Before she left the house, she baked spaghetti and placed it in the oven. She decided to wait on the garlic bread so it could come out of the oven hot. The tossed salad was in the refrigerator along with a pitcher of fresh brewed tea.

Bernard had signed his release papers and had been given his at home care instructions. Rhonda sat next to him on the bed waiting for someone from transportation to come. Although he wanted to walk, it was hospital policy that he is wheeled out in a wheelchair.

"I love you Bernard. I can't wait to get you home. I've really missed you. Having you away from me and laid up in the hospital has made me realize how much you mean to me."

"I love you too Baby." He squeezed her hand. "There is so much we need to talk about once I get out of here. There are so many things I wish I could change Baby. You have really stuck by me and I am going to spend the rest of my life being a good husband to you. You deserve nothing but the best." Bernard looked away from Rhonda. He deeply regretted getting involved with Nikki. She had been a thorn in his side. Rhonda had her faults, but he should have tried to work things out with her. Instead, he found himself in the arms of another woman who was controlling, deceitful, and manipulative.

Rhonda leaned over to kiss her husband when someone knocked on the door. "Finally! Transportation. Come in." She stood up."

A woman walked into the room. "Bernard Simpson?" She asked.

"Yes." He nodded. "What can I do for you?"

The woman extended her hand, first to Bernard and then to Rhonda. "Hi, I'm Ms. Cutshaw from the Department of Social Services; Child Protection Division. May we speak in private?" She asked Bernard.

Bernard looked at the woman in total confusion until he remembered the incident at the school. A student had come to him about an issue of abuse. He sent the student to the Guidance Counselor. By law, they are required to report any suspected cases of abuse to the Department of Social Services.

"Oh no! It's fine Ms. Cutshaw. This is my wife Rhonda. You may speak freely in front of her. We're waiting on transportation. I am being discharged today."

"Your wheels have arrived." A nurse walked into the room pushing a wheelchair. She pushed it to Bernard's bed and he climbed in.

"Mr. Simpson, I'll tell you what. How about if I give you a minute to get home and get settled in. I didn't know that you were being discharged today. I'll meet you at your house in... let's say, about an hour. Does that work for you?" Ms. Cutshaw asked.

"Sure. We'll see you in an hour." He answered.

Once they were in the car, Rhonda questioned Bernard. "Honey, what was that all about?" She asked him.

"I'm not sure Boo but I think it is about a student. Her name is Brianna. She came to school one day and was very withdrawn. At first, I didn't think much of it because we all have our bad days. When her bus was called at the end of the day, she wouldn't move. I told her that she was going to miss her bus and asked her if she heard them call her bus number.

She told me that her mom was not going to be home and she didn't want to be there with her step dad because he beats her. She showed me a large bruise under her sleeve. I took her to the Guidance Counselor. There's not really much that I can tell Ms. Cutshaw. The Guidance Counselor can help her better than me but I'll talk with her."

"Damn. It's just hard telling these days." Rhonda said. "I mean like sometimes these parents do go too far with hitting and abusing children; but there are also the children who really need to have their asses torn up. My parents whipped my ass and I am still here. If anybody had come to my house from Social Services and seen some of the whelps on my ass, they would certainly have gotten my folks."

"Tell me about it." Bernard agreed, "It's nothing like it used to be. Parents can barely chastise their child now because of the laws. Then they send them to school and expect us to be able to do something with them."

Rhonda pulled up into the garage and helped Bernard out of the car. "I love you Bernard. I have to bring you up to speed on everything that has been going on. First, let's get in the house and eat. I'm starving."

Bernard sat patiently while Rhonda pulled the pan of baked spaghetti out of the oven and put the garlic bread in. She poured him a glass of tea to drink while she set the table and prepared to serve him lunch.

He enjoyed his meal and couldn't seem to take his eyes off of Rhonda who had changed into shorts and a tee. "Baby, it's been a long time. Doc says I'm as good as new. After Ms. Cutshaw leaves, I'm going to show you how much I love and need you."

He was stretched out on the couch when Ms. Cutshaw rang the doorbell. Rhonda spoke into the intercom to let Ms. Cutshaw know she would be right there. She opened the door and welcomed Ms. Cutshaw.

"Come in and have a seat. May I get you something to drink? A nice cool glass of tea?"

"No thank you Mrs. Simpson." She walked over to the wing back chair and had a seat. Bernard picked up the glass of tea Rhonda had fixed for him and took a sip.

"Ahh! It sure is good." He said to Ms. Cutshaw.

"Mr. Simpson, I'll be as brief as possible. I'm here concerning your daughter."

Bernard dropped the glass of tea he held in his hand. Glass shattered over the marble floor. Rhonda sprang to her feet as Bernard sat there speechless gazing at her with a solemn look on his face. "Daughter? What are you talking about? My husband doesn't have a daughter!"

"Ma'am, I'm sorry. I had no idea that you weren't aware of the child. I assure you that your husband has a daughter. Paternity was established after her birth."

Rhonda looked at Bernard for some kind of explanation. He continued to gaze at her, mumbling, "I'm sorry. I wanted to tell you. It was an accident."

"Accident? Accidents don't just happen. You whoring ass son-of-a-"

"Whoa!" Ms. Cutshaw stood in front of Bernard who was still seated. "I see that you have a few things to discuss with your wife. I also realize that this is not the ideal time for what I have to say."

Bernard stood up. "What is it? Does that bitch want more money? I give her more than any Judge would ever order me to pay. I take care of her house payments every damn month and along with cash money, I have the child on my insurance. What else does she want? Blood?"

Rhonda was in total disbelief. She wanted to cry but nothing came out. How could her husband have a child and she not know? The shit didn't make any sense. "Who's the child's mama?" She screamed.

Ms. Cutshaw looked at Bernard before answering. "Ma'am her name is Nicole Harris."

"Nikki! That bitch Nikki? Oh my God. Oh! I hate you." She shouted.

"I'm sorry. I don't mean to put added stress on an already stressful situation. However, we have removed Bernadine from the home. We received a call from Camp Slumber. They noticed several bruises on her body and she seemed to be in pain when she was touched. The child refuses to tell us what caused her injuries. Bernadine was taken to the hospital and examined. Her ribs are cracked. She has had unexplained injuries in the past. There is an investigation but I must be candid with you. It doesn't look good. I doubt seriously if your daughter will be placed back in the home any time soon, if at all.

"So what are you saying? What does that have to do with us? What the hell do you expect us to do?" Rhonda asked through sobs.

"Bernadine was taken from the hospital and placed with a foster family. She is being taken care of. This visit is an attempt to place her with a family member. We always strive to do what we think will be in the best interest of the child. I understand that the two of you will have to discuss this before making a decision. I will return in forty-eight hours. At that time, I will need an answer so I can proceed to the next step."

Before walking out the door, Ms. Cutshaw handed Bernard her card. "If you have any questions, please do not hesitate to contact me."

When the door was closed and Ms. Cutshaw was gone, Rhonda ran upstairs towards their bedroom. Bernard ran behind her. "Wait Honey. We need to talk. I'm sorry Baby. Please. I'm begging you to forgive me. Let's talk about this."

Rhonda didn't answer her husband. She continued towards the bedroom. Bernard figured that she was going to lock herself into the room. He tried to stop her. "Please don't shut me out Baby."

When Rhonda went into the bedroom, she walked over to Bernard's closet. She opened the door and snatched his clothes off the rack. "Get out! Get the fuck out!"

Chapter Thirty-Eight

◇◇

Brandi's head felt like someone had stomped on it wearing army boots. She sat up on the side of the bed and pressed her hands onto her temples. Her eyes surveyed the room for Tylenol, Aleve, or any pain reliever that would stop the pounding.

On the nightstand next to her bed was an empty bottle of Grey Goose; a reminder of the previous night. Anthony's letter lay on the floor where she had dropped it. Brandi grabbed the bedpost to steady herself as she reached down to pick up the letter. The paper trembled in her hands as she read over it for the fifth time.

Brandi,

> *Check dis out. If ya wanned a toy, ya shoulda gotten ya a baby doll. Don play no fuckin games wit me cause I'm not down wit dat shit. I told ya how much I love ya and ya claimed to love me too. I guess ya were just tellin a damn lie. Who is the nigga ya got out there in yer ear and in ya damn bed? I'm not stupid. I thot ya wuz diffrent from da rest of dem whores but ya are just like dem. Ya tell a nigga ya gone stand by him but wen the shit get hard, ya ready to go. Well I don need ya. I can do dis shit by my damn self. I just don*

*ppreciate bein played. Ya messed wit da wrong one. Ya will
live ta regret fuckin over me. I promise ya da shit. Karma is
a muthfucka. Trust me.*

Anthony

Brandi tossed the letter on the bed. She stumbled into the bathroom
to check the medicine cabinet. She grabbed the bottle of Tylenol from
the top shelf. It felt nearly empty. Brandi opened it and removed the one
Tylenol, which was left in the bottle. She went to the kitchen and got a
glass of water to wash down the pill. Brandi sat at the kitchen table and
rested her pounding head in her hands. She ignored the ringing telephone
and let the answering machine pick it up while she listened.

*Brandi, its Rhonda. You must be in the shower. I'm on the way over.
See you in a few.* She had completely forgotten about Rhonda who had
called the night before needing to talk. Rhonda had sounded like she had
something heavy on her mind but Brandi was in no mood to help anyone
with their problems. She had lied to Rhonda, telling her that Erik was there
and asking if it could wait until morning.

She dragged herself into the shower before slipping on a pair of jeans
and a tube top.

Pain was written all over Rhonda's face when Brandi opened the door
to let her in. Her eyes were red and swollen. Her clothes were wrinkled
like she had slept in them all night and she had on bedroom slippers. She
looked nothing like the petite, well-groomed friend Brandi was used to
seeing.

"Come in Rhonda. What's wrong? Is it Bernard? Did he have a backset
after he got home or something?" Brandi asked.

"Or something is more like it." Rhonda answered. She told Brandi
about the visit from Ms. Cutshaw, and about Bernard's illegitimate child.

"I'm sure that muthafucka doesn't expect you to raise his child. It
would be a constant reminder of his infidelity. Tell him 'HELL NO' and

don't even entertain the thought." Brandi was having a difficult time with what Bernard had done. All of the girls had bragged about how Rhonda had it going on and they thought Bernard was the most faithful husband, a woman could possibly have.

"I am having a hard time with this shit. I can't believe it. He has a child and I didn't know about it." She cried.

"Are you sure that the child is his?" Brandi asked. "You know how these women will put a child on the man who they think can provide more for them."

"It's his. Paternity tests were done after the child was born. There is no doubt that the girl is his. Now that I think about it, she looks like him too." Rhonda answered.

"You've seen her?"

"Yes, I've met her but at the time, I didn't know she was his child. I did notice a familiarity about her but I just didn't put it together." Rhonda sat down.

"Damn! You've been faithful as hell to that cheating ass bastard. Of all the whores running around out there he chooses to cheat with one that is smiling in your damn face. No wonder her ass was at the hospital all the damn time. She was checking on her man. The bitch!" Brandi walked into the kitchen. "Can I get you a cup of coffee? I have a fresh pot."

"Yes. Thank you. Cream and three packs of equal." She wondered what kind of sick game Nikki was playing. Why would she lay up with her and try to act like she was so in love with her while hiding the fact that Bernard fathered her child? Why was she so fixated on her? What the hell did she want?"

"Hey! Snap out of it." Brandi snapped her fingers in front of Rhonda's face. "Where did you get to? I lost you for a minute there."

"I don't know Brandi. I asked Bernard to move out of the house but he wouldn't. He moved into one of the guest rooms. We talked. He said that he wants our marriage to work but I don't see it. How can I ever trust him again? I hate him for doing this. I hate him for putting us in this situation." She took the cup of coffee Brandi handed her.

"Thank you."

"What are you going to do? Don't tell me that you are considering taking that child Rhonda. Don't be a fool." Brandi pleaded with her.

"She's innocent. She is really a sweet child. It's not her fault. She's a victim just like I am. Damn! I hate him!" Rhonda cried. "How can he love me and do me like this?"

Brandi put her arms around her friend to console her. As she held Rhonda, she thought about her own painful situation. She didn't like the tone of Anthony's letter. *Was he planning on doing something to her? He wouldn't do anything stupid would he?*

"Rhonda, I know that it's not all right but eventually, it will be. Only you can decide what to do about your situation. I love you and I am here for you no matter what you decide. If it were me, I couldn't deal with raising the child; but that's just me. You and I are different people. If you decide not to take the little girl, I will understand, and if you decide to take her, I will do everything I can do to help you. You need to sit down with Bernard and discuss it. Remember that you are on a time schedule."

"You're right. Thanks." Rhonda said.

"Anytime. What are friends for?" Brandi smiled. She wanted to be supportive of Rhonda but she silently hoped that Rhonda would not take the child. She didn't want to see her friend hurt.

Rhonda had only walked down a few steps towards her car when her cell phone rang.

"Hello. What? What happened? Thanks. I'm on the way. Bye." She turned around and faced Brandi who was standing in the door. "Get your shoes on. We have to go. That was the hospital. Shemeka is there. She's been there all night. I don't know what happened. The woman only said that Meka needs for someone to come and that she shouldn't be alone."

Rhonda was worried. She prayed that Robert had not come back and done something to Shemeka.

"What the hell has she gotten herself into? I should have stayed. She was so upset about that he-she. I hope that she didn't take any pills or anything. What do you think?" Brandi wondered if Shemeka was more distraught than she had realized.

"Hell no! She wouldn't be that stupid. Shemeka is not suicidal." Rhonda jumped in the driver's seat of the car.

"We'll know soon enough. Say a prayer." The two women headed to the hospital.

Rhonda and Brandi dashed through the sliding glass door of the emergency room.

Brandi approached the woman behind the desk. "We're looking for our friend. She came in last night. Was there an accident or something?"

"Hold on! Hold on there young woman. Slow down. What's your friend's name?" The nurse asked Brandi.

"Her name is Shemeka." Before Brandi could blurt out her last name, Shemeka came running down the hall at a fast pace. Black streaks from running mascara had dried on her face.

"What the hell happened? We thought you were hurt." Rhonda asked her. "She placed her hand on Shemeka's shoulder. "Tell us. What is it?"

"That crazy ass bitch." She cried. "Nikki. She came to my house. She was goanna kill me."

"I don't doubt it. You need to stay away from her. She is very unstable." Brandi told Shemeka.

"Yeah. More than we realized." Rhonda added. "And I just found out that she and Bernard have a child together. He fucked that bitch but it's a long story. I'll tell you about it later. Where is the bitch? Did you fuck her up? Is she in surgery? They are not going to charge you are they?" Rhonda noticed the police officer standing down the hall.

"No! It's not my fault. She tried to blame me for everything. She pulled out a gun."

Brandi took Shemeka by the hand and led her to a chair. She collapsed in the chair and rocked her body back and forth. Through sobs, she continued. "Robert...oh my goodness...he...he... jumped in front... of me. He...oh Lord, he has to be okay. Pleeease God! He saved my life."

Brandi put her arms around Shemeka. "Honey, I'm sure that Robert will be fine. He's strong and he's young. Pray for him. We'll all pray for him." Brandi didn't realize what she was saying until she had said it. She was referring to Robert as if he were a man knowing full well that he was a female. She hoped that Roberta would pull through. It was clear that Shemeka had strong feelings for her.

"Where is that lunatic at now? I hope they lock her up and throw away the key."

Rhonda noticed that the officer had not left his post down the hall. "I don't know. She left before the police and ambulance arrived." Shemeka said.

"Do you mean to tell me that bitch is on the loose?" Rhonda screamed.

"Calm down Rhonda. I'm sure the police have her by now. There is nowhere for the bitch to go. I'm going to get Shemeka some water. Would you like some?" Brandi asked.

She didn't hear Brandi. Rhonda wanted Nikki caught and put away. Nikki had played her. Bernard and Nikki both. They had played the hell out of her. Coaxing her into a threesome. Bernard making love to Nikki like it was the best pussy he ever had, moaning and jerking like a damn fool while he shot his slimy sperm into her welcoming pussy.

"RHONDA!" Brandi raised her voice. "Did you hear what I asked you? Can I get you anything?"

"Oh. I'm sorry. No thank you." The only thing she wanted was Nikki's head on a damn platter. It should have been Nikki in there fighting for her life instead of Robert.

"The doctor!" Shemeka jumped up and met the surgeon as he walked towards them. He pulled his facemask down and removed his surgical gloves. Before speaking, he shook his head. "I'm sorry. We did our best to save her. She had lost an extensive amount of blood. The bullet perforated her aorta. Her heart stopped beating on the operating table and we weren't able to bring her back. I'm sorry. Are there any questions I can answer for you?"

"No! Nooooo! No!" Shemeka screamed repeatedly. "Please God. No!" Rhonda and Brandi each placed a hand under one of Meka's arms and helped her to a chair to prevent her from falling.

"Shemeka, I know it's hard. Cry as much as you want to. Go ahead and let it out.

We're going to get you out of this hospital. Where did you park? Brandi can drive your car and I will follow." Rhonda put her hands in her purse to retrieve her keys.

"I didn't drive. I came with Robert in the ambulance. I can't go home. Robert got killed there. And suppose that bitch is still out there?"

"Shemeka, I doubt if she is still out there, but we'll take you to my house." Brandi offered.

"I'll pull the car around." Rhonda told them.

"No! I want to see him. Please let me see him." Shemeka begged. "I have to."

The doctor nodded to the nurse who took the women to where Robert lay. He looked perfectly innocent. His body was covered from his feet to his neck. Brandi and Rhonda watched silently as Shemeka said goodbye to him. She kissed him on the forehead while a single tear dropped from her face to his face. "I love you." She whispered. "I'm so very sorry. You're at peace now." She covered his face with the sheet before walking out of the room. Rhonda and Brandi followed.

During the short drive to Brandi's house, Shemeka was silent. Robert had saved her life. Not only had he proclaimed to love her but also in the end, he proved it by giving his life for hers. She had treated him so badly when she found out that he had deceived her but he didn't hesitate to take a bullet for her.

When they got to Brandi's house and everyone was inside, Shemeka wanted to take some of the focus off her. She felt bad enough about how she had treated Robert. She might as well as spit in his face. Now he was gone and there was no way for her to make things up to him. No way to undo the past. She had to make sure that Nikki paid for this.

Shemeka looked at Rhonda. "So how did you find out about Bernard? He is the last man in the world that I would have suspected of cheating."

"You think that you are shocked?" Imagine how shocked I was when a woman from the Department of Social Services came to inform me that Bernard had fathered a child by that bitch."

"That says a lot about your husband. I don't mean any harm but he went up in that bitch raw. He's lucky that he only came out with a baby. He could have come out with a damn disease. Kick his ass to the curb. You don't need that."

Rhonda didn't respond. She had mixed emotions about the situation. Bernard was wrong as hell but she had not been faithful herself.

"Damn! I'm sorry Rhonda." Shemeka told her. "It seems that we are both dealing with a lot. I am numb right now. I can't feel anything. Things with Robert happened so fast. I can't help but to wonder what it would have been like if he had been straight up with me. Maybe he and I could have been good friends."

Brandi looked at her. "Can I ask you a question?"

"Sure what?" Shemeka asked her.

"Did you love him?'

"I don't know." Tears started to form in her eyes. "I loved Robert, or the person I knew as Robert. I never got the chance to know Roberta. All I know about Roberta is that she was wounded as a child."

Brandi hated to see Shemeka hurting. There was nothing she could do to ease her friends' pain. She didn't know how Shemeka felt because she had never experienced anything like that before. She never understood how Shemeka allowed herself to be deceived. "I'm so sorry for your loss. I didn't get to know Robert well but from what I saw, he really was a nice person and it was obvious that he loved you."

"Brandi, you seem to be the only one of us who has their life in order. Here we are up in your crib with all of our problems and you're straight. I'm glad that at least one of us has it together." Shemeka continued. "We both gave you hell about Anthony and you're more content in your relationship than either of us."

"You're right about that. I certainly don't have a relationship. Any time your husband fucks around and gets a damn baby on you, that pretty much sums it up. I should never have said shit about Anthony because Bernard has never been locked up and look how he did me."

"Stop! Anthony and I are not like that. There's been so much going on with all of us that we haven't touched base. I've been seeing Erik and it feels great." Brandi was happy to finally be able to share her news with the girls.

"I remember Erik. I'm happy for you. This was probably a hard decision for you but at least Erik is a free man. How did Anthony take the news?" Rhonda asked.

"Not too well, I'm afraid that it's like the quiet before the storm. There was something in the letter he wrote me that made me feel a little uneasy. You know that he has no one he can depend on but me. I hope that he doesn't get out and try to kill me. He said that I will live to regret it."

"He's not that damn stupid. Once he gets out of there, I'm sure he won't be trying to go back in. Besides, I never thought that he was just sitting in there communicating with only you." Shemeka told her.

"He's not going to bother you," Rhonda added. "Anything he said in that letter is only prison talk." She felt like Brandi was being overly dramatic. It was great that she wasn't wasting any more time on Anthony. It was time for her to be happy. In fact, it was time for all of them to be happy.

"I agree with Shemeka. Anthony is not stupid. He is going to go on about his business when he gets out. Don't even worry about that shit. Enjoy Erik and have the time of your life. You have a few more years to think about what Anthony will do. I betcha that he'll have him another woman in no time."

"If he doesn't already have one. Those guys know how to play the game." Shemeka added. For a minute she had allowed her mind to focus on someone other than Robert. Looking around Brandi's living room brought her thoughts back to why she was there. She gazed at the walls and wondered how she was possibly going to get through this tragedy.

"I know it's too early to make arrangements for Robert but, does he have any family?" Rhonda could sense where Shemeka's mind was.

"I don't know. That bitch who shot him is his cousin. That's all I know. I hope they put him in a nice suit. He looked so handsome in suits." Shemeka started to cry again.

"Honey, you have to prepare yourself for anything that might happen. If he does have family, you can't be sure how they felt about his lifestyle. They may wish to bury him as Roberta. No matter what happens, we'll be there." Brandi stood. "Let me get yall something to drink. I don't know where my manners are. A night like this calls for something strong."

"No thank you." Shemeka answered. "What I want; I can never have."

Chapter Thirty-Nine

B ernard opened his wallet to remove the picture he had of Dean. He felt like a failure. Not only had he failed his wife, but he had also failed his daughter. They both deserved so much more than he had given them. Rhonda had been a real trooper. The money, cars, house and diamonds were all material things. She needed a faithful husband. He wondered how or if he could ever make it up to her. She had agreed to let him stay, but leaving could not have been any worse than seeing the pain in her eyes.

The doorbell startled him. Bernard placed the photo in its original place in his wallet and pushed the speaker button to ask who was at the door. When he got no answer, he slowly walked to the door. He looked through the peephole to see Nikki. She looked extremely wild with her hair all over her head and her face pale. He felt as if she was probably stressed but she didn't deserve any sympathy from him. She was the cause of most of his problems. Bernard swung the door open and she raced in.

"What the hell did you do Nikki?" He asked her. "DSS has been over here and the woman said they took Dean. Rhonda is having a damn fit. She might even divorce my ass. You ruin everything you touch. Anyone in your path gets destroyed."

Nikki looked from Bernard to the ceiling. She was silent. Her eyes rolled around in her head as if someone was performing an exorcism on her. She slowly swung her arms around from behind her back. Bernard stumbled backwards falling over the ottoman. Nikki walked towards him pointing the gun to his head while he remained speechless.

"Who the hell do you think you are talking to punk? I'm calling the damn shots. Now I know damn well you don't think I'm going to let you take my baby from me do you? DO YOU MUTHAFUCKA?" She screamed.

Bernard was afraid to speak. He was afraid to breathe. Nikki smacked the side of his head with the gun. "Answer me you son-of-a bitch."

"No Nikki. I'm not trying to do anything. DSS is trying to do that. I told them that you are a good mom and you take good care of Dean." He lied. "I know that you would never intentionally hurt her."

"Liar, where is your wife? Call her downstairs." Nikki demanded.

"She's not here. She left earlier. I don't know where she went. I told you that she's upset about that damn lady from DSS coming by here."

"Do you love that bitch? "Nikki asked him.

"Yes I love my wife. What kind of question is that? Nikki put the gun down please. It's just the two of us here." Bernard felt uneasy with the gun in Nikki's hand. What if she hit him with it again? What if it accidentally discharged and shot him?

"Do you love me?' Nikki looked at Bernard with pleading eyes. He wasn't sure what answer she was expecting. Nikki was so unpredictable that any answer he gave might be the wrong one. She was waving the gun freely. "Be careful how you answer."

"Yes Nikki, I love you too. I love you and Rhonda. We share a child together. How can I not love you?" He prayed that Nikki was not about to flip on him when she moved closer to him.

"Take off your clothes. Take them off right now." She instructed Bernard.

He wondered what Nikki had in mind. It couldn't be anything good. Maybe she was going to get him naked and shoot him so Rhonda could come home and find him dead. He didn't put anything pass her. He wondered who in the hell allowed someone as unstable as Nikki to have a permit to buy a gun. That was ludicrous.

"I want to see how hard it is." Nikki put the gun under his chin and slid it in a spiral motion down his chest and rested it on his zipper. "I said un...damn...dress."

OH SHIT! Bernard thought. *She's going to shoot it off. I need to get to the phone. I need to call the police. How in the fuck can my magic stick get up under all of this fuckin pressure?*

"You've got three damn minutes to get your damn clothes off and two of those minutes have expired. I suggest you get them the fuck off right now. I want to see how much you love mama and how much I excite you."

Bernard hurried to get his clothes off. He didn't trust Nikki. She would probably shoot him and think nothing of it. "Okay. Okay. I'm doing it but you know that I can't be but so hard with all of this steel aimed at me."

"Ha...ha...ha!" Nikki lifted the gun to her own head. "Are you talking about this? Stop being such a damn pussy."

"Nikki please! Let's talk. Please. Just put the gun down and I'm sure that we can work this out." Bernard was desperate to calm Nikki and get her relaxed enough to put the gun down.

"That's what I want. I want a workout. I've lost everyone I love and it's your fault. You spoiled it. Didn't I ask you not to spoil it? Now slide my pants down. Do it slowly and don't try anything. If you try anything at all, I'll kill you."

Bernard wasn't thinking about trying anything. He knew who he was dealing with. He was thinking about Rhonda. He didn't know when she was coming home and he didn't want her to come in and find him there naked with Nikki. He wanted to get things over with so she could leave and hopefully he could live to tell the story. Bernard slid Nikki's pants down to the floor. She kicked her feet to step out of her pants.

"Ouch! Shit!" Bernard grabbed himself while bending over in pain. "What the hell did you do that for?" Nikki had kicked him in the groin with her knee.

"I thought you said that you love me. It seems like you need a little help to get your sorry ass equipment up and working. Do you think I am playing with you muthafucka?"

"No Nikki I'm sorry. I'm just nervous. Shit! You have a fuckin gun."

"The police are probably already looking for me. I have nothing Bernard. Nothing except the baby your sorry ass is about to put in me. So you have five minutes to get that damn dick working or I'm going to blow it to kingdom come. You don't need it if it doesn't work." She fell back on the couch and spread her legs. "Get your ass down here and eat this pussy. And pray that it gets your dick ready for mama."

He dropped to his knees. Balls of sweat dripped from his face. Nikki pointed the gun at him. "If you hurt my pussy the least little bit, I swear that I'll splatter your brains all over this nice Persian rug. NOW EAT!"

Bernard tried to steady his nerves while he devoured Nikki. He put one hand between his legs to massage his magic stick. *Please get hard.* He thought to himself. *All I have to do is calm down. Imagine the gun is not there. The gun is not there. I want this pussy. I can do this.*

"Who's got the best pussy you ever put your damn lips on?" She asked him.

"You do. Yours is the best I've ever tasted." His magic stick was semi hard. Bernard stood up. "I'm ready. Let me put it in. Put the gun down. I'm ready for you."

"I'm not putting shit down. Do you think I'm crazy? I'm not fuckin crazy. Put your damn dick in me and replace the baby you are trying to steal from me." She demanded.

Bernard could not get his nerves together. He prayed that his magic stick would not go down before Nikki got off. No matter what she said, he was not going to cum in her. He would never put another baby in her crazy ass. He got off the floor and moved to Nikki who lay wide legged on the couch. He entered her and put one leg over his shoulder. She pointed the gun at his chest.

"Tell me it's good muthafucka." She pressed the gun against his chest.

"It's good Nikki. Damn it's good." He told her.

"I know it is. Your wife told me it was good. You know that she's been my bitch don't you? We had a fuckin good time while you were in the hospital fighting for your life. Why didn't you die?" Nikki smiled at Bernard. She wanted to expose Rhonda. How dare that bitch choose Bernard over her?

Bernard let her leg down. "You're a lie. Rhonda would never go behind my back like that. You will never make me believe that lie." He let his magic stick fall out of her. She was doing all she could to try to destroy his marriage but he was not going to fall for that shit. She didn't know how he had to coerce Rhonda into that second threesome. Nah! That had to be a lie. Bernard stood to look Nikki in her eyes.

"Muthafucka she did it and she enjoyed it. She couldn't get enough of my damn pussy. You don't think you satisfied her do you? At least she said that you didn't. She told me that she loves you but the dick isn't shit. Hey! And I know from experience." She laughed out loud.

He looked away. There was something about the way Nikki spoke that told him she was not lying on Rhonda. He wasn't sure of the details but Rhonda had been fucking with Nikki while he was fighting for his life. How could she have done that?

"Now finish what the fuck you started before I blow this little thing off." Nikki continued to laugh while moving the gun from his balls to the head of his dick. "FUCK ME NOW!"

Bernard's magic stick had gone to sleep. "Nikki can you suck it for me? I want-"

They both heard the key when it turned in the door. Nikki pointed the gun at Rhonda when she stepped in the door. "Come on in Baby. Welcome home. Mama missed you."

Chapter Forty

Shemeka woke up and looked around the room. She rubbed her hands over her face as she recalled the events of the previous day. To her left Brandi lay sound asleep on the loveseat with one leg hanging over the edge. An empty liquor bottle was on the floor. Shemeka slowly stood.

"Brandi! Wake up Brandi!" Shemeka tapped her friend on the shoulder. "I'm going to get ready to leave. I have a lot to do today."

"Um…my head. Get me a beer out of the fridge please and two eggs." Brandi lifted her head.

"A beer? Brandi, you killed an entire fifth by yourself last night." Shemeka really wanted Brandi to get some help with her drinking. Sometimes she acted like she couldn't handle pressure without a drink. It had to be a bit frightening going into a new relationship. The unknown was always scary. But she had to learn to depend on herself and find her inner strength. Maybe she was truly afraid of Anthony but what could he do while his ass was locked up? Her problems were minor compared to Shemeka's.

"I know Meka. I feel awful. I already have a glass. Come on now. It's going to make me feel better. You don't know how many times I have done this." Brandi said.

"No I don't, but I can imagine." Shemeka went to the kitchen to get a clean glass from the cabinet. She opened the refrigerator and took out a beer along with two eggs. She poured the beer in the glass, cracked the two eggs and put them in the glass before handing the glass to Brandi, who drank the contents straight down.

"I need to leave." Shemeka told Brandi. "Thanks for everything. I need to see if I can find out what kind of arrangements are going to be made for Robert."

"Hold up. Let me get myself together and I'll go with you. Besides, you don't have a car. Remember? You rode in the ambulance with Robert. And you don't need to walk back in that house by yourself." Brandi's head was hurting but she knew that Meka would have a breakdown if she walked in that house alone and had to relive seeing Robert get shot.

"Yeah! I dread walking back in there. Blood was everywhere. I have to clean it up. I keep having flashbacks. It was awful. Robert saved my life. The bullet was meant for me. That bitch intended to kill me." Shemeka rested on the recliner. "He jumped right in front of me. Robert took my bullet."

"What is wrong with that woman anyway? What did she say after she shot him?"

"She never let go of the gun. I thought she was going to shoot me next but I had to call the ambulance for Robert. While I was on the phone, she was telling him how sorry she was and that she loved him. She begged him not to die. I heard him whisper something to her about her secret being safe and then he lost consciousness. She got up and ran out the door. I think she thought he was dead."

"But why?" Brandi asked. "It doesn't make any sense that she would want to kill you. She doesn't even know you."

"It makes sense if her ass is crazy. The bitch is insane. She said that I was trying to take Rhonda from her and that she would kill me before she let me spoil it."

"What? Take Rhonda from her? That bitch needs to be in the nut house. She's crazy as hell. Do you think she is gay or something? She might have a crush on Rhonda. Maybe it runs in the family." Brandi had a habit of running her mouth without thinking.

"Oh damn! Oh Meka. I'm sorry. I don't know what I was thinking. Forgive me." She put her arms around Shemeka, "I would never be insensitive towards your feelings. I didn't mean it the way it came out. Robert loved you and no matter how he chose to live his life, he made you happy." Brandi was apologetic. She would never intentionally hurt her friend. Although she didn't fully understand Meka's pain, she knew it was real.

"Let me wash my face. I feel sick as hell."

"As a child, Roberta was molested by her dad. When Nikki moved in, he molested her too.

Roberta retreated to take on the persona of a man and Robert emerged from that. I guess that Nikki just snapped. I don't know. Robert blamed himself for not being able to protect Nikki.

He was older and felt like it was his fault for not getting Nikki out of that situation."

Brandi yelled out of the bathroom with toothpaste spit in her mouth. "That wasn't Roberta's fault Meka. She was only a child herself. I can't imagine what they went through." She spit the toothpaste out and rinsed out her mouth.

"I know. It had to be awful Brandi. Being abused by the very person who is entrusted to care for you. Robert told me that he would sometimes lie there and pretend to be sleep until his dad got finished. Nikki used to cry when she was molested but got to the point where she would just lie there with a straight face and pretend it was not her but a different person who was being molested by that lowlife bastard. It's really sad.

Robert said he would sometimes offer himself to his dad in order to save Nikki but the old man would not go for it." Shemeka sat on the couch.

"And check this out. He was a deacon in the church. He'd molest Robert on Mondays, Wednesdays, and Fridays. Nikki's days were Tuesdays,

Thursdays, and Saturdays. They were not allowed to switch days but on Sundays, they got a break from his filthy ass because he said it was a sacred day. He would always snatch his dick out to keep them from getting pregnant. He would shoot his nasty sperm all over their body." Shemeka told Brandi. "Robert hated him."

"That bastard had to be one more sick ass dog. How any sane person could hurt a child is beyond my imagination." Brandi came out of the bathroom wearing a pair of sweats and a pullover shirt. "I'm going to help you sanitize your place. Let me call Erik and cancel for tonight."

"No Brandi. Don't do that. I don't expect you to put your life on hold for me." Shemeka stood. "Just give me a lift. I have to face it sooner or later. Might as well be sooner.

"Stop being silly Meka." Brandi told her as she picked up the telephone to dial Erik's number. "I'd never let you go through this alone. You know better than that. You'd do the same thing for me. I know you would." She waited to see if Erik would answer his cell phone."

"Hello Baby. Listen, I have a situation. I'm not going to be able to keep our plans for tonight. I'll explain it to you later. Rain check? Thanks Boo. I love you. Mmm…Wah!" She hung up the telephone.

"Brandi, you know that you didn't have to do that." Shemeka told her.

"I know that I didn't have to but I wanted to. You don't have to go through this alone.

Not when you have Rhonda and me. What kind of friends do you think you have?"

"Thanks Brandi. I'm goanna face this head on. I'm not ready for it but I don't have much of a choice." Shemeka was grateful that Brandi was going to be with her. She was always the weakest of her friends and without any support, she felt like she would crumble.

"Let me call Rhonda. I know that she'll want to come. It will help her to get her mind off of Bernard. I'm still having trouble believing that shit. He fooled the hell out of me."

Brandi picked up the telephone to call Rhonda's cell number but it rolled right into voice mail. "Damn. Rhonda is the worst when it comes to keeping her phone charged." Brandi said to Shemeka. "I'll try her home phone." She dialed Rhonda's home phone and got a busy signal. "I thought that everybody had call waiting. Her phone has to be off the receiver. We'll swing by and pick her up. I'm sure she's ready to get away from Bernard for a while anyway."

Brandi knew that Rhonda was the calming one in the group. If Shemeka went to pieces; Rhonda would be able to handle it and know the right things to say. She would be more of a comforter. It's not that Brandi wasn't compassionate, but she wanted some backup. She picked up her keys from the table. "I'm ready. Let's go get Rhonda." The two women headed out the door.

Chapter Forty-One

R honda was exhausted from being up all night. It had been one more horrific experience. Nikki had pointed a gun at her as soon as she came in the door.

Bernard and Rhonda both felt like they had been tortured at the hands of a crazed woman. Nikki was out of control. Rhonda's mind recalled the events of last night. Her husband was naked as hell when she got home and she immediately thought that she had interrupted him fucking his whore. She thought Nikki pulled the gun on her out of fear of her tripping but she soon learned that was not the case at all.

When Nikki forced her to undress and made her get a pair of panty hose to tie Bernard's hands behind his back. Rhonda knew that she was in trouble. He sat on the wing back chair with his hands behind his back and his eyes on Nikki and the gun.

"Eat my pussy Rhonda. Do it like you did when he was in the hospital. Make mama feel good." Nikki smiled at Rhonda after tracing her lips with her tongue. Bernard sat in silence with a look of bewilderment on his face. Rhonda knew that she was busted but there was nothing she could say to dispute Nikki. She had cursed Bernard out and made him feel like scum for fucking around with Nikki when she too, had been creeping with the bitch.

Nikki relaxed on the couch with a pillow propped behind her back while Rhonda dropped to her knees and began eating her. "Don't play Bitch! You better eat this pussy like it's fried chicken. Yeah! Put your finger in it while you eat it. Um...that's it Baby. That feels good. Mama loves you." She put one hand on Rhonda's head but never released her grip on the gun.

On the wing back chair, Bernard's dick got bone hard. He couldn't understand why he was getting excited while being held hostage at gun point. His dick was throbbing and he wanted it in something. He thought it was strange that, he was turned on by Rhonda eating Nikki. He didn't care if his dick was in a pussy or a mouth but he needed to nut.

Rhonda thought that Nikki would loosen her grip on the gun but the more she pleased Nikki, the tighter she gripped the gun. When she was on the verge of cumming, she slapped Rhonda across the face with the gun. When Rhonda fell to the floor, she got up and walked over to where Bernard was seated and with her back to him, eased his stiff dick into her wet pussy. She pointed the gun in Rhonda's direction as she rode him cow-girl style.

Although Nikki was in control and he didn't know what she might do next, Bernard enjoyed the ride. He wished that his hands were not behind his back. He thought to himself that it would be nice to hold onto Nikki while she rode his dick. It felt so damn good and he wanted to moan in pleasure but he dared not do it with Rhonda there on the floor. She had not moved from the spot after Nikki hit her with the gun.

"Damn! Give me this dick muthafucka. I know you are enjoying it. Is this the best damn pussy you have ever had or what?" She asked him.

"Yes! This damn pussy is good." Bernard was not saying it for Nikki's benefit. The pussy felt damn good.

"Do you want to cum in it? Do you want to shoot your juices in Mama?" She asked him.

"Yeah!" Bernard answered. He wanted to yell, *Hell yeah!* But he didn't. If Nikki didn't get her ass off of him soon he was going to shoot a load in her. It wasn't his fault. Rhonda couldn't blame him this time. Nikki's pussy was wet and hot as fire.

"Talk to Mama Muthafucka. Let me know what you're feeling."

Bernard didn't know how Rhonda would react or what she would think. They both knew that Nikki was crazy. What choice did he have when she had a gun pointed at his wife? "Oh Mama...umm...umm... daaaaaym! This pussy is good. Give it to Daddy. I want you Nikki. You feel good." He was being straight. His dick felt good in Nikki's pussy.

Although she was in control, he felt the power. He wished that Nikki would tell him to fuck her in the ass. He wanted to put his dick in her tight ass. Just thinking about it aroused him even more and he couldn't hold back. "Fuck me Nikki." He begged. "Fuck me."

She rode him fast and hard. Bernard gripped his hands together and let out a loud yell. "Ugh...ugh...Oh damn!" His body jerked in the chair as he shot a load of his sperm in Nikki's juicy pussy. She sat there on his dick while his sperm traveled. When she felt his manhood deflating, she climbed off his lap.

Rhonda never said a word. She observed from the floor unable to believe what was happening. This had to be a nightmare. When was the alarm clock going to ring and wake her up? This shit only happened in nightmares and in the movies.

"Get a washcloth and clean mama up." Nikki had said to her. "If you try anything Rhonda. I will kill your husband."

Now Rhonda was in her living room recalling the tragic events and wondering how her perfect life had spun out of control. Once she didn't have a care in the world. Now, she was uncertain of her future. A future that once looked bright and promising.

Nikki was dressed and Rhonda prayed that she would leave. She had been up all night long and Rhonda knew that the lack of rest could possibly add to her deranged behavior.

"Nikki, you know that you can't stay here don't you? They are looking for you. Also, Mrs. Cutshaw from the Department of Social Services will be here this evening. Let Bernard and me give you some money so you can leave. Take my car. The keys are right there on the table."

"Just leave huh?" Nikki held her stomach as she laughed. "That's what I plan on doing. You and I are going to leave. We're going to get the hell out of here. Mama loves you Rhonda. I can't do this without you." She started to cry. "I'm sorry I hurt you. Forgive me. It won't happen again. Do you forgive me?"

"Yeah Nikki. I forgive you, but I don't think I should go with you. You don't need me. You'll do better traveling alone." Rhonda didn't want to be with Nikki running from the police. She knew that Nikki would not hesitate to use her as a shield and she wasn't ready to die. She needed to convince Nikki to leave alone. "It's going to be best if I stay here. If you take me with you, they will be looking for two women. You wouldn't get too far."

Nikki walked up to Rhonda slapping her across the face with the gun twice. Rhonda's head hurt like hell and she was tired of Nikki's shit but she was powerless to do anything. Nikki's voice became deep and satanic. "Did I give you a choice Bitch? Get the fuckin keys. I know you are not trying to choose your punk ass husband over me." Her eyes were red from being up all night. She looked like a maniac and Rhonda was afraid that if she refused, Nikki would kill her.

Bernard didn't comment. He tried to free his hands, which were tied behind his back. He knew that he had to stop Nikki but he wasn't sure how. Reality had set back in. He wondered what he was thinking last night. How could he think about busting a nut in Nikki under those circumstances? That was crazy as hell. His dick should not have gotten hard. Maybe he was as crazy as Nikki. What was Rhonda thinking while she observed? At the time he didn't care, he just wanted Nikki's hot pussy but now, he wondered if Rhonda would ever forgive him.

Rhonda picked up the car keys from the table and walked to the side door with Nikki. With one hand on the gun, Nikki used the other hand to squeeze the cheeks of Rhonda's ass. She stuck her tongue in Rhonda's mouth and kissed her. "I'm sorry for hitting you Baby. Why did you make me do that? I don't like to hit you. Rhonda, you are going to have to behave for Mama. Why do you keep upsetting me? I forgive you this time but I can't let you spoil things. That wouldn't be fair to either one of us. Let's go Boo. You drive."

"Where are we going Nikki?" Rhonda asked her.

"Don't fuckin' question me Bitch." Nikki raised her voice. "You know I don't like that shit. Shut the hell up and open the damn door."

Rhonda opened the door and proceeded to the garage. Nikki made her slide in from the passenger's side of the car. Nikki slid in beside her and pressed the gun in her side.

"You know that I don't want to use this Boo, but I will if I have to. We are going to get out of here and stop by the bank before they start looking for you. It should be a while before they find Bernard so we'll have a head start. Remember Rhonda, you have to be good. Okay?"

"Okay." Rhonda answered. She was glad that Nikki was letting her stop by the bank. There had to be a way to alert someone that she was in trouble.

As soon as Rhonda opened the garage door with the remote, six policemen ran into the garage with guns drawn. One had a loud speaker. "Step out of the car please with your hands in the air."

Nikki gripped her pistol and pointed it to Rhonda's head.

"Ma'am, drop your weapon and put your hands in the air. You are surrounded."

"Nikki please!" Rhonda begged. "Please put the gun down. If you don't they will kill you. Throw it out the window. I don't want to see anything happen to you."

"You don't care. You don't love me." Nikki cried.

"I do Nikki. Trust me. Please." Rhonda could feel the pressure of the gun as Nikki held it to her head.

"Ma'am, this is your last warning. Drop your weapon." The officer shouted.

Nikki tossed her gun out the window and both women stepped out of the car with their hands up. One of the officers kicked the gun away and placed Nikki's hands behind her back. While he read Nikki her Miranda Rights, another officer checked to see if Rhonda was hurt. Nikki looked confused.

"Ouch! That's too tight. You're hurting me. What's this about anyway? I haven't done anything. Why are you treating me like a criminal?"

"I know. That's what they all say." The officer answered.

While Nikki was being placed in the police car, Shemeka and Brandi ran up the sidewalk. They all embraced. "Thank God you are all right." Brandi said.

"We knew something was wrong when we saw that bitch's truck out there." Shemeka blurted out.

"She's crazy." Brandi added. "I didn't know what she might do. She's capable of anything. We called the police and waited for them to arrive."

"Thanks." Rhonda told her friends. "I don't know what I would have done. I love y'all. She has been here all night. It was hell. At one point, I thought she was going to kill Bernard and me."

"Mrs. Simpson?" One of the officers walked to where the women were standing. "We'll need for you to some down to the station and give us a statement."

"Can't it wait?" Brandi asked. "She's been through a lot. That monster has been torturing her all night."

"Sure. We already have an outstanding warrant for her arrest on murder charges. We'll take her down to the station and book her but we will need for you to come in later."

"I will. Thank you." Rhonda was exhausted but she would make it her business to get there. They watched as the police cars drove away.

Chapter Forty-Two

◇◇◇

B randi and Shemeka left Rhonda to handle her business. She had been through a lot and still had to deal with the issue of Bernard's illegitimate child.

They stopped by the Coffee Shop before going to the Funeral Home. Brandi ordered tuna on wheat while Shemeka ordered grilled chicken. "I appreciate you wanting to keep an eye on me Brandi but you didn't have to cancel your plans with Erik. I'll be fine."

"I know that you'll be fine but you don't need to be alone. What are friends for? If I can't be here for you when you need me then what good am I to you as a friend? You have lost someone very dear to you. Robert made you happy. Rhonda and I could not only see it on your face but we could hear it in your voice." Brandi knew that Shemeka loved Robert. He was her entire conversation. He had been the one person to renew her belief in love. Whether he was male or female, he had brought her out of her shell.

"You have problems of your own to deal with. You jumped out of one relationship and right into another one. I know that you still love Anthony. This is a man that not too long ago, you were contemplating marrying. By the way, I'm not sure it was such a good idea to jump right out there with Erik. You need a cooling down period." Shemeka looked at Brandi. "I know that I gave Anthony a hard time but damn! Look at how Bernard fucked over Rhonda. These men out here in the streets have just as much game as the ones who are locked up; if not more. I might have been too hard on Anthony. It's easy to judge others but I'm realizing now, that we shouldn't judge anyone. Live and let live."

"But the fact remains that he is not here with me. I do love Anthony but after a while, the toys get old. I'm young Meka. I need a warm body next to me. If he didn't have that extra time, it would be different. These men who have more than a few years should not expect a woman to put her life on hold for them. That just isn't fair." Brandi tried to convince herself that she was right in her decision.

Shemeka couldn't argue that point. She had spent many nights alone until Robert came into her life. It seemed like he was the answer to her prayers. He was everything she had hoped for in a meaningful relationship. As she used to hear her teachers say, *If it seems too good to be true, it usually is.*

Brandi took a bite of her tuna sandwich. "There is a whole world out here waiting to be explored and I can't do that if I'm living in a box. Anthony committed the crime but I swear those bastards at the prison acted like they wanted to punish me. And for what? My only crime was loving him and trying to stick by him. They made things as difficult as possible for me. We developed our own distinctive lifestyle, roles and behavior norms. You would never believe what it was like unless you were in the struggle yourself." Brandi thought about all that she had gone through with Anthony.

"Brandi, you did go through hell with that system. I sometimes think it is designed that way. They claim that our men are incarcerated for reformation, deterrence and rehabilitation but I don't see it. Prison doesn't rehabilitate a person. What it does do is destroy the family unit. How many women do as you have done? How many throw their hands up in the air and say they can't do it anymore? That's why it makes me angry as hell when a strong black woman stands by a man and he gets out and fucks around on her. I think that's grounds for her to fuck his ass up without penalty." Shemeka seemed to be getting in her feelings. Brandi didn't understand if it was out of pain from losing Robert or if it was a new revelation.

"Are you saying that I am wrong for wanting more? When is it going to be my time?" Brandi asked.

"Hell no! I would never tell you that you are wrong for the way you feel. If you can't handle it then you did the best thing by walking away. It's just that sometimes, good people make bad choices and they need to have someone stick with them and by them. They need that support. I didn't do that with Robert. I tore into him like a pit bull tearing into a child's throat going for the jugular. How can I make it up to him now that he's gone? I can't." Tears rolled down Shemeka's face. She pushed her half eaten grilled chicken sandwich away. "I don't have an appetite. We can check with the Funeral Home whenever you are ready."

Brandi left enough money on the table to cover both meals and a nice tip for the waitress. She knew there was nothing she could do to ease Shemeka's pain.

When they arrived at the Funeral Home, the Director informed them that Robert had a great aunt and a host of cousins. His body was being shipped to Florida. Shemeka would not be able to see his body. She slid to the floor as her cries echoed from the hollow walls.

Brandi took Shemeka home with her and fixed her a cup of hot herbal tea. "I don't think we need to worry about going back to your place Meka. I'm going to call a cleaning service that I have used in the past. We'll give them the key and have them to clean your house. You've had enough to deal with. They are reputable and I assure you they will do an excellent job. The spare room is made. Why don't you lie down and take a nap?" Brandi offered. Meka didn't seem to be in a mood to talk and she didn't want to press the issue.

"Thanks! I just want to rest a while. So much has happened in such a short amount of time. We can't ever take anything for granted. I'll just lie across the bed. My head is throbbing." Shemeka walked in the direction of the spare bedroom. "Do you have anything for a headache?"

"No, I took my last Tylenol. Just lay down and make yourself comfortable. I need to go to the store anyway. I'll pick up something for your head while I'm out." Brandi picked up her keys and left the house. She decided that rather than shop for groceries, she would pick up a bottle of Tylenol from the pharmacy. That would allow her to get back to Shemeka sooner. She didn't want to leave her alone for a long period of time.

As she passed the medical building, she noticed that Erik was still at work. Brandi felt bad about having to cancel on him. *Why not?* She asked herself. *I'll at least drop in and say hello, get a kiss and bring him up to speed on what is happening with Shemeka.*

She pulled into the parking lot, parked her car and entered the medical building. Erik had to be working late on something. The building was quiet. No screaming babies, no little old ladies in wheelchairs, no pregnant couples, just silence. Brandi stepped off the elevator on the fifth floor hoping that she would not find Erik buried deep in paperwork, or examining patient charts.

As she got closer to his office, she heard it. It sounded like someone slurping up an icee. As she rounded the corner, Brandi froze when her eyes fixated on them. They were in a lip lock; tonguing each other down like they could not get enough of each other. She couldn't believe what she was seeing. Brandi rubbed her eyes and looked again. She wanted to run but her feet would not move. Erik unzipped the man's pants and pulled his dick out. Once Erik dropped to his knees and put his P.A's dick in his mouth, Brandi threw up.

"Oh my God! Brandi!" Erik called out to her as she rushed to the elevator. She frantically pushed the down button until the doors opened. *What the fuck was that shit?* Brandi asked herself? Just as the elevator doors were closing she saw Erik trying to stop the elevator. "I'm sorry Brandi." He yelled. "Wait! Let me..."

Chapter Forty-Three

"I really don't understand Rhonda. You made me feel like shit. You acted like I was lower than a snake. While you were kicking me in the gut, you never once revealed that you had been with Nikki." Bernard told Rhonda. "You were with her while I was fighting for my life. You could have easily said that you got caught up in threesome and went back to explore. I would have understood that. But you were just as guilty as me."

"Bernard, it's not the same and you know it. I was wrong for messing with Nikki but do you realize what you did? It was you who brought that bitch into our home. You talked me into having a threesome with a bitch who you had not only been fucking with but one with whom you fathered a child. That was totally disrespectful to me. I didn't know anything about a damn Nikki until you invited her to our bed. I didn't have any thoughts of being with a woman. This was all your doing." Rhonda knew that she was wrong too but it never would have happened if Bernard hadn't brought her into their bed.

"Baby, it was supposed to be a one-time affair. You were not supposed to carry on with her behind my back." Bernard was not going to let Rhonda make him feel totally at fault when she shared in the problems with Nikki also. She was not going to act all innocent when she had enjoyed Nikki just as much as he had. She had actually deceived him because he was under the impression that Rhonda wasn't into a woman like that.

"Behind your back? Muthafucka you have a daughter by that bitch. You fucked her raw. You didn't have enough decency to wear a condom. Then you bring her to me like it's a damn first time experience. Now you expect me to help raise a child that the two of you conceived. Don't you think that's asking a bit much?" Rhonda stood. "This is not what the fuck I signed on for. You made a damn fool out of me."

"Rhonda, I was wrong. My goodness. I'm human, and I sometimes make mistakes. The thing with Nikki just happened. I was angry with you, I had a little too much to drink and Nikki was there. One thing led to another." He wanted Rhonda to understand.

"It wasn't like you picked up some damn whore at a bar, fucked her and then left it alone. You went back for more. You have been fucking this woman for at least four years and we are coming up on our fifth wedding anniversary. So that means that you have been fucking her for almost as long as we've been together. She started to cry. Bernard didn't realize how badly he had hurt her.

"Baby please forgive me. What do I have to do?" I'm begging you Rhonda. I don't want to lose you." Bernard loved his wife. He had made a mistake but it had nothing to do with his love for Rhonda.

"How do you think I feel knowing another woman has a part of you? She has given you something that I haven't given you. And you act like I'm supposed to go on with life as normal." She screamed.

"Listen Rhonda." Bernard got on his knees and held her hand in his. She quickly snatched it back. "I love you woman. I was wrong. Please forgive me sweetheart. Please!"

Rhonda wanted to forgive Bernard because she could not stop loving him. She wondered if the relationship could survive all the betrayal. How could she ever trust him again? More importantly, how could she raise his child? In reality, they had both been wrong.

"Bernard, this is hard. You hurt me. Do you think it is fine for you to destroy my life? Am I supposed to forget about what you've done? Do you think this shit can be fixed with an I'm sorry?"

"No Baby. I realize that I have not only hurt you but our marriage. There is nothing you can say to me that I haven't already said to myself. Just give me a chance and I'll spend the rest of my life making it up to you."

"You weren't the only one wrong." Rhonda began to cry. "I had a part in this fiasco. I'm not sure if we can get through this but I love you enough to give it a try. We've been through too much to throw it all away. So what do you want to do about your daughter?"

"Baby, she is not a bad child. It seems that she has been through a lot. I know that Nikki has mood swings but I never thought she would go so far as to abuse Dean." Bernard got off the floor and sat beside Rhonda.

She understood what Bernard meant by Nikki having mood swings. She had witnessed it firsthand. She had also been on the opposite end of Nikki's abuse and couldn't imagine someone as small as Dean being the victim of Nikki's anger. "I know that she is not a bad child Bernard. I've met her and she was polite. She appears to be shy. I don't know if it is because of all the hell she has gone through or if she simply doesn't trust people. You need to tell me what you're thinking. Do you want to bring her into our home?" Rhonda asked.

"It's your call Baby. I can't disrespect you any more than I already have. I don't want to do anything that is going to hurt you. Dean is my child and I would hate to see her end up in foster care when we have this big ass house here. If you can't deal with it, I understand and I'll call Ms. Cutshaw."

Rhonda took his hand in hers. "No Boo. We are not going to let your daughter go into foster care. I love you and she is a part of you. I won't lie and pretend that I am not hurt. I hurt like hell. But it's not her fault. She didn't have anything to do with this and I can't blame her. Somehow, we'll get through this.

"Are you sure?" He put his arms around Rhonda. She nodded her head indicating that she was sure of her decision. He kissed her on the forehead and his mind drifted to Nikki. She really did have some deep-rooted problems. He remembered the night of the threesome. He had been stupid as hell for not using a condom when he went up in Nikki.

He wondered how he allowed himself to be so turned on by her. He only wanted his dick in her pussy. The load he shot in Nikki should have been going in Rhonda. At the time he wanted to bust a nut so bad it didn't matter. Now he was begging God. He prayed that Nikki was not pregnant. To ask Rhonda to raise one child by another woman was bad enough, but to ask her to raise two? Nah!

Chapter Forty-Four

◇◇

A nthony was wide-awake when they opened the doors at 5:30. He was anxious to get out of that hellhole. He had been locked up for a long time and had anticipated being locked up for much longer. God had looked out for him and he would not forget it. He'd go to church every Sunday. It was the least he could do after God worked things out for him. He never had any respect for snitches. In fact, he hated a snitch, but his situation was different. It was all about survival and freedom. He was ready to get the hell up out of there and if being a snitch was what it took, a man had to do what a man had to do.

He had no idea that things would happen so fast but cooperating with the feds had its benefits. "Bulldog," his ex-cellmate had confided in Anthony about how his case would never go to trial. He had gotten rid of two potential witnesses in his case and the only other person who could hurt him was his ex-girlfriend. Even though he wanted to trust her, she was weak. If she was pressured enough, she would break and tell everything she knew. The last time he spoke with her was at a visit. She told him that she would keep her mouth shut but she was moving. She gave him no forwarding address and stopped writing or visiting him. He couldn't trust her. She may have already rolled on him. She may be sitting in court on his trial date waiting to testify. He didn't know what to think but he knew what he had to do.

He gave her parent's information to an inmate who was being released. He furnished the address and a layout of the house. The inmate was to go there on a Wednesday night while the couple was at Bible Study. The instructions were to ransack the house, wait on the couple to return, and then he would tie them up and kill them making it look like they walked in on a burglary. The death of his ex-girls' parents would bring her out of hiding and make it easier to kill her before she could testify.

Anthony let the feds know he was privy to certain information and made a deal with them. After he furnished them with the date and time that things were expected to go down, he gave them the names of those involved. The couple was alerted to what might possibly be a dangerous situation and were taken to a Safe House. Undercover cops were stationed outside the house as well as three on the inside of the house. The gunman broke the back window and entered the house. He was in the process of ransacking the house when an officer stepped up behind him and identified himself. "Police! Freeze."

The lights were turned on and the other two police surrounded the intruder. "Get on the floor, spread your legs and put your hands behind your back." In his possession were two ropes, tape, and a 357 Magnum. The information provided by Anthony had prevented two innocent people from being killed, one potential witness from being killed and a dangerous drug dealer from being released.

He thought about Brandi. She had been a big source of disappointment for him.

Anthony had thought she would stand by him through thick and thin. She had promise to have his back but obviously she was not the strong woman he had thought she was.

It hurt him more than he had been willing to admit. He knew that he was a strong man but even men with the strength of Tarzan had a weak moment from time to time. He wasn't going to front like it didn't matter to him because he loved her. When they first broke up, he thought of ways that he could hurt her. He wanted her to feel as much pain as he felt if that was possible.

Eventually, he calmed down. He knew that dealing with the prison system had taken its toll on Brandi. It hurt him to know that sex was the main reason she had bailed on him. She had several toys. After talking with some of the other inmates he began to cool down. There were different opinions.

"Man, you mean that bitch had the nerve to tell you she had another man? She's bold as hell to come out of her mouth with some shit like that." Clint didn't realize how close he came to getting busted in the mouth. No matter what Brandi had done, no one was going to disrespect her by calling her a bitch.

"Back the fuck up man, ya out of line." Anthony gave him a pass but he'd better watch his mouth.

T-Bone jumped in the conversation. "Well to be honest with you, most of them fuck around man, including my ole lady. I don't deceive myself by thinking she's keeping that pussy for me. I have twenty more years to do. But she knows not to let me hear about that shit. It's all about respect."

"Yeah, but she takes care of you Dude. She's been riding with you for about seven years now." Clint patted T-Bone on the back.

"Hell no!" Anthony protested. "The thot of some damn man out der wit his dick up in my woman makes me sick. I don give a damn. Either she's wit me or she's gainst me. There is no damn in between. I don need fer her to visit me or put no money on my books if she's out there bein a fuckin whore. I'm not down wit dat shit."

"To each his own Bro. I'm just thankful that my woman hasn't cut me completely off. A lot of guys in here don't have anyone looking out for them." T-Bone looked at Anthony. "If my lady needs some dick, I can't give it to her, so what's she going to do?"

Following that conversation, Anthony had spoken with some of the other guys. To his surprise, a lot of men agreed with T-Bone. Only a few agreed with Anthony. They couldn't forgive a woman if she cheated on them. If she was supposed to have their back, they meant for her to have it completely. If they even thought she was giving up the pussy, they said that would be the end of it. They would rather ride it out by themselves.

Now Anthony was in conflict with himself. He wondered if he should call and share his good news with Brandi. Should he try to win her back from the man she chose over him? Would she want him back? Could he forgive her?

After pondering over the situation, he decided not to call. He would not let her know that he was being released. He was not contacting her. Brandi was the one who chose to bail on him. He would call his mom to pick him up. He wouldn't put her name on his visiting list at the Halfway House either.

Anthony thought: *Fuck her. I'd neva put my dick in dat whore agin. It wodnt askin too much fer her to keep her damn legs closed. Any whore can open her legs and let some man cum in her. If she truly loved me like she claimed, then all of dem niggas wud hav ben off limits. If she was real, she neva would have done nunthin to jeopardize us. Hell no. I don wan her no more. Ima survivor. I can make it. I will make it.*

Chapter Forty-Five

◇◇

Shemeka loaded the last box into the truck. She took one final look at the place she used to call home, before climbing into the driver's seat of the U-Haul she had rented. Bernard had sent some of his friends to help her move and they were following the U-Haul.

She knew that she could never live in that house again. The memory of Robert clutching his chest as he fell to the floor would always haunt her. She couldn't stand to walk through that living room daily, stepping over the place in the carpet where Robert laid bleeding and clinging to life.

It had been a welcome relief when Brandi suggested she move in with her. They could share the expenses and Shemeka could get herself together while she was waiting on her house to be sold. There were too many memories. Not only were there the bad memories but there were also good memories. She wanted to block out the way Robert made her feel. He would always be Robert to her. She could never bring herself to think of him as a woman.

She felt fortunate to have a friend like Brandi. Even though Brandi didn't understand how she had been deceived about Robert's gender, she didn't judge her. Robert loved her and she had fallen in love with him. If he had not died they may have been able to make a life together. No, she wasn't gay but she had fallen in love with him. He loved her enough that he was willing to have surgery. He would have done anything to make her more comfortable with the relationship. How many men would go to such lengths to make sure their woman was happy and content? How many men would die for their woman?

When Shemeka arrived at the storage, the men took their time while unloading the truck and were very careful while handling her things. Brandi had a bedroom suit in her spare room and she decided not to impose on Shemeka any further by asking to bring her own. A fresh start would be better anyway. Less memories. When the last of her items were unloaded, a tear rolled down her cheek as she locked the storage building. It seemed as if everything had happened so fast. Her life had fallen apart at the blink of an eye. One minute she was happy and on top of the world, enjoying her soul mate. The next minute, she was miserable, in a pit of despair, and without anyone to love.

When Shemeka got to Brandi's house, her friend seemed to be deep in thought. She wondered why Brandi was so withdrawn. It probably had something to do with Anthony. After debating in her mind as to whether or not to say anything; she decided to at least see if Brandi wanted to talk about it.

"Brandi, you know that you made the right decision don't you? I know that it is a hard transition but your future is going to be so much brighter with Erik."

At the mention of Erik's name, Brandi burst into tears. She took the pillow from the end of the couch to bury her head in. Shemeka was sorry that she had said anything. It was never her intention to upset Brandi. She walked to the couch. Brandi slowly removed the pillow from her face.

"I've made the biggest mistake of my life." She cried. "I fucked up. I told Anthony that I would be there with him until the end. But what did I do? I bailed on him as soon as Erik showed me a little affection. I was lonely Meka. I should have been stronger than that."

"Where is all of this coming from Brandi? Did you get another crazy ass letter from him? Don't let Anthony cause you to second guess your decision. Erik is a standup guy. You did what was right for you." Shemeka said.

"Did I? What did I do?" What's right for me?" Brandi threw the pillow on the floor.

"Brandi, stop it!" Shemeka shook her. "Get yourself together. I'm the one who should be torn to pieces. Not you. Erik is a wonderful man. He's everything a woman could imagine and more. On top of that, he is free. I know that you care for Anthony and you probably feel sorry for him but he'll never be the man Erik is."

"You can say that again." Brandi cried. "I should never have rushed into a relationship with Erik. He doesn't want me. He just wants me to be away from Anthony. Do you think Anthony will ever forgive me for hurting him?" She ignored the ringing telephone.

Shemeka walked to the table and looked at the Caller ID. "Good! It's Erik."

"I don't want to talk." Brandi said quickly. Shemeka had already answered the telephone. She placed her hand over the mouthpiece of the telephone.

"Come on now Brandi. You will feel better. Please! Talk to Erik." She begged.

"Hang up the telephone Meka. I don't have anything to say to him." She turned her head.

"Erik, I'm sorry." Meka spoke into the telephone. "Brandi is not feeling well at the moment. It's probably something she ate. If you don't mind, I'm going to have to ask you to call back later." She hung the telephone up. "Brandi what was that about? You're wrong as hell for that. You can't treat Erik like that just because you doubt your decision. Anthony has nothing to offer you. Are you ready to spend the next few years traveling up and down the highway?"

"I'm tired Meka. All I want to do is soak in a hot tub. I had a key made for you. It's on the table. Not exactly your ideal first night in a new place is it? Sorry. You know where everything is. Goodnight."

Brandi filled the tub with water and watched as the bubbles rose to the top. After pouring in the skin-so-soft bath oil, she stepped in. The water was soothing, almost tranquil as she laid her head on the back of the tub and closed her eyes. Images of Erik and his lover danced around in her head. Brandi wanted to explain to Meka what was going on. She wanted to tell her what she had seen. She wanted to tell everybody. She and Erik had been the best of friends for as long as she could remember and she never would have guessed he was gay.

Erik had condemned the way Anthony treated her but he had treated her no better. At least Anthony wasn't a fake. She knew who he was. She knew what she had in him. How could she have let anyone cause her to abandon Ant? He wasn't perfect by a long shot. He had a temper and he sometimes said things without thinking, but who wouldn't, given his situation? He was like a caged animal with no means to escape his captors. He was frustrated.

As Brandi washed her body, she told herself, *I'll move on. I won't tell anyone what I saw. There is no need for me to ruin Erik's reputation because the truth of the matter is that I am the one who came on to him. He didn't ask me to be his woman. I rushed into it. Maybe he thought he was helping me to get over Anthony. I don't know. He might have thought I would judge him. Now it makes sense what he used to say. I remember him telling me that he wasn't against inmates or anything but the prison should provide condoms for those guys. He couldn't condemn inmate men fucking each other when all the time, he's doing it. He doesn't need to call me anymore. He doesn't owe me an explanation. He only owes it to himself to be true to who he is.* Brandi stepped out of the tub and wrapped the towel around her. She looked in the mirror. *Mirror, mirror on the wall, who's the biggest fool of all?*

Chapter Forty-Six

<<<<<<<<<<<<<<<<<<<<<<<<<<<<<<<<<<<<<<<<<<<<<<<<<<<<<<<<<

T he sun was bright and the morning warm. Birds chirped and butterflies flew. It was a wonderful day to smell the flowers. Anthony walked into his mother's waiting arms. He was not only blessed, but he was also determined. Too much of his life had been spent behind the wall. Some of the guys he was leaving behind would never get a second chance. Others would get a second chance only to mess it up and return to the very prison system they claim to hate and despise. He was determined to take full advantage of the opportunity he was given. He swore to himself that he would never return. He would go to school, get his GED and he would succeed.

It was 8:35 a.m. and he was ready to get home to some of his mom's home cooking. The Feds had worked it out for him. He would be able to sleep in his own bed tonight, stay up as late as he wanted to and sleep in tomorrow morning. Anthony could report to the Halfway House at 8:00 a.m. but he had until midnight before he would be considered AWOL. His mom had gotten everything he needed including quarters for him to use the pay phone. He would not be allowed to have a cell phone at the Halfway House.

Anthony didn't mind the stipulations. He knew this was another step in his route to freedom. He was required to get a job and would get a bus pass so he could start his job search. In order for him to be reintegrated with the community he had to become a productive member of society-one who contributes to the general well-being of the whole.

This was different from what Anthony had previously envisioned. He had envisioned that upon his release, Brandi would be there and he would swoop her up in his arms, giving her a wet tongue kiss. As much as he wanted to hate her, he couldn't, but neither could he forgive her. She had been good to him through it all but why had she gotten weak on him? He had seen it time and time again. A woman would start off strong, and declare that she was in it for the ride. Then the letters would become few and the visits would become fewer. He always took Brandi to be stronger than that. She caved in for what? Some dick? Some cuddling? Damn! Was it worth it?

He didn't claim to be a saint. He had jeopardized her by having her bring in contraband. Even though he tried to justify it by saying he was helping her, he knew that he was wrong. It didn't mean he loved her less. It meant he had been stupid and succumbed to the pressures of prison. He had to deal with other inmates daily. Some acted like they were his buddy while others acted like they could not stand his ass. For the most part, those who acted like they were his buddy did so because they wanted something from him. Most of them were manipulative. He had to stay on top of his game so the last thing he needed was to wonder what his woman was out there doing.

His mom had not been there for him like he thought she should have. She didn't visit him and only put money on his books occasionally. However, Anthony knew that she loved him. It was her way of showing tough love. She didn't want to enable him.

When they arrived at his mom's house, there were cars parked on both sides of the street. He walked into the living room, which was filled with balloons and relatives. The aroma of country ham filled his nostrils. Everyone took turns hugging and kissing him. His grandmother cried. He cried with her. She was ninety-two years old and he had prayed to

God each night that she'd live to see him get out of prison and turn his life around.

"Enough of this sobbing." His uncle said. "Let's eat before these grits get cold. I hate cold grits." They all laughed as they headed to the kitchen.

"Dis is what I call eatin. I'm telling ya Mom, ya cooking is what I missed da most. I can't wait to dig in. Dat slop they serve ain't gud enuff fer pigs." Anthony washed his hands before filling his plate with scrambled eggs, grits, red-eye gravy, smoked sausage, and hot biscuits.

"I'll get it." His mom said when the doorbell rang. Jessica walked into the kitchen looking like a million bucks. Anthony froze with his fork barely touching his mouth. It had been years since he had seen or spoken to Jessica. She still looked good. He checked out her full figure body in the Apple Bottoms jeans she was wearing with the Apple Bottoms shirt. He stood to embrace her. She was soft and warm. The scent of her White Diamonds perfume drowned out the aroma of country ham. As he felt his manhood growing, he released her and held her back to admire her beauty.

Anthony could hardly believe she was there to welcome him home. His mom must have arranged it. She was the last person he had expected to see. They dated for four and a half years. The relationship ended when she came to his house unexpectedly and found him in bed with Brandi. She was supposed to go to Georgia for the weekend with her girlfriends but they cancelled out at the last minute for some reason. She decided to surprise Anthony and showed up at his crib with strawberries, cool whip, and dressed in a cape with nothing on underneath. She had a bottle of wine in her hand when she entered the bedroom. It shattered on the floor when she walked in the bedroom and saw Anthony pulling his dick out of Brandi, cum dripping from his penis. She turned and ran out the door. He was busted. He never tried to contact her, never tried to explain. He moved on with Brandi, but always regretted hurting Jessica. Three months later he got locked up.

"Hi Anthony. Welcome home. Your mom invited me for your homecoming breakfast.

Sorry I'm late."

"No! No! I'm glad to see ya. I don know too many people who would agree to come to breakfast at midday. Well dis is more like a brunch. Sit down. Make yaself at home." He told her.

When everyone had finished eating, Anthony walked out on the porch with Jessica.

The two strolled over to the porch swing and sat down. There was so much he wanted to say to her. How could he explain being unfaithful? He had been right in his letter to Brandi. Karma was a muthafucka. He started to wonder if that was why Brandi had fucked over him. Maybe it was his payback. If it were then he had been paid in full.

"Jessica. I wanted to call ya. I wanted to apologize to ya. I'm sorry. I know dat I hurt you.

She looked him square in the face. "Yes Anthony. You did hurt me. I loved you and I was faithful to you. Men tried to holla at me but I always made it clear that I had a man. Or at least I thought I had one. What I thought was something special turned out to be nothing but it's all good. I'm here to welcome you home. I've always gotten along with your mom so when she asked me, I couldn't say no to her."

He couldn't look at her. Anthony looked away as he squeezed Jessica's hand. "I was wild and out der doin my own thin witout no regard to nobody's feelins. I was young and stupid." He looked at her. "I've growed a lot Jessica. I'm in a different place now. Bein locked up gives a man time ta think. Time ta realize wat is important. So who is da lucky man that has you now?"

"I'm not seeing anyone at the moment. I was seeing this guy named Ray but it didn't work out. He wanted to put his hands on me. I don't play that shit. Oh! He apologized and all but I know enough about abuse to know that if he did it once, he'd do it again. I ended things right away."

Anthony slid closer to her. "Jessica. I'd like ta have a chance ta make things up ta ya. If ya give me a chance, I promise ta never hurt ya again." He told her.

"I don't know Anthony. I'm a good woman and you took advantage of that. You tore my world apart." She answered him.

"Please Jessica." He begged. "Just give me a chance."

"Anthony you were a playa. When you went in, I found out about all kind of women you had been sexing behind my back. One night stands, sticking your dick in a whore just to be able to say you had hit it. I'm not with that shit."

"I was caught up in da game Boo. I was dealin drugs. Girls would suck my dick and do all kinds of shit fer a hit. I'm not blamin dem but it's the life I led. I'm beyond dat now."

Jessica had never stopped loving Anthony. "One chance Anthony. One mess up and I'm out. No talking, no it only happened one time, no it was a mistake, no nothing." She warned.

Anthony stood and pulled Jessica up from the chair. He whirled her around and kissed her. "Ya won be sorry Babe. I promise ya won."

As he released Jessica, Brandi walked up the sidewalk. "I don't believe it. I see it and I still don't believe it. I heard that you were getting out this morning but I didn't believe you would come home without letting me know." She glanced at Jessica. "What's up with this?"

He put his arms around Jessica who stood there silently. "Dis is my woman. Ya've moved on and so have I. Brandi, I hope dat y'all be happy. I know dat I will."

Brandi couldn't say anything. She had brought it on herself. Anthony was a good man. She had let him down as well as let herself down. Now, she had no one. She and Shemeka were both traveling Heartache Avenue. Somehow, she thought, they'd both get through the pain. She wanted Anthony to be happy, and wished him all the luck in the world. Brandi watched as Anthony and Jessica turned their backs and went in the house.

Chapter Forty-Seven

<<<<<<<<<<<<<<<<<<<<<<<<<<<<<<<<<<<<<<<<<<<<<<<<<

Brandi and Shemeka went inside the crowded courtroom. They looked around and spotted Bernard and Rhonda on the second row. "Let's sit back here." Shemeka told Brandi. "I really wasn't expecting it to be this crowded."

"A bunch of damn spectators. Most of them are here to be nosey." Brandi responded.

"Yeah, I know." Meka agreed. "The newspaper did so much publicity on it that people wanted to see things first hand. I'm glad they didn't bring Dean. She didn't need to be here."

"I hope they put that bitch away for life." Shemeka spirted out angrily. "I hate her.

She should never be allowed to walk the streets again."

They both looked up in time to see Nikki being led into the courtroom. There was a deputy on both sides of her leading her to the defendants table. One of the officers removed her handcuffs. Nikki looked decent; almost professional. Instead of being in an orange prison jumpsuit like they had expected, she wore civilian clothes. She had on a navy blue skirt, white blouse and navy jacket. Her navy and white pumps enhanced the look of her suit. She wore pearl earrings and a pearl necklace adorned her neck. From her outer appearance, Nikki could have easily passed as a teacher or a lawyer. Shortly after her appearance, everyone stood for the judge.

When they were seated the courtroom remained quiet while the charges were being read.

"You are charged with Murder in the 1st degree, kidnapping, assault, and holding persons for hostage. How do you plead?"

Her lawyer stood. "My client pleads not guilty your honor."

"Not guilty?" Brandi whispered to Shemeka. "How can she plead not guilty when you saw her ass?"

"I hope they hurry up and call me to testify." Shemeka whispered back. "I'm ready to get it over with."

The spectators were quiet and attentive when Rhonda took the stand to be sworn in. She was nervous about her testimony; not quite sure what Nikki had revealed to her lawyer. Bernard was a schoolteacher and well known in the community. She didn't want anything to come out that would damage his standing in the community.

Rhonda tried to be lenient enough in her testimony to pacify Nikki. She had never shared with Shemeka and Brandi that she and Bernard had indulged in a threesome with Nikki. This was not how she wanted them to find out about it. She tried to stay middle ground because if she were too lenient, it would be like a slap in the face to Meka. After all Nikki was a murderer and had killed her man. She could always use the excuse that she was trying to protect Dean.

She explained she had met Nikki through her husband and that an affair the two had, led to a child who they were now raising. She spoke of the kidnapping but lied and stated that Nikki promised to let her go as soon as she reached a safe destination.

Nikki sat quietly throughout Rhonda's testimony. When Rhonda stepped down from the stand, Nikki looked at her and licked her lips. Rhonda pretended that she didn't see Nikki and walked on to secure a seat next to her husband.

When Bernard was crossed examined, he stated that Nikki had held him at gunpoint before his wife came home. It was the first time the courtroom and jury got a chance to see Nikki perform.

"Gunpoint? You begged me Bitch." She stood as the judge banged on the podium. "You wanted my pussy. You still want me!"

The judge banged his stick with a warning. "Control your client Mr. Davis or I will have her removed from my courtroom."

"I apologize Your Honor." Mr. Davis whispered in Nikki's ear as she sat down. She looked at Bernard and blew him a kiss. He tried to ignore her as he explained that he was afraid for his life not knowing what Nikki might do to him.

When Mr. Davis cross-examined Bernard, Nikki smiled. "You feared for your life from a woman whom you had an affair with, whom conceived a child for you, whom you snuck away from your wife in the middle-"

"Objection! I object. Mr. Simpson is not on trial." The prosecutor stated.

"I withdraw." Mr. Davis said. "No further questions."

Shemeka could barely contain herself as she told the jury how Nikki had shot Robert in cold blood in an attempt to kill her. She described Nikki as being unstable and a threat to society. The Courtroom was quiet as Shemeka spoke between sobs.

"Did the defendant come to your house to kill Robert?" Mr. Davis asked.

"No! She came to my house to kill me. She would have succeeded if Robert had not jumped in front of me. He saved my life and now he is dead."

"Didn't she ask you to stay away from Robert, the only lifeline she had?"
"No she didn't."

"Isn't it true that she was abused as a child? Didn't she think you were taking her protector?"

The prosecutor stood. "Objection! Hearsay. Miss Eller wasn't there. She can only testify as to what she was told."

"This leads to explain my clients' state of mind and things that led up to the shooting." Nikki's lawyer said. "This will help the jury to understand some of her actions."

"It's Hearsay!" The prosecutor argued.

"Sustained!" The judge said. "Jury, you will disregard those remarks."

"Not likely." Bernard whispered to Rhonda. "How can they disregard what they have heard?"

In his closing remarks, Nikki's lawyer painted the picture of her as a wounded lamb, trapped inside a barbed wire fence, not knowing how to escape. He spoke of a troubled childhood without the guidance of a mother and being raised by an abusive uncle. He didn't try to excuse her behavior but instead tried to explain the reason for her behavior.

Mr. Davis spoke to the jury. "She is more of a danger to herself than to anyone else. She is battling demons within her. Don't you for one-minute think that she didn't love Roberta Holloway, because she did. Roberta was her cousin. The state wants you to find her guilty of 1st degree murder. This death was an accident. There was no malice or forethought. The gun simply discharged accidentally. Miss Harris was scared. She ran to the Simpson's house. They are the only other people in town who she knows. She didn't harm them. She had a gun but she didn't use it. She could have killed them both, took the car and been out of the state before anybody realized she was gone. Mrs. Simpson said by her own testimony that she was going to let her go as soon as she reached safety. Most importantly, the prosecution has not proved its case. They have not proved anything except that my client held two people hostage out of fear. The burden of proof is on them."

Mr. Davis walked closer and looked at each juror. "If they have proven to you beyond a reasonable doubt that my client is guilty of these allegations; if they have proven to you that she shot and killed Roberta Holloway with malice and forethought, then you have no choice but to find her guilty. But if they have not; if you have the slightest doubt in your mind, then it is your obligation and your duty to find her not guilty."

The jury deliberated for three and a half hours before returning with a verdict. "On the charge of assault, how do you find the defendant?" The judge asked.

"On the charge of assault, we the jury find the defendant. Guilty."

"On the charge of holding persons for hostage, how do you find the defendant?"

"On the charge of holding persons for hostage we find the defendant Guilty."

"On the charge of kidnapping how do you find the defendant?"

"On the charge of kidnapping, we find the defendant, Not Guilty."

"On the charge of 1st degree murder how do you find the defendant?"

"On the charge of 1st degree murder we find the defendant Not Guilty."

Nikki smiled at the jurors. The judge asked, "Did you consider the lesser charge?"

"On the lesser charge of 2nd degree murder, we find the defendant Guilty!"

"Suck my pussy Muthafuckas!" Nikki screamed at the jurors. "Take my cum! Ha…ha…ha!" She laughed.

The judge banged his gavel stick on the podium. "Someone get this woman out of my courtroom. Sentencing will be held Tuesday morning at 9:00."

"Want some of this good pussy, Your Honor? It's hot. I bet your wife can't do it like me." Nikki lifted her skirt.

The judge nodded to the deputies, "Get this woman out of here before I impose sentencing right now!"

As the deputy took the handcuffs from his belt, Nikki leaped over the front row of seats to the second row where Bernard and Rhonda were seated. The officers subdued her as she tried to lick Rhonda's face. They handcuffed her and removed her from the courtroom as she kicked and screamed. "I'm sorry Baby. I'll keep this pussy for you. Don't worry. I'll be back!"

Outside the courtroom, Rhonda and Bernard shook their heads as they walked towards Shemeka and Brandi.

"She's truly sick" Shemeka said.

"Well maybe now, she'll get the help that she needs." Rhonda could not help but feel sorry for Nikki.

"It's over now." Bernard told the women. "At least we can get on with our lives now. Why don't the two of you come over tonight for a drink?"

"Not a bad idea." Brandi answered. Her mind went back to Anthony. "We'll drink to closure."

Chapter 1

◇◇

A t 2:15 a.m. the halls were quiet. The patients were asleep and the only movement was of a few employees shuffling. Lance scurried down the hall quietly. He was supposed to be making his rounds. It was time for him to check his patients and make sure everyone was breathing and had no complications. He unlocked the doors leading into the green zone.

Lance unlocked the door to room #341. Miss Blackwell was asleep with her face turned towards the wall. He tipped past her to her roommate.

"Pssst…pssst! Wake up. Are you ready?"

The patient rubbed her eyes and sat up on the side of the bed. He took her hand and led her to the bathroom. She was very compliant.

Lance recalled the day she was admitted. She walked into the dayroom and stood by the calendar on the wall. Her dark chocolate skin was smooth. Her thickness and the way she swayed her hips when she walked made him stand at attention. There was something different about her and Lance wanted to know what her story was. She seemed like a fish out of water. Her demeanor and the way she carried herself was one of a totally sane woman, yet she was locked away in a mental institution with women who had lost touch with reality.

When Lance introduced himself and explained to her that he would be working on her ward, she flashed him the most beautiful smile he had ever seen. After extending her hand to him and introducing herself, she told him that a misunderstanding had occurred and she was there for an evaluation.

Although he knew her story to be fabricated, he couldn't help but to be attracted to the confident black woman who stood before him. The following night, he pulled a double shift. While on third shift, he came into her room to do a patient check. Lance had not expected her to be awake when he entered her room but as soon as he walked over to her bed, she sat up.

"Can't sleep?" He asked.

"No! I'm hungry." She answered.

"The kitchen is closed. Maybe I can find you a pack of crackers or something to snack on." He responded.

"It's okay." She grabbed his crotch. "This will do just fine."

Lance did not resist when she unzipped his pants and pulled out his manhood. It had come to life with her touch. When she took him in and out of her hot mouth, he grabbed her head. Third shift was a wonderful shift to work over on and he must do it more often. What was it about the muscles in her mouth? It had not been five minutes and he was about ready to explode. Lance prayed that her roommate would not wake up but there was no way in hell that he was going to stop her.

"Mmm…Damn!" He tried not to be loud. "Yes. Ugh!" He held her head tighter, "I'm cummming… Ughhhh!" Lance tried to pull out so he wouldn't put all of that in her mouth. He'd shoot it in his hand. She grabbed the base of his manhood tighter as he moaned and she drained his fluids in her mouth.

"Ahh!" He whispered. "Damn, that felt good. Thanks Nikki."

Nikki licked her lips. "Can a crazy woman make you feel like I just made you feel? That was nothing. I can do so much more."

"I need to make my rounds. Thanks again." Lance zipped his pants up and hurried out of the room. He locked the door and continued to check on his patients. Nikki had made him feel better than his wife ever made him feel. Her mouth was amazing.

After that night, he and Nikki started kicking it on the regular. They could sneak in a session while he worked third shift but soon he went to third shift permanently. Lance was beginning to think there was actually nothing wrong with Nikki. Whenever anyone was around she knew how to be discreet. She never let on that she had any interest or involvement with him.

Now she was in the bathroom bent over, letting him take her in the ass. She had spoiled the hell out of him. It felt good to stick his manhood into her tightness. She took it like a pro. Nikki welcomed his stiff rod. He held her tight around the waist as he stroked long and deep.

"Harder." Nikki whispered. "What are you scared of? Give it to me."

Lance held her tighter as he stroked harder. "Augh! Augh! Nikki!" He couldn't hold back. He pulled his rod out of Nikki and shot cum all over her back. Then Lance beat the head of his rod on her back and finished draining his fluids.

Nikki turned around and kissed him. "Baby it's been a few years now. I'm ready to get out of here. You promised that you would help me. You know for yourself that I don't deserve to be in this place. Am I out of touch with reality? Do I talk to walls? Do I sit in a corner talking to myself?"

Lance shook his head. "No Nikki. You don't do any of that but you're taking your meds on the regular. I just need a little more time. I'm going to have to find you a place somewhere that nobody will think to look. Just be patient. I'll get you out of here. These things take time Sweetheart. This is not something I can just jump up and do overnight. This has to be carefully planned or it won't work." Lance kissed her before locking her in for the night. Nikki made him feel good. Everything he was missing at home, he had found in Nikki. He knew that he was taking a chance by dealing with her. If he ever got caught that would be the end of his career, his marriage and possibly his freedom.

He wondered if she would continue to service him after she got out. There was a possibility she would forget about him. She might return to her kids and her previous life.

Lance wondered why Nikki never talked about her kids. She had given birth to a son while she was there. The staff had whispered about how she showed little or no emotions when the baby was taken from her. He wondered if it were too painful for her to talk about.

One thing for sure, Nikki had her mind set on escaping. He knew from everything he had read in her file that Nikki was not a woman he could cross. He had to find a way to make that happen. Although Nikki made him feel good, he knew there was another side to her.

ABOUT THE AUTHOR

Joli lives in a small city in North Carolina with her two children. She has a Masters degree in Criminal Justice and a Masters degree in Psychology. Writing has been her passion since youth. Joli is the author of erotic fiction. Presently Joli is not revealing her name.

Printed in the United States
By Bookmasters